I0713315

MOON CAUGHT

Written by:

C. M. CONNEY

Published by
Ace Lyon Books
January 2018

Also, by C. M. Conney

The Real Deal

Take the Shot

Copyright© C. M. Conney September 2017

All rights reserved. No part of this book may be used or reproduced in any form or by any means, electronic or mechanical, including photocopying, recording, or by any information storage and retrieval systems, without written permission of the Publisher or Author except where permitted by law.

Published by
Ace Lyon Books
Acelyonbooks.com
First Edition
Cover Design by S. M. Savoy
Moon Caught C. M. Conney

ISBN 978-1-947122-18-5

This is a work of fiction. Names, characters, businesses, places, and incidents or events are either products of the Author's imagination or are used fictitiously. Any resemblance to actual events or locales or persons, living or dead, is entirely coincidental.

Contents

MOON CAUGHT

One

May

Stacy?" Kelly's mother, Alice, called from the foot of the stairs.

"She isn't up here, Mom," Kelly called back as she felt for her sneakers beneath the bed.

"That girl," her mother muttered so loudly Kelly heard her from a floor away.

A glass bottle brushed Kelly's fingertips, and she frowned at the half-empty bottle of Jack Daniels she pulled from beneath her bed. She threw her sneakers on and grabbed the bottle. It seemed like Stacy was getting into trouble every time she turned around, but she wasn't taking the rap for her stash.

A quick peek showed an empty hallway, so she darted to Stacy's room across the hall and slid the bottle beneath her bed where it clinked against others. Kelly winced as she dropped to her stomach to peer under the bed.

"Jeez, no wonder it was under my bed; she's got no room left." A scowl lined her brow as she thumped down the stairs.

"What's got into you?" Her mother tweaked her ponytail and handed her a paper bag.

"Nothing." She pasted on a smile and gave her mother a hug.

"Go past the Palmers old place and see if your sister is there. If she is, shoo her home."

Kelly grabbed an apple from the bowl on the worn countertop and shined it absently against her shirt as she spoke. "I'll check, but you know she won't listen to me. Abby and I will be back for dinner. She can sleepover, right?"

Her mother's frown changed to a smile, and she took the apple from her and cut it in half. "You eat half, and yes, Abby can sleep over. Stay off the roads though and stick together!" her mother called after her as she darted out the door.

Her pony, Flit, greeted her with a happy whicker from the corral right beside the main barn. She rubbed his nose and feed him his half of the apple before saddling him.

"I'll be too big to ride you soon," she said as she pulled futilely at the stirrup. The buckle was already in the lowest hole and all her yanking just produced an annoyed flick from Flit's tail.

She bit her lip and glanced back at the house. Money had been tight since her mother was laid off, and while she liked having her mom around, it meant no new horse for her.

"Not that I want to replace you." She patted the horse's neck and led him from the paddock before swinging up. Her feet dangled almost to the ground. She was tall for thirteen and stick thin.

For sure this would be the last summer with Flit, she thought sadly as the pony ambled down the narrow path behind the barns.

Cows milled beside the pasture gate, hoping for a handout, but she ignored them and headed west to the trail that cut through the state forest.

Flit balked at the beginning of the steep path that led past the tumbled down house. She urged him forward with soft words. She didn't like this place either. It smelled of stale beer and cigarettes, and the boys that came here were rude and scary. Kids came from all over to hang out here, usually at night though.

Flit stood, flicking his ears and sidling when she dismounted to stick her head in the door, hoping the entire place wouldn't come crashing down. The back half of the building had already fallen in, and the roof sagged with a gaping hole above the front room.

Broken bottles glittered in the dim light beside a stained mattress to the right of the front door. Kelly didn't go any further, but she called her sister for a minute before running back into the sunshine. No one was around, but the quiet made her uneasy. Flit still stamped and sidled, so she hurriedly checked his feet to make sure he hadn't stepped in glass or picked up a needle before leading him forward.

"What's gotten into you, silly boy? Smell a snake or something?" She kept her gaze on the path, hoping it wasn't a snake, and yanked Flit forward. "Probably better to walk you anyway. I'm getting too big to lug up these hills, aren't I?"

Flit followed easily for a minute before sidestepping and shaking his head hard. He jerked to a stop and reared on his hind legs.

Shocked, she jumped away from his slashing hooves. Flit screamed an equine cry of fear and strained hard, lashing out with both front feet. The reins slipped from her grasp, and he bolted back down the hill, crashing and snorting through the brush.

Uneasy now, she glanced around.

A low coughing snort came from her left. The hair on the back of her neck rose at the odd sound. She'd never heard anything like it. Pine scent filled the air as a low branch rustled, and her wide-eyed gaze caught on the shine of an animal's eyes. She began backing away one slow step at a time.

She screamed as the beast leaped, seeing only brown fur and long teeth as she turned to run. White-hot pain grabbed her leg, and she screamed again as she fell, catching herself with her hands and scrabbling back.

A wolf slavered and snapped at her face, then ripped again at her leg. Sobbing and crying, she smacked at its head as it ripped a hole in her jeans, taking a hunk of flesh with it. Blood sprayed in a hot arc, and the wolf growled savagely.

She kicked at it with both feet, and it bit down hard before releasing her to lick the bloody wound.

Pain raced up her leg, but she knew she would die if she didn't get away. Forcing herself against the pain, she thrashed wildly as she searched the ground for a weapon.

On her stomach, she dragged her leg behind her, reaching for a broken limb. The wolf grabbed her by the shirt and dragged her back, but she'd managed to grab the branch and turned to hit it. It snapped at her face, then ripped the stick from her hand.

Tears blurred her vision as it knocked her back and stood on her chest. She lifted both arms and tried to strangle it while blocking the teeth gnashing for her throat, but it was so much bigger than her, she couldn't budge it. Warm breath, smelling of her blood and rotten meat, wafted her face. Salvia and blood dripped to her cheek as the wolf licked her, its warm tongue scratching from her chin to her forehead.

She shrieked and heaved with all her might. The wolf bounded away, leaving fur in her hands, tail wagging, almost prancing. Bile rose in her throat.

It's playing with me like a cat with a mouse. As she thought that, it spun and pounced, knocking her back and rolling her over. Pain made her head spin, and when it cleared, the wolf was eating her leg. The pain was like nothing she'd ever imagined, and she screamed shrilly and kicked feebly with her good leg.

A gunshot made them both jump, and she screamed again, this time for help. The wolf whirled and crouched as if prepared to pounce at whoever approached, then whirled back to lick her face again.

Loud voices called, but Kelly couldn't distinguish the words through the blood pounding in her head. The wolf stared into her eyes a moment before bounding away.

She stared after it, still clutching a handful of its reddish-brown fur. Her leg had stopped hurting, and a tingling warmth suffused her body. Her eyes fluttered shut.

When she opened her eyes again, her leg throbbed, and her mother leaned over her crying.

"Oh, thank God."

"Flit?" she managed to ask.

Her throat felt raw, and her head pounded.

"Safe at home," her father said and kissed her brow. "You had us so worried."

"My leg?" Pain burned the length of her leg, pulsing into her hip, growing brighter every second.

"You'll need another operation, but the doctors think you'll walk just fine. Maybe a limp for a while but we can worry about that later."

She began to cry, and her father hugged her tightly.

"It tried to eat me. It was going to eat me alive."

Her crying became hysterical, and the doctor came and gave her a shot. The world drifted away.

Her last thought was she hoped someone killed that damned wolf.

Two

Early October
Two and A Half Years Later

Sunlight filtered through the floor-to-ceiling windows of Richard's office, giving the dark, hardwood furniture a rich luster. The room smelled of books and old leather, and Mark stopped to sniff appreciatively.

Richard waved him into the room and pointed at his computer screen. "That makes six girls now. I'm certain it's our feral. I've sent teams to the neighboring states, but I want you to head to Minnesota. From his pattern, he's heading straight north. The Dakota packs are on alert, but won't be leaving their territories. You smell another wolf, it's our bad guy."

Richard frowned irritably at his computer screen as he said, "If he sticks true to form, he'll avoid cities and head for the nearest state park. My guess is he'll head to Sibley State Park. It borders a large lake with miles of forest and is surrounded by farmland. Plus, he might be familiar with the area from his childhood. Delmont's pack ran there for a few years when the feral was young."

Mark perched on the edge of the desk. "All his victims were attacked while hiking or riding in the woods in broad daylight. Witnesses took pictures at two of the attacks, but I wasn't able to get them."

Richard tapped the screen, and Mark leaned closer to peer at the blurry images of a hundred-and-twenty-pound reddish-brown wolf. He didn't ask how Richard had gotten the pictures. His gaze caught on the terrified expression of the little girl.

"Jesus!" Mark turned away from the screen.

He'd been to each crime scene but hadn't seen the victims. He'd followed the scent, but the wolf wasn't stupid and always lost him by heading to water, avoiding bus stations and airports.

Only once had Mark caught his scent at a rental agency but he'd lost him again when he found the abandoned car at a train station. He knew the feral had jumped a train, but he could've jumped off anywhere.

Richard spoke, bringing Mark back from his reminisces.

"My guess is he wants a mate younger than himself. He has a type he goes for; thin, tom-boyish with long dark hair. Two of the girls he killed were thirteen, three fourteen, and one was twelve. She looked older though, so maybe he thought her mature. Who knows what this sick fuck thinks? Stop him permanently. The attacks are escalating in violence too. The last two girls were raped and partially eaten. The police think they might have a serial killer using dogs to terrorize and dispose of his prey, and they wouldn't be wrong. He is a serial killer whether he means to be or not. The feral hurt them bad enough they never regained consciousness until they died of the injuries. The doctors called it massive infections."

He tapped the screen again and smiled in grim triumph. "Within two days of every attack, police were called to bar fights within ten miles of his victims. Fights that ended in robbery and death. I think that's how he's funding himself, picking fights in bar parking lots. He kills the men quickly and with weapons. He isn't looking to make a friend."

Richard tapped the screen again, and the picture changed. On the right, a smiling, freckled-faced boy of about twelve with reddish-brown hair and a mocking grin; on the left, a wolf with the same reddish-brown hair and the same devilish grin beneath narrowed, golden eyes.

Richard leaned back in his swivel chair and stretched. "That's the last official picture we have of him taken five years ago. Audrey has convinced me to send teams to make sure he left no living victims, but I've been combing police reports from the last two years, and no other bites were reported that I'm not certain were domestic dogs. This last attack was only one month from the last. He's escalating rapidly, and I'm afraid he's left more dead behind him, girls reported as missing."

"I better get going then." Mark hitched his pack

higher on his back and headed for the door.

"Shoot his ass. Don't take stupid chances," Richard called after him.

Leah, Richard's mate, stopped him at the door. Mark breathed deep of her scent and held her close for a minute. She smelled like home.

"Take care of yourself, Mark. He's just a pup, but a dangerous one. Rainy called me. He was one of Delmont's pack. He left, they thought to seek out a new pack because theirs had no young females, but, except for his parents, they were glad to see him go. Word has it he had a temper and was vicious, liked to play with his kills, lost himself in the scent of blood. Rainy offered him a place in her pack, but he turned her down. She's worried he's going to come back and make a stab at killing her mate to become Alpha and force one of the young girls to be his mate, and she thinks he might do it the coward's way and shoot him. She won't let any of her pack leave. They've closed ranks and are patrolling their territory. This isn't a shocked human, but a boy who knew what he would become and is reveling in it."

"I'll stop him." Mark kissed Leah's brow. "And don't be so worried. I'm not looking for trouble."

She stroked his hair. If he'd been a cat, he would have purred. Leah's touch soothed like none other. He pushed her away before longing for a mate of his own overwhelmed him.

Human lovers are good enough for me, he told himself firmly.

Mark patted the holster beneath his navy-blue windbreaker with Montana Fish Wildlife and Parks emblazoned in white on the left breast pocket and across the back. He showed the stewardess his badge and handed her the lockbox containing his gun before settling into the first-class window seat.

"A bit far from home, no?" the man beside him asked.

Mark opened his briefcase and withdrew a stack of maps. "We occasionally leave our jurisdiction to help our fellows. I'm on the trail of a serial poacher." He handed the man a stack of photos, most of endangered species, but all had been beheaded and the bodies left to rot. "The bastard is a headhunter, and I think he's moved on to Minnesota."

The passenger handed the grisly photos back and wiped his hands on his pants. "I hope you catch him."

"Oh, we will. Arrogant bastards like him always slip up. We're real police and take this kind of thing very seriously."

That was true. Mark was a real game warden, and that was his real badge. But he wasn't hunting a poacher. Donald, another werewolf, and a good friend, would be covering him on his job at home. Not that he really cared if he lost it. He enjoyed the job, it let him live peacefully on the ranch, but he'd done many things in his long life.

"I envy you that job. It must be nice to spend your time outdoors instead of in an office."

Mark chuckled and opened his laptop. "Everyone says that until the first day they go to work and it's five below. Rain or shine we're out there, and believe me, there seem to be more lousy days than nice ones."

The passenger laughed politely and turned to his own laptop. They didn't speak again until the plane landed.

"Good luck, young man." He offered his hand, and Mark shook it, trying to keep the grin off his face. He had a good hundred and fifty years on the man.

The stewardess returned his gun, and Richard, or maybe Leah, had arranged a jeep for him. He was on his way to the state forest in minutes. This time, the little shit wouldn't get away. He'd know his scent, and now he knew his pattern. Richard would call him the second the boy killed, and Mark would be on his ass. The wolf within him wanted to run and sink his teeth into their enemy.

Soon, he promised and stepped hard on the gas.

He slowed when he reached town. A shiver of excitement rippled his spine. This was exactly the type of place the feral preferred. A small main street with houses set far apart and well back from the road.

He slowed further as he reached the state park and pulled into the gravel lot of a bar that sat by itself on the outskirts of town. Forested hills behind the bar were the edges of the state park.

Flickering lights, half of them out, lit a faded sign proclaiming, 'Moe's.' Pines grew right up to the back door, and the lot was narrow and wrapped around the building. From the worn marks in the grass, customers parked along both sides of the street and in the scrubby lot across from Moe's.

The perfect place for a slash and grab, Mark thought as he stepped from the car. He hadn't taken two steps when he smelt wolf.

"Fucker is already here." Shocked, he snatched his cell and called Richard.

"He's here already. Have there been any murders within the last week?"

"Jesus." Key clicks filled the line. "None. I figured you had at least a month, maybe more. You sure it's him?"

"I'm sure. And the scent is fresh. He's likely scoping the place out. He'll smell me too if I go nosing around. I'm going to follow from here."

"I'm sending backup. We can't afford to lose him."

"I won't fucking lose him."

Mark slipped his phone back into his pocket and headed toward the scent. A scent he shouldn't be able to smell so clearly. He eyed the dried urine on the side of the building thoughtfully. The feral was marking his territory. He was getting cocky. He had to know there would be hunters on his trail. Mark squatted to sniff the stain. The feral was aroused.

The thick scent of male musk and a hint of blood underlay the stronger urine smell.

He sauntered to the door and pretended to drop his keys so he could sniff the handle. His eyes narrowed, and he straightened and headed to the forest at a jog. The feral hadn't gone inside. Whatever had aroused him had been outside, and it had been less than two weeks since his last kill. The speed at which the feral was moving worried him. It seemed to Mark as if this punk had a plan and knew exactly where he was going. A full moon loomed, and he wondered if the feral had decided his odds were better if he attacked while the moon was full. That meant he had mere hours to find the bastard.

He knows hunters are tracking him. Maybe he thought he could lure me in?

Mark slowed his advance and stepped off the trail to strip. He stuffed his clothing in the bag and with a practiced wriggle positioned the pack on his shoulders, keeping the strap in his mouth. The ground felt cool and moist beneath his knees, and he welcomed his wolf.

Fur rippled over his body, his muscles twisted and his bones reformed with a feeling of release. He shivered in delight. Some hated the feeling of being remade, but he loved it.

He yanked the strap with his teeth, and the pack settled to his back. The smell of earth and leaf decay wafted from his paws as he stretched and dug his claws into the earth. Claws longer and harder than any natural wolf sliced deep furrows into the leafmold. He had to resist the urge to roll, not wanting to dislodge his pack, but he scratched hard, enjoying the ripple of his muscles before lowering his nose to the ground.

Gotcha, he thought with savage satisfaction and raced after the tantalizing smell.

Three

$\mathcal{B}$ranches caught in his fur and the smell of pine deepened. The feral didn't look away from the girl in his arms. He didn't appear to sense the danger, and the wolf almost couldn't blame him. From thirty feet away she smelled delicious.

Mark eased closer and glanced up. The full moon had risen, and he could smell the boy's sweat as he fought the change. The girl in his arms kissed him then pushed away.

"My father will kill me. I got to get home."

The boy tightened his hold and pushed her to the ground.

"Stop," the girl said, sounding scared now.

And she should be scared, the wolf thought, but it was too late for her. From her smell, she'd already been bitten. His golden eyes narrowed as the boy roughly yanked her jeans to her knees while she struggled and pleaded with him to stop.

But, if she'd been bitten, how was she resisting the change? A new wolf would have no control. The moon would call her, and she'd have no choice but to listen.

Mark snapped at a limb beside his face, breaking it in his teeth with a sharp crack.

The boy rose his head, and even from where Mark hunkered in the trees, he could see the animal shine in them. The feral released the girl who ran away crying. Already shirtless with his shoes off, the boy let his jeans fall to his ankles and embraced the change.

Mark waited for the boy to shift, it was easier to hide a wolf corpse than a human one. His eyes narrowed at the speed with which fur sprouted across the boy's torso. If he could already shift so quickly, he'd grow into a powerful wolf, an alpha for sure. And a ruthless one with no humanity. He was the type to kill every other alpha in his pack and steal unmated females, just like Mark's father's alpha had been.

A low snarl burst from Mark's lips, and he hoped the girl kept running and didn't look back. The feral whined and crouched.

Mark clamped down on his pity. It wasn't the boy's fault he was the way he was, but it sure as shit was his fault for not accepting the pack's help.

His first snap missed. The boy was limber and twisted away, but Mark's second snap connected. The boy snarled when Mark ripped away a chunk of fur and muscle. A coppery odor of fresh blood covered the scent of pine and rotting leaves.

The two wolves circled each other, snapping and snarling. Countless fights both playful and real over the last century gave Mark the advantage. The boy's head hung low, and he darted glances around, seeking an escape.

There would be no escape, the older wolf thought in satisfaction and leaped.

He made it quick, ripping the throat out in one swift move. Blood gushed over his face and chest as the boy's paws scrabbled at the earth and his bowels voided.

Mark dropped the corpse and howled. Then he dragged it away beneath a dense stand of pines where he dug a deep hole, grateful for his sharp claws and strong muscles that made it easier.

It took him a few hours to satisfy himself no one would stumble on the corpse, or notice a fight had taken place. Not that it should make much difference if they did find a wolf corpse, but if the girl brought searches here it was better to avoid questions.

No human man could dig beneath the pine branches like he could. His scent would discourage predators from digging up the corpse, but he painstakingly gathered rocks, and half dragged, half carried them in his jaws to lay atop the grave. He added some loose pine limbs and peed over the top. Not in desecration, but to embellish his scent to discourage predators.

Back in the clearing where they'd fought, he

gathered the bloody leaves with his teeth and stuffed them in the boy's sweatshirt. He wished he could shift back to human form to better gather the leaves, but the full moon still rode the sky, and he would be stuck a wolf until the moon set.

He shredded the boy's boots with his teeth and claws and slunk beneath a low-growing hemlock to bury them along with shirt-fulls of bloody leaves. Once he was satisfied only light traces of wolf blood remained, he snatched the shirt and jeans in his teeth.

The pants snagged on limbs and brush as he loped through the woods. He let them fall and continued to a small trickle of a brook he'd crossed earlier in the day to dump the sweatshirt. Tepid water barely reached his shins, and it took him ten minutes of rolling in the water to wash the blood from his fur.

He returned to the clearing and scattered fresh leaves before finally letting himself follow the tantalizing aroma of the girl. He doubted she would be able to send police to this exact spot, but even if they came, they'd find nothing except light traces of animal blood.

Head to the ground, he wrinkled his nose and inhaled deeply. The scent of fear hung heavy about her obscuring the earlier scent of her arousal. He tracked her through the woods and across a hay field. The cows in the next field lowed and scattered from him. He barely spared them a glance.

She'd run straight home. The lights in the

downstairs windows of the two-story farmhouse remained off. He didn't think it likely she'd told her father about the would-be rapist. The faint sound of running water drifted through the open windows when he circled the house, and he wondered if she showered. He circled the house three times before he was certain she had neither left again or shifted and killed her entire family and was snacking on the corpses.

Now he wasn't sure what to do. *Maybe the boy hadn't bitten her yet?* Maybe the delicious scent of her had drawn the boy, and she was safe. The chances of another wolf finding her were slim. As far as he knew, there were no packs in Minnesota. Sure, a rogue wolf, like the boy, could stumble across her, but the chances of that were small. Pack law forbade taking humans without their consent and the consent of your alpha. Only a feral would try it, and normally a feral kept away from pack territory.

Some wolves preferred to live alone, but they asked for permission to cross pack lands. A strong alpha could force a feral or unbonded wolf to become pack, and an alpha would kill to protect the unmated females in their packs. Ferals lacked the control to be around female wolves. Wolves without packs might be tempted to steal a female and force her to mate to start their own pack, which was why if you didn't want a pack to kill you, you told them you were coming.

Sharp branches caught in his coat again as he

wriggled beneath a coarse scrub brush in her backyard. He lay there until dawn lit the treetops. The house had remained quiet, and he was still perplexed as he headed back to the woods.

The cows again mooed and shuffled away from him when he leaped the fence. It was a simple matter to retrace his steps and find his clothes and pack, and it only took him a few seconds to resume his human shape. He grabbed the cell phone from his bag and made a call before he dressed.

Richard answered on the first ring.

"Mark, everything go okay?"

"I caught him, and took care of it, but there's a problem."

"He bit someone?"

"I don't know. He was with a girl, and I never smelled anything like her."

"When you say a girl, do you mean literally, or was she a woman?"

"I'd say fifteen or so."

"Fifteen?" Richard sounded puzzled now too. "And she didn't change? Were they having sex?"

"Kissing. I interrupted him. She didn't want him, and he was going to force her."

"Jesus, did she see you?" Richard sounded angry now.

Mark winced, half annoyed and half worried. The more he thought about this impossible girl, the more worried he became.

"Of course, she didn't see me! What do you take me for? The boy will disappear, and she'll be grateful to never see him again."

"Unless he bit her. Then she won't be so grateful. We lost him for over three years when he first ran away, and bodies only started showing up two years ago. Fifteen is old, but some girls mature late. He could have bitten her when he first ran and been waiting for the change. God knows it's what I would do."

"So, what do I do?"

"Make friends with her. Find out if he bit her, and if he did, bring her to us— before the next full moon."

"Sure, I'll just walk up to this kid and ask if she wants to be friends."

"Jesus, Mark, we don't have time for this shit. She changes without a pack, and she'll rampage. You want to have to track her down and kill her? Yeah, it'll suck for her if she was bitten and you have to kidnap her ass, but she'll understand, and she can go back and work something out with her parents when she's in control. You think she'll thank you if you let her kill them or some random stranger?"'

"Fuck, I know that…" Mark closed his eyes and rubbed the bridge of his nose hard.

The problem was her scent. She smelled so fucking good Mark was afraid he might bite her himself, and he sure as shit would bed her if she gave him a chance, and she was too damn young. In the pack, young girls who were about to hit puberty spent the full moon with their wolf parents far from anyone unless they'd already chosen a mate.

"Can you handle this?" Richard asked. "If she's turning, she can't mate."

"I fucking know that."

"Not just with a wolf, dumb ass."

"I know," Mark growled. The thought of her mating with a human boy rose his hackles. She was meant to be a wolf. She was meant to be his wolf. The thought shocked him speechless for a moment. When he next spoke, a growl laced his voice.

"What do I do if she does?"

"Does what? Changes or mates?"

"Both."

"Stay with her. I'll send—"

"No!"

Richard chuckled. "Bring her home first." He faltered and then said in a hesitant voice. "You're an old wolf, and I thought a confirmed bachelor. To pick a woman who doesn't even know of us… A mate is a lot of work at the best of times. They change your life in ways that can't be explained. She won't be like your human lovers."

"I get that. I'm not stupid. If she's going to change, she's mine."

"Look, Mark, don't do anything stupid. If she's going to change, bring her home, even if there's just a chance."

"She's mine," he growled again and snapped the phone closed.

He'd left his rental car a mile away in Moe's parking lot. The closest motel was twenty miles away. He took the room; he had no choice. He dumped his bag, taking only his cell phone and headed to the nearest high school.

Lurking outside the school proved harder than he'd thought it would be. He wasn't there five minutes before three teachers approached his car and asked his business. They left when he told them he had car trouble but stared from the doorway.

He finally resorted to laying a toolbox on the curb and crawling beneath the car. He smacked his head hard when she walked by in a gaggle of other girls. Her scent mingled with theirs but still pulled him like a magnet. From where he lay, he couldn't see her face just her worn white sneakers and equally worn jeans. He didn't know if it were a fashion statement or if she was just poor. Half the kids wore ratty clothes. All the girls she stood with wore jeans with holes in them and all except her wore tight tops. She wore a baggy pink sweatshirt with her long brown hair caught up in a ponytail. He wished she'd turn so he could see her face.

He growled and banged his head again as a group of boys stopped to talk to the girls. The girls laughed and flirted, tossing curled hair and batting made-up eyes. Somehow, he had a feeling she didn't wear makeup. He grinned at her shyness. She didn't join in the flirting, and he wondered how the boy had talked her into a kiss. She couldn't have known him long at all. His grin died, and a frown replaced it.

Or maybe she wasn't shy but traumatized from

last night.

She disappeared inside the building, and he crept out from beneath his car.

He slapped a sign on the front window, 'broken down went for a part please don't tow.' And jogged to the nearest diner. This was a hick town with few stores and fewer strangers.

The waitress asked his name and made small talk as if she knew every customer, *and she probably did*, he thought ruefully.

He'd need an excuse to be seen around town, something that the girl would believe. He pursed his lips and considered his flannel shirt and white t-shirt.

While he didn't look his true age by any stretch, he didn't look eighteen either. He glanced around the diner, and his frown deepened. He could pass for early twenties, but here, in this town, he'd be arrested for sure if they suspected he was after such a young girl.

"Fuck," he muttered and dropped a twenty on the table.

Four

It took him a week to find a reason to be near her. He'd debated trying to get a job at her school as a janitor or something, but people would notice if he singled out a student to talk with.

For that same reason, he gave up on the idea of hanging out where her friends did. Not that she hung out a lot. In the week he followed her, he learned her name was Kelly Anderson and that she spent two hours in the library and three at a mall with five girlfriends. The rest of her time she spent at home. She had a pony she spoiled to death, and it inspired him.

Three days later, Richard sent him a beautiful mare from the ranch. Used to wolves, the mare didn't sidle and prance like other horses did when he approached. Richard also sent him the name and address of a woman who'd died three months ago.

Mark bought the first house the realtor showed him that met his criteria, a fast sale and a cellar. Finding a used truck and a beat-up horse trailer was easy. Then he headed to Kelly's house and knocked on the front door bold as brass.

Her mother answered the door, and he took the opportunity to examine her. Tall, with long, dark hair and thickly lashed brown eyes like her daughter, the resemblance ended there. Kelly had inherited her father's high cheekbones and narrow chin. It was plain she'd grow into a beauty although she was gawky now, too thin and awkward in her skin.

Her mother smiled pleasantly enough, the smile brightening when he said why he came.

"Marge at the diner said you might be willing to rent me a stall for my mare, Marigold. I can pay a thousand a month, plus her feed and vet bills, but that'll have to include someone mucking her out for me. I can't get here every day. Marge says as how you might be willing to exercise her too. Not every day, like, but enough to keep her gentled if I'm busy with work."

"What work do you do, Mr. Miller?"

"I'm new to the area. My great aunt died and left me her house. I haven't been back in years, but it seems like fate that she'd pass when I'd just lost my job to cutbacks, so here I am. I've always wanted to try carpentry, and this feels like a good time while I settle my aunt's estate. I plan to buy a spread of my own one day, but meanwhile, Marigold needs a home."

"I'll have to talk it over with, John, but I'm sure he'll agree." She bit her lip and looked worried.

"We've got just the one pony, my daughter's horse. Does your mare get on with other horses?"

"She's a good girl; never had a problem before." Mark handed her the references Richard had sent.

Mark had never been to Tennessee, but he had no doubt if she called this number, the person who answered would sing his praises. He also didn't doubt that if she went to the address, there would be a farm with horses exactly like Marigold. When Richard made a cover, it was tight.

"Well then, if you'll leave your number, I'll get back to you."

Mark stiffened, the breeze bringing him Kelly's scent.

"Soon please," he said and had to clear his throat, he sounded so breathless. "I'm keeping her in my backyard right now, and I'm afraid the neighbors will complain."

Kelly's mother laughed, and her glance passed him. He was surprised by the frown that replaced her smile.

"You're late," she called and gave him a half-smile while shaking her head at her daughter. "Mister Miller has asked to board a horse and needs someone to clean and exercise her." Her frown disappeared as her daughter beamed at her, completely ignoring him.

Sweat trickled down his back and soaked his shirt as he stood there trying to appear disinterested.

"Really? That's great? I'll do it. Flit will love the company. Want to see the barn?"

Her voice was sweet and lower than he'd thought. Fear had risen her voice three octaves. The thought made him angry, and he clenched his hands hard and spoke rougher than he'd meant to.

"Honestly, any place will do for now. I need her out of my backyard pronto."

Kelly narrowed her eyes at him. Clearly a horse lover, his blithe disregard didn't sit well with her. Her mother smiled though.

"It isn't fancy, but it's clean and well-kept," she said. "You're welcome to take a quick look, but no promises until I talk to my husband."

"He'll agree though, won't he, Mom?" Kelly turned her excited brown eyes to him.

He caught his breath sharply and had to fake a cough to cover it.

"How long are you looking to board, Mister?"

"Call me Mark, and I'm not sure. Depends how my business goes."

Kelly was practically vibrating with eagerness. Her mother laughed and shooed her away.

"You can only ride her when he says you may. This isn't your horse," she called after her and shook her head. "As you can see, you'll have willing help."

Mark grinned, shook her hand, and then trotted after Kelly. Her pony ran to the fence when it saw her, but shook its head and sidled away when he approached.

"Flit is normally really friendly." A frown etched lines across her brow.

"Maybe it's my clothes." Mark held out his arm

and sniffed. "I was cleaning earlier, and I'm afraid I smell sort of bleachy."

She stepped closer and sniffed his arm.

"Maybe," she said doubtfully.

He frowned at her, and she nervously turned away. A faint but clear scent of wolf hung over her. She should be able to smell it on him. Standing this close to him, she should be able to tell what he had for lunch as easily as he knew her last meal was bacon and eggs with coffee. He hastily cleared his expression and gestured to the barn. "Looks good from here."

He watched her cross the gravel drive, taking in her slim hips and narrow ass. She had no curves to speak of. Her baggy sweatshirt made it hard to tell how big her breasts were. He knew they were small but she had them, or maybe she wore a padded bra.

"How old are you?" he asked when they entered the barn.

"Fifteen and a half but I'm real reliable. I'll take good care of her. We don't have a saddle or anything for a horse, but I know how to ride."

"I have everything I need for her. No riding until I say though."

She nodded so hard her hair flew into her face. It took effort to resist the urge to smooth it back. She pointed out the empty stalls and again tried to entice her pony to him.

"This looks great. I hope your parents agree," he said and forced himself to turn.

"I hope so too," she called after him.

Back in his new, old truck he'd bought for the worn look it had, he had to take several deep breaths to compose himself. He had twenty-eight days to decide what to do. He didn't need to ask her if she'd been bitten by a dog. His entire body knew she'd change soon. The question was, was it better to take her now, or lock her up on the full moon and let her change, then take her once she knew what she was.

"Fuck," he muttered and slammed his hand on the steering wheel.

The curtains twitched on the front window. So he grabbed his phone and pretended to talk a minute before driving away. Her mother would remember any weird things he did if her daughter went missing and sure as shit talking to himself was weird enough to get remembered.

He pulled into the first parking lot he passed and laid his head on his folded arms. If he took her, he'd have to stay behind for a few months at least. He was bound to be a suspect in her disappearance. She'd be without friends surrounded by young wolves eager to make her acquaintance. And even if she believed him, and took the news well, it would be traumatic and might empower her wolf, letting the wolf make decisions for her. But her reaction to him, or rather lack of reaction, proved she had no clue what was happening.

Puberty would hit her hard. Her first period would change her life, and by the looks of her, it would happen any day. He'd never heard of a woman bitten so far before puberty before. Normally, if a male werewolf tried to make a mate, the woman was already fully grown, and it seldom worked. Werewolf bites were toxic, and most died from it. That boy he'd chased had been trying to make mates and left a string of dead behind him; but say he bit her first, thinking her a woman and she wasn't yet?

He'd only heard of one girl bitten before puberty, and she'd lived but been feral for years. Her wolf had taken her hard and kept her, but she'd been bitten and become a wolf in the same month before the bite even had time to heal.

Damn it, I need to know when Kelly was bitten. He almost turned the car around.

"She'll think I'm a nut for sure." He smacked the steering wheel again and drove home to call Audrey.

Audrey answered on the first ring, sounding happy to hear from him, and he promised himself he'd call more often.

"Hey, Mark, Richard told me you might have found a live victim."

"She smells of wolf, and the boy was for sure one of us. But I swear she doesn't have a clue."

"I didn't either until that first change hit."

"You never sensed it?"

"No, but I had severe injuries."

"She doesn't smell of pain or wounds, she smells like spring air and sunshine."

"Got it bad, huh?" she said teasingly but with a

hint of worry.

"I really want her," Mark admitted.

"How old is she?"

"Fifteen."

"Jeez, Mark."

"I know."

He hesitated then asked, "If I bring her to the ranch, will her wolf roll her and force her?"

"Maybe. I wish I could say no, but maybe. In fact, it seems likely. The boys here will smell good to her wolf. The change will be traumatic. Hell, finding out we're real will be traumatic. Trauma will empower her wolf. We'll try to keep her from them, but if she's determined…."

Audrey was silent a moment. "I get you want her, but keeping her there is a bad idea. Sooner or later her menses will start, and when they do, that full moon is going to release an untrained wolf. She'll be scared, and her wolf will grab that fear and make her run. And then she'll be hungry, and the wolf will make her eat, and she won't care what."

"I know." He sighed hard and ran his hands through his hair. "I think I have a way to see her daily. Soon as I smell her, I'll get her away."

"That's quite a risk. What if she goes away a few days with a friend or on vacation or something?"

"She's mine," he said in a strangled voice.

"Be careful and at the first hint take her. Don't let the moon catch you off guard. I don't know how you'll manage this. The moon will be calling you too."

"I'll manage. I have to manage."

"I can't believe I'm going to say this, but if you just have to have her, bring her here and take her."

"I'm not a rapist." The fact that he considered it sickened him. He, of all people, knew how futile that was. If he wanted her, he'd have to make her love him.

"Isn't that better than letting her rampage? I assure you, I'd have rather been raped then kill my entire family."

"Oh, Audrey, I'm so sorry." He closed his eyes and rubbed his forehead, sorry he'd called and woken painful memories. "I swear, I won't let her."

"Should I come to you?"

He opened his mouth speechless. It took him a second to say, "Thank you, but no. I'll be fine."

He winced when she sobbed.

"Really. Stay there in the mountains, and I'm sorry I called."

"I would come."

"I know, but there's no need. I love you."

"I love you too," she said sadly.

He hung up the phone and almost cried. That Audrey had offered to leave her home floored him. He'd never expected her too. It hadn't even occurred to him, and he hated that he'd upset her peace. A hundred and twelve years after Richard had found her and brought her home and she still hadn't once left the ranch. The idea of seeing humans terrified her. That she'd offered humbled and worried him.

Of all people, she knew the full horror of

rampaging, but he'd never be able to bring himself to rape. The idea of it cramped his stomach. Wolves mated for life. Biology made it so. To have sex would bond them with an unbreakable bond that even death wouldn't ease. Their bodies would become one and having sex with another would be extremely painful.

He rose his hands to his head as if to block the screams he heard in memory and sank to the floor. He would never resort to that. The echoes of long-gone screams shivered his skin. His mother had hated his father so much she'd tried to take another mate, a wolf she'd loved, and she'd died trying, leaving him an orphan at thirteen.

Two packs had been decimated by his father's actions, and the hell of it was Mark knew his father had loved his mother. He'd been sorry, but she'd never forgiven him. No, Kelly would have a choice if it killed him, but he needed her to choose him. He jumped to his feet and headed to the hardware store. He had a cage to build.

Kelly's mother called him the next day. "Mister Miller, if you're agreeable to the terms we discussed, my husband says you can bring the mare today."

"Thank you so much. I really appreciate this, Mrs. Anderson. I can be there around three-thirty if that's okay."

"Call me Alice, and that's fine. You can come whenever you like between nine and seven. If you want to ride at night, or early, please arrange it first."

"No problem. Afternoons are good for me. See you at three."

He hung up and practically danced across the room before running back downstairs to finish his 'wine cellar.'

There was no chance his house wouldn't be searched if Kelly disappeared, willingly or not, so his cage needed to not look like a cage. Hopefully, when he was finished, it would appear to be a home theater with a small wine cellar and bar, the insulated walls and locked door completely explainable. He'd make a few friends and have a few parties, and he could keep her here for her first full moon. And once she knew what she was, they could decide what was best.

If she agreed, he could tie her in the woods or keep her caged here, but he hoped she would go to the ranch with him. If he had just a few months, he was sure he could charm her, and then, if her wolf rolled her, the wolf would want him, the familiar friend.

"That isn't rape," he told himself firmly. "Why not me if the wolf forces her?" His conscience had no answer or at least none that he liked.

He worked on his basement until two-thirty, then took a quick shower before loading Marigold into the horse trailer, and he couldn't contain his grin as he drove away. He made a mental note to send apology letters and beer to the neighbors, although none had complained.

"Get a grip," he muttered as he backed his truck down the long driveway.

He couldn't wait to see her.

Five

"What's got your panties in a twist," Abby asked as she slapped Kelly's jittering knee.

"We're getting a horse today."

"Really?" Abby's eyes widened and then narrowed. "Why the big secret?"

"He just came by yesterday, and my dad said this morning he could board her there."

"Ahh, a boarding horse. I thought you meant your own. Not that that's not cool," she added hurriedly.

"It's so cool. I know we can't afford one of our own, but I get to ride this one, and who knows, maybe we can board more, and then I will be able to get my own."

"I'd rather get a car," Abby said and returned her attention to her magazine.

Kelly grimaced at the beautiful woman in the skimpy, red bikini on the cover, and her hand dropped to the scar hidden by her jeans.

Abby caught the movement and frowned harder.

"Does it still hurt?"

"Aches sometimes."

"I hope whoever bought that damn dog got bit too."

"I'm lucky it didn't kill me."

Abby squeezed her hand and flipped the magazine closed. She was one of the few people who understood the extent of Kelly's terror.

"The scar looks lots better," Abby said.

"Pfft. It's an ugly mess, but who sees it?"

"Kell, it doesn't make you ugly. Boys will still like you."

"Sure, they'll drool all over my huge breasts."

Abby giggled and slapped a hand over her mouth, glancing guiltily at her generous curves. "Not every guy likes big ones," she said and laughed so hard at Kelly's disgruntled expression she grabbed her side.

"Sorry, Kell, some girls just develop later."

"Whatever."

Abby grabbed her book bag from the floor of the bus and rose as the bus turned onto her street.

"Good luck on the driving test," Kelly called after her.

"I don't need luck; I've got style," Abby said over her shoulder as she hurried down the aisle.

Kelly grinned after her and absently rubbed her thigh as she stared out the window. Her heart thumped hard when they reached her street. Marigold had arrived. Mark's black truck sat in the driveway with the horse trailer still attached. She ran to the barn, dropping her bag by the front steps as she passed.

The mare pranced in the paddock beside Flit who looked offended.

"Oh, she's beautiful."

"Mark," the man said and grinned at her. "My name is Mark, and this is Marigold. Let me show you her gear, and you can ride her on the lead."

Kelly grinned and jumped the fence. Flit whiffled warm horse breath over her hands, and she giggled as Marigold nudged her.

"Does she have a favorite snack?"

"I haven't noticed her have a preference for food. She's a bit of a beggar, so no more than three treats a day. She enjoys being brushed though."

The mare stepped daintily. Mark let Kelly take the mare's lead and peered over her shoulder as she checked Marigold's hooves. She watched enviously as he rode in slow circles around the paddock. He grinned at her and jump to the ground.

"Okay, your turn. Go slow though. Your parents will kill me if my horse hurts you."

"You won't, will you beautiful?" The horse lipped Kelly's hair and blew grassy breath in her face, making her laugh.

"In the paddock, only," Mark said gruffly when she swung into the saddle.

She kept to a sedate walk and kept a nervous eye on Mark who frowned at her.

"Promise you won't take her out of the paddock until I okay it. Marigold is gentle but still an animal."

"You can trust me. I'll take real good care of her." She slipped from the horse's back to feel its legs. She hated to admit it, but her leg twinged. The scar pulled. She'd have to work up slowly. She hadn't ridden since the attack.

"Did you hurt yourself?" he asked anxiously.

She dropped her hand and flushed.

"Nope. Well, not recently. I have a scar on my leg, and it hurts sometimes, but it's nothing to worry about." She gazed at him anxiously. She could tell he was worried she'd get hurt, and he'd get blamed, and she couldn't really blame him. Her mom would freak.

"Marigold has been pastured for a few months, so she'll need to be handled and eased back into trail rides. Let's take her for a walk and settle her in. You can take her out tomorrow but twenty minutes tops and stay in the paddock," she finished with him, making him laugh.

He lifted his hand as if he were going to ruffle her hair, but dropped it before touching her. The small gesture saddened her. She missed her sister.

He let her lead Marigold down to the crick behind the cow pasture and nodded approval when she made Marigold a deep bed of straw to sleep in.

"I'll drop by tomorrow to check her. Not that I don't trust you," he added hurriedly.

She headed back to the house after rushing through her chores.

"Well?" Her mother glanced up from the cutting

board where she was busily chopping carrots.

Kelly swiped one and poured herself a glass of milk. "She's beautiful, Mom. And real sweet. I'm sure Mark won't mind if you take a ride too."

"Mark, huh?"

"He said to call him that. Want to go see Marigold?"

"Tomorrow. Supper in an hour. And, Kelly, don't fall behind in your homework or chores, or the horse will have to go."

Kelly winced and ran the last few steps to her room. Her mom could suck the joy out of anything. Her constant corrections in the pursuit of the perfect daughter were getting old.

She did homework until dinner and felt bad for her earlier harsh thoughts when she got downstairs. Her mom had made her favorite, vegetable lasagna with extra crunchy garlic bread.

She cleaned the table afterward without being asked while her parents settled before the television.

"Night," she called as she headed back up the stairs.

"I'll be checking your homework in the morning," her mother called after her.

Kelly grimaced but said nothing even though she wanted to yell, I'm not Stacy. She passed Stacy's closed door and paused. Footsteps on the stairs hurried her to her room. She'd been forbidden to go into her sister's room or speak to her, and now she had something to lose. Her mother wasn't above using Marigold to ensure good behavior.

She showered and threw on old sweats and laid in bed staring at her ceiling wondering what had turned Stacy so crazy— drugs and boys and sneaking out at all hours until finally their parents kicked her out and told her to never come back. Stacy would be expecting her Thursday in the library. She didn't know how long she could keep sneaking her lunch money, but she couldn't let her sister starve.

How could their parents turn their backs on her?

Kelly agreed Stacy made bad choices but she was still family, and a small part of herself thought Stacy acting out might be her fault.

Stacy had begun sneaking out when Kelly was in the hospital and her parents busy. The pain pills Kelly brought home had disappeared. Stacy stole them to sell. A fact that both angered and worried her. Her leg hurt, but it hurt more that her sister didn't care and used her pain for profit.

When she finally fell asleep, she had nightmares all night. In her dreams, the brown wolf stalked her. The police had told her it was a German Shepard, but she knew it was a wolf. She felt it rip her flesh and drool on her face. Her dream self began screaming and kicking, knowing it was going to eat her. Her screams seemed to echo in the woods, and no hunters came this time. She jerked awake crying and lay awake until her alarm clock rang.

Her stomach and back hurt when she woke, but she didn't tell her mother, afraid she'd put the kibosh on riding Marigold later.

Mark was riding and waved a greeting when she got home. Flit greeted her as he always did and she was happy to see he wasn't running from Mark now. Marks' smile died as she drew closer, and Flit cantered to the far end of the paddock.

"You have got to be kidding me. I just can't catch a break," Mark muttered as he slid from the horse.

"What's wrong?"

He gave her a tight smile. "Nothing at all. I just remembered I left my, ahh, welder on. Can you bed her down for me tonight?"

"Sure."

He handed her the reins and vaulted the fence with effortless ease. She stared after him wistfully. Abby would swoon when she met him. Mark looked like a man from an old cigarette ad with his rolled t-shirt sleeves revealing tanned, muscular arms and a five-o'clock shadow barely darkening his cheeks. He was rugged, handsome, and sure of himself, comfortable in his jeans and cowboy hat, unlike half her classmates who wore their clothes like props.

Flit nudged her arm, and she turned back to the paddock, blushing. No way would a man like him be interested in a skinny girl like her. Abby maybe, she looked older than sixteen, and Mark was probably twenty-three or so not so old that he wouldn't date an eighteen-year-old.

Flit nudged her again and shook his head, clearly impatient for his dinner.

She laughed and hugged his neck, breathing deeply of his clean, horsey scent.

"You love me, don't you, boy?"

Flik snorted and lipped her hair.

"He's out of Abby's league too."

Flit bobbed his head as if agreeing, making her laugh.

Marigold snorted and strained to reach the bale of hay right outside the paddock. Kelly laughed again and went to feed the horses.

The next day after school, she met Stacy in the library like she did every Thursday. "You look like crap," her sister said as a greeting.

"I feel like crap," Kelly said but grinned at her sister and leaned closer. "I got my period last night."

"About fucking time. Mom should've brought you to the doctor years ago. I was starting to get seriously worried." Stacy ruffled her hair and gave her a hard hug. " Is everything, ahh, okay? Do you need anything?"

Kelly blushed and pretended to examine the book she held. "Nope. There's still supplies in the bathroom. I didn't tell Mom yet."

"Tell her before she sees blood, or she'll go on a rant."

"How are you doing?" Kelly glanced up from her book and eyed her sister uneasily.

In her opinion, her sister wore too much makeup, and it made her look old and tired. "You look tired."

"I was up late." Stacy bit her lip and wrung her hands together.

Kelly handed her the envelope containing her lunch money before she could ask. "Take it. I wish I had more. I don't know how you survive on this."

"I have friends," Stacy said, but she blushed and looked away.

"I'm sure they didn't mean it—"

"They meant it," Stacy said flatly and rose.

"You can't live on the street."

"I'm fine. Who needs them anyway. Don't you be stupid though. Keep your grades up and finish school. Get a good scholarship and a good job. Make enough to take care of yourself. Don't depend on any man."

"I'll make enough to take care of us both."

Stacy ruffled her hair again, but her eyes were sad. "I can take care of me. Me and Jamie are going to be heading to California. Ask Abby if I can write to you and send the letters to her."

"California?"

"The land of opportunity. I'll be a model and make millions."

Kelly hugged her sister hard. "Come home," she whispered knowing it would make her mad, but unable to stop herself."

"Catch you later, kid."

Stacy grabbed her huge, purple purse and sauntered from the library. Kelly felt like crying. She slumped in an empty seat in the magazine section and fanned her hot cheeks. This couldn't go on. *Her parents had to forgive her, they had too.*

"I saw Stacy today," she said as soon as her mother picked her up.

Her mother's lips tightened, but she didn't glance over.

"Mom, she needs help. Please, won't you please let her come home?"

"Did she say she wants to?"

Kelly bit her lip and shook her head. "But that's only because she thinks you don't want her. You still love her, don't you?"

"Kelly… it isn't that simple. And it's none of your business. Stacy and I have our own relationship and—"

"It is my business. She's my sister, and I love her. How can you just turn your back? She's starving to death for crying out loud."

Her mother sighed hard and pursed her lips into that tight, disapproving expression Kelly hated.

"She isn't starving. She's doing drugs. How would taking her in help? You want her to steal our television or Flit? She would you know. Why do you think we put in the alarm? Drugs make people crazy, and you can't help them until they want to be helped. I blame myself for not being harder on her when I first noticed. I should've cracked down the very first time I caught her in a lie. I won't make the same mistake again," she finished and gave Kelly a pointed glance.

"She took drugs. She didn't kill anyone. Can't you forgive her?"

"Your sister is a bad person. I'm sorry, but she is. She's a liar and a whore. God knows what drove her to it, but you can't believe a word she says."

Kelly stared unseeing out the window.

"I got my period," she finally said as they pulled into the driveway.

Her mother parked the car and sat staring at her hands clenching the staring wheel. "So, you're becoming a woman."

Kelly laughed bitterly. "It isn't a bad thing."

"It is if you become the kind of woman your sister did. Please don't break my heart like that. Your father and I really couldn't take it."

"I'm not a liar or a whore, and I never took drugs," Kelly said in a choked voice.

Her mother patted her hand. "I know. You're a good girl." She gave her a sickly smile and hurried from the car.

"Why can't you just love us?" Kelly asked as her mother ran into the house. Tears burned her eyes, and she rubbed them angrily. "She loves me," she whispered and began to cry.

She didn't notice Mark's angry frown.

Six

Mark stared after Kelly as she ran into the house crying. Something was wrong with her family, and it didn't take wolf senses to see it.

He groomed Marigold and released her into the paddock. He'd need time to shower and change. There was nothing he could do for Kelly anyway. She wouldn't believe him if he told her she would become a werewolf in three weeks; he'd have to force her to stay even if he transformed to prove it. His cage wasn't finished yet, and his cover wasn't in place.

She'd just have to be unhappy a few more weeks, he told himself firmly and drove away without looking back.

Moe's was busy, busier than he expected from its rundown condition. Country music blared from a jukebox in the corner, and men and women danced on the small dancefloor. A bar to the left of the door went the length of the room, and patrons sat and stood there two deep. Every table was full. Mark breathed in deeply. The air smelled of hard liquor and sex.

He ordered a beer and drank it while listening in on the conversations between the groups of women. His interest was piqued when one woman complained about night shifts, and another disagreed, saying she liked them. Lovers who worked nights were always his first choice.

He stepped closer and sniffed but it was hard to sort the scents, the people were packed so close.

The woman who liked night shifts was pudgy with a sweet face, and limp, dirty-blond hair pulled back in a tight ponytail. Her eyes widened when he smiled at her. She nervously smiled back and stared down at her drink.

"Can I buy you another?" he asked.

Her friends tittered. The woman next to her nudged her shoulder, then grinned at Mark. "She drinks strawberry margaritas."

He smiled and nodded his thanks, giving the woman a wink that made her blush, before pushing through the crowd at the bar to order a pitcher of strawberry margaritas.

The women made space for him at their table, and he offered the dirty-blond his hand.

"I'm Mark Miller."

"Jessie Adams."

"Nice to meet you, Jessie. I'm new in town. What's fun to do here?"

She gazed at him with wide eyes as if she'd never been spoken to at a bar before.

"Jessie likes fishing," her friend said.

Jessie gave the woman a puzzled glance, then smiled at Mark. "Lots of fishing around here," she said then bit her lip and took a big gulp of her drink. "Do you like fishing, Mark?"

"Sure. Maybe you could show me a good spot for walleye."

Jessie glanced at her friend again with desperate eyes.

Her friend said, "Oh sure, my husband and I fish for them all the time at Lake Andrew, but they don't start biting good for another month."

Mark grinned at her, surprised she knew fishing seasons. Jessie obviously had no clue, but she seemed game to try it.

"Trout is good." She flushed and took another big drink.

Mark took pity on her.

"I love trout. How about we see if we can catch a few and have a picnic?"

"I'm off Monday," Jessie said as if not believing he'd asked her. "I work nights," she blurted.

"Monday, it is." He took out his phone, gave her his number, and they poured over the tiny screen together, picking a spot to meet. Her drink relaxed her, or maybe it was her friend's cheerful teasing, but soon she talked comfortably with him and seemed disappointed when he rose two hours later.

"I had a good time and am looking forward to Monday." He wished he'd worn his cowboy hat so he could tip it. Her eyes burned into him as he sauntered out, and he heard them burst into laughter as the door closed. He grinned and tossed his keys into the air.

"Gotcha."

The next day, Kelly's mother yelled at her to come inside as soon as she stepped foot off the bus. When she showed up at the paddock, lines of strain bracketed her eyes, aging her five years.

"Everything okay," he asked lightly.

"Yeah."

She clearly didn't want to talk about it, so he dropped it and offered her the new curry comb he'd bought.

Her smile returned as she groomed Marigold, and he left her happily riding in small circles. He headed to the local gun range, shot a few rounds, and talked bows with some locals and got invited to a tourney shoot. He accepted and asked for fishing hole tips, telling them he had a date, and soon a group of men surrounded him, arguing over the most romantic fishing spots.

He called Jessie Saturday to confirm their date. She sounded nervous and excited, and he felt bad, but he promised himself he would treat her nicely.

It would be four dates tops, hardly enough to break her heart, he told himself forcefully as her eyes lit when she saw him beside the lake on Monday.

He baited her hook and tried not to laugh at her

inept casting.

She giggled when her line got caught for the second time in a tree twenty feet behind her.

"The fish are safe from you," he said and grinned at her as he restrung her line.

"Honestly, I haven't fished since I was a kid."

"Yeah, I got that." He winked at her and expertly casted his line. "We don't have to fish now either if you'd rather do something else."

"This is fun. I don't mind watching. You catch 'um, and I'll cook 'um."

"Are you a better cook than fisherman?"

She giggled and sat on the small fishing stool, examining the tackle as she spoke. "I'm a great cook. I worked at Dot's Dinner for three years, putting myself through nursing school. That's what I do now."

"I'm a carpenter." Mark told her the same bullshit story he'd told Kelly's mother.

Jessie was a good cook and good company. If he hadn't already met Kelly, she'd have made a fun companion, but he wouldn't date her. She was the type who wanted commitment. He chose lovers who had their eye on something different. Some were career women, some had gypsy souls, and some were just looking for a quick lay.

He didn't want to leave a heartbroken woman behind him, and Jessie was the heartbreak type. Guilt made his voice rough when he asked her to the movies for the next date.

He closed his eyes tight when he kissed her

goodbye, not wanting to see the hope in them, and felt like a shit for leaving her staring after him.

He spent his days finishing the basement and with Marigold, and his evenings at the range and the bar. He changed his mind a hundred times a day, reaching for his cell, then putting it back unopened. He knew he should call Richard and get someone else here, someone who wouldn't mind forcing Kelly to the ranch, but he couldn't make himself call.

His wolf wanted her so badly it left his hands shaking when he left her farm. Leaving her behind grew harder by the day, and it sickened him how much he wanted to run away with her. The conflict was tearing him up. He had no business being interested in such a young girl, and he couldn't deny he wanted her. In sudden decision, he grabbed his phone and called Leah. She could come, and he'd go far away, maybe become his wolf and live in the woods. The world didn't need another pedophile.

"Mark," Leah said, and he realized she'd said it twice already. Misery made all his reactions feel slow.

"Sorry, yeah, I'm here."

"Whats wrong?"

"Kelly will turn this month."

"You're sure?"

"Yes."

"Bring her home."

"I can't. She smells so fucking good, and if I bring her there… I just can't. God, Leah, what kind of sick fuck wants a fifteen-year-old girl?"

"She isn't a girl."

Mark growled.

"No, I mean it. She isn't a girl; she's a werewolf, and it isn't you that wants her, it's your inner wolf. You aren't a pervert. Think about it, Mark, what do you want to do with her?"

"Run," Mark said slowly.

"See?"

"I want to curl up with her and feel her breath. I want to hunt…"

"Exactly. It isn't sex you want."

"I want that too," Mark said in a strangled voice.

"As an abstract or are you lusting over her body?"

Mark opened his mouth, then snapped it closed. He slumped as a weight left his shoulders. "No, you're right. I picture us making love, but she isn't a kid in my dreams. She's a grown woman."

Leah laughed. "I shouldn't laugh. It's hard on wolves when they meet their mate and it happens instantly. It can be shocking, even overwhelming. Most expect to meet and fall in love like humans, and it happens that way too, but sometimes you just smell them and know, like Richard and I.

"Some try to talk themselves out of it. Sometimes, they don't like them, like your parents, or are in love with someone else, or, like you, they think their mate is too young or too old, but fighting your inner wolf is pointless. Relax and love her. I don't mean sexually, but let yourself fall in love. It might be harder than you think, the wolf loves her already but to love her for herself—"

"She's an amazing person."

Leah laughed quietly, the sound easing Mark's heart.

"I'm glad you've found her, Mark."

Mark closed his phone and clutched it to his chest; his heart soared. He could do this. He could love her without it being about sex. Much more cheerfully he headed to the bar.

He got three of his new friends to help him carry his new big screen television into his basement, and they hung around drinking beer and eating pizza afterward.

Men greeted him by name now when he entered the bar and gun club. His cover was in place and not a moment too soon. Friday was the full moon.

Kelly greeted him Thursday afternoon with an easy grin.

"You're in a good mood today," he said.

"Mom agreed to go see my sister."

"I didn't know you had one." His brow lifted in surprise. He'd never smelled anyone except them when he asked to use the bathroom.

"She left home a year ago." Red crept across her cheeks. "She got kicked out," she blurted.

"For what?"

"Drugs and stealing mostly. They fought all the time, and my parents are constantly on my back now. God, I hope she comes home." She turned sad eyes on the house.

"Does she like horses?" Mark asked to change the subject.

Her revelation troubled him. Her parents were going to lose another daughter, and this one loved them.

Seven

Mark glowered at his finished basement. He was going to break Kelly's heart. He'd never seen someone try so hard to get approval, and it didn't take wolf senses to see Alice's disapproval. He understood Alice's worry but couldn't understand how she missed her daughters fear of rejection. Kelly was terrified her mother would turn her back on her too.

And yet, despite her fear, she tried to help her sister. His girl was brave and loyal. She was going to be an amazing woman.

"A woman worth waiting for," he said and shook the decorative grill hard.

It barely rattled. Six, quarter-full cases of wine lay outside the cage stacked against the wall in their decorative wooden shelves. He'd practiced, and he could get the shelves behind the gate and the floating shelves on the wall with the liquor bottles and glasses repositioned in under three minutes. Right now, the eight-by-six space contained a bucket behind a sheet, bedding on the tile floor, and the sink for the wet bar.

He slapped the last piece of noise insulating foam against the windows and turned the surround speakers up as loud as they could go, then ran outside.

While standing on his rickety front porch, he could feel the vibrations but heard only the faintest sound as if a radio were on low in the house. From the street, even that faded. He had a tranquilizer gun, wolves could be fucking loud, but hoped he wouldn't have to use it.

The tricky part would be getting her here unseen. A glance at his watch showed he had less than eight hours to put his plan into effect.

Kelly greeted him with a grin that he returned, hoping she couldn't smell his nervous sweat.

"For you," he said and handed her the doctored orange soda." And for my girl." He handed her the bag of peppermints. "And Flit of course," he added as the pony trotted up.

He'd shamelessly bribed the pony, giving it so many treats it had put on weight, which he blamed on the grain he fed both Marigold and Flit.

She laughed and gave a candy to both horses.

"I can't stay. I just stopped by to tell you the vet will be coming Sunday to float her teeth. If Flit needs any work, or your dad's cows, it'll be cheaper to do it then."

"Maybe," she said doubtfully.

"Take her for a long ride today, and Saturday,

and I'll have the vet check her feet too."

She nodded eagerly, and his guilt ratcheted up a notch.

"I'll go ask your mom if she needs anything done."

She began to saddle Marigold. He kept an eye on her as he banged on the kitchen door. Alice answered the door wearing a worried expression.

"I have the vet coming Sunday to float Marigold's teeth, and thought, if you had work that needs doing, since I'm already paying the house call fee, it would be a good time."

She smiled and glanced at her daughter. He followed the glance and grinned as she took a big sip of soda, riding with one hand on the reins.

"That's kind of you. I'll ask my husband."

"Have him call and let the vet know if he needs to bring any supplies." He glanced at his watch. "Got to run. I've got a date."

She watched him get in his truck. He was careful to drive normally although his palms sweat and his entire being urged him to hurry. His wolf knew he was worried about Kelly and wanted out.

He parked his truck a mile away in Moe's parking lot and jogged down the street, then cut through the woods and began running as fast as he could. He was in the field behind her house six minutes after he left, and following her trail a minute after that. She'd already tumbled from the horse. And Marigold, being the friendly sort, munched bushes nearby.

The horse whickered in greeting and didn't try to run when he grabbed her reins. He threw Kelly over the saddle and lead the horse at a jog down the trail. He'd already picked out a good place to tangle the reins. Marigold should be content there for a while browsing the shrubbery before even trying to pull away. He dropped a peppermint for her, grabbed Kelly, and ran.

His heart thundered in his chest. This was the first time he'd really touched her, and both he and his wolf were almost overwhelmed. Veins strained in his neck and arms he was forcing his wolf back so hard. She'd hurt herself in the fall. Blood trickled from a gash on her forehead but her pulse was steady, and the change would fix her right up. The thought didn't reassure his wolf at all. It wanted to sniff her and lick her wounds.

He reached the edge of the forest and hesitated. He didn't want to put her down. His soul cried out for him to run with her. But if he let his wolf have its way, he'd take her with or without her consent, and she was too young to make that sort of decision anyway. He ruthlessly slapped down his wolf and concentrated.

This was the tricky part of his plan. He had no idea how long she'd be out, and he'd debated tying her and then going for the truck, but he'd never be able to explain her tied body. So, he laid her beneath the bushes right off the road and ran back for his truck.

Every second it took to circle around felt like a

year. Mark's wolf fought him hard, making him stagger and fall repeatedly as it tried to force him to change. And the wolf was strong. A new moon loomed, and it knew. Sharp pains made him grimace. It felt as if his wolf tried to claw its way from his chest.

The cab of his truck felt stifling, and it took effort to drive the speed limit. Every atom of his body urged him to run; his wolf knew he'd left their mate alone, hurt, and defenseless, and clawed beneath his skin for release until he whimpered with the pain of it.

His heart pounded so hard by the time he reached her, he thought he might faint and had to take a few deep breaths to calm down. Traffic was slow on this road, and he didn't have to wait to throw her on the floor of his truck. His inner wolf calmed as soon as he picked her up. It didn't relax completely, but he was able to drive with some semblance of calmness. A mixture of excitement and dread made him giddy.

She began to stir before he reached his house and he longed to go faster but couldn't risk a ticket. By the time he reached his garage, she was moaning.

"Sorry," he said as he crammed her into the refrigerator box to bring her inside.

"Mark." Her voice was weak, but she knew him when he took her from the box a minute later.

"You're okay. You had a spill from the horse."

"I got dizzy," she mumbled and moaned. "I

think I'm going to be sick."

"I'm so sorry."

She didn't seem to realize where she was, and she wasn't alarmed. His wolf rejoiced, and he almost sagged in relief when the pressure eased. He carried her down the stairs and laid her on the blankets.

"Don't be scared. I swear to God I won't hurt you."

"What?" She opened her eyes and glanced around while grabbing her head. Her eyes widened, and she pushed away from him.

"Where am I? What is this?"

"I'm sorry, sweetheart, but I had too. Tonight is the full moon, and I couldn't—" His cell rang, and he growled in frustration.

"I'll be back to let you out. Nothing bad is going to happen. This is for your own protection. Don't bother screaming or trying to break free. I really don't want you to hurt yourself."

He winced as panic filled her eyes. A sour odor of fear bloomed, and his wolf went berserk. It felt as if his soul was trying to flee his skin. He groaned and grabbed his head, staggering under the ferociousness of his wolf's attempts to get free. To her, this was a massive betrayal and terrifying. She watched with terrified eyes as he strained against his wolf. Never before had he pitted his will against his inner wolf so hard.

To his relief, the wolf subsided quickly, but he felt its impatience. It would try again, he was sure of that. She must think him a crazy man, but he had no time to explain. He made sure the door was latched before he ran up the stairs to answer his phone.

It was her father, as he'd known it would be. He'd hoped it would take longer for Marigold to wander back but this would work too.

"Did Kelly say where she would be riding today?" John asked as soon as he answered.

"The lower trail I think. She planned to go for a long ride. The vet—"

"Your horse came back without her."

"I'll be right there. Did you call the police?"

"Yes, and they're sending men to search."

"I'm so sorry—"

"Not your fault. That's a nice horse, but even nice horses spook if they see a dog or something."

The fear in John's voice made Mark's guilt worse. John's daughter had been attacked once in the woods, and that memory must haunt him.

John hung up without saying goodbye. Mark ran back downstairs. Kelly backed away from the gate and rose her bloody hands to her face, her wide, terrified eyes locked on him, and his heart constricted.

"Stop," he moaned as he crashed to his knees when he scented her fresh blood. He knew his contortions as he fought his wolf must be scaring her, but he couldn't afford to change.

He finally pushed his wolf back enough to rise panting to his feet. "I'm so sorry I'm scaring you.

You're going to think I'm crazy, and I wish I could stay to help you, but I can't. Your parents think you're lost in the woods. Marigold returned without you, and they'll be searching. Tomorrow, you can return and tell them you fell and knocked yourself out and got lost or something."

He wasn't sure she heard him. Her breath came so fast he thought she might hyperventilate and pass out.

"Okay, this is the hard to believe part. You're a werewolf." He smiled when puzzlement replaced fear. The smile was a mistake. Her slow tears turned to a torrent.

"I know it sounds crazy, but tonight you'll change for the first time, and it can be dangerous, so I locked you up. We can talk more when I get back, and I'll answer all your questions but I need to go, or they'll come here looking for you." He opened the small refrigerator right outside the gate and dropped the quick-charred steaks into the cage.

She stared at him like he was crazy now, but her eyes held a tinge of hope.

"I'll let you out first thing in the morning, I promise. Hell, maybe I'm wrong, and you're a normal girl," he added, not because he believed it for a second, but to let her have hope he wasn't going to keep her, that he was a harmless nut.

He ran back up the stairs and locked that door too. In his car, he called his date. She answered on the fifth ring like always, and he wondered, as he had before, if she did that to all men so she wouldn't appear eager.

"Hey," she said cheerfully.

"Sorry, Jess, I have to cancel. The kid where I board my horse took her for a ride and the horse came back alone. I'm going to go help search."

"I'll come help."

"Only if you can be ready by the time I pass your place."

"I'll be ready."

He slapped the phone shut both proud and ashamed of himself.

Jessie was waiting in jeans and a flannel shirt, carrying two flashlights and a first aid kit when he pulled in.

"How old is she?" she asked as she strapped her seatbelt.

"Fourteen or so. Kelly's a nice girl. God, I hope Marigold didn't kill her."

"It isn't your fault." Jessie squeezed his knee.

He said nothing. When he arrived at Kelly's house, police cars and an ambulance lined the drive. Red and blue light lit the darkening sky and glittered on Alice's tears.

Volunteers had arrived behind him. He was surprised at the quick turnout. Alice grabbed his shirt the second he stepped into the yard and burst into tears. "Marigold came back alone, and I knew something bad happened. She would be back by now if she weren't badly hurt. The police found blood on the saddle. Dear God, this can't be happening. Do you think it was dogs again?"

He patted her shoulder, not knowing what to say. To his surprise, Jessie took her arm. "She probably hit her head on a branch. We'll find her. Don't you go worrying about dogs. The dog warden hunted and set traps. There are no more feral dogs around here."

An older woman arrived and made tsking noises as she led Kelly's mother away.

Jessie watched her leave with sad eyes. "That poor woman. I didn't want to say it, but if Kelly hit her head hard enough to knock herself out, it might have killed her."

"I've taken hard knocks, and they make you sick. She might just be laying there miserable."

Jessie patted his arm and handed him a flashlight. "It isn't that cold out. So, there's that at least."

The hiked for hours calling for Kelly. In the distance, flashlights waved, and others called for Kelly, and he felt like a shit. All these people were really concerned. It was after ten when he brought Jessie back to his truck. Volunteers milled in the yard, handing out coffee and fresh batteries, comparing notes, and offering encouragement to her mother who stood frozen on her front porch.

Mark counted quickly and it looked like half her high school had shown up. They headed into the woods in pairs of three as he watched. The moon hung low in the sky and called him hard. He couldn't hold it off much longer.

"Thanks for coming out. Sorry I wrecked our

date," he said as he pulled Jessie to his truck.

"Hey. Don't be crazy. I get it, and I'm willing to stay and keep looking.

"I'll call you in the morning, or sooner if I hear anything, but it's silly to keep looking when we can't see a thing. I'll come back at dawn with fresh eyes."

"Makes sense. There's enough people here searching. We must have walked right past her." She shivered and pulled her flannel shirt tighter. He gave her a quick hug and kissed her cheek. They said nothing as he drove her home.

"You could come in," she offered hesitantly when he pulled up before her house.

"Thanks, but I need to catch some zs if I'm going to be awake at dawn."

She nodded and hopped from the truck. Mark knew he should escort her to the door or kiss her goodnight, but his skin felt like it was going to crawl from his body. He waved and floored it. All the police were busy; he sped all the way home.

Eight

Downstairs, in the cage, a gray wolf crouched trembling in the corner. Clothing was scattered across the floor of the cage. He wanted to speak to her and offer reassurance, but the moon called him hard. He shifted before he had time to strip, something he hadn't done in over a hundred years.

A howl burst from his lips, and he crashed hard against the bars before he regained control. His wolf wanted her fiercely.

Her teeth showed in a soundless snarl, and she crouched with her forepaws spaced far apart and her rump in the air. She was ready to fight him but scared to death. A puddle of urine grew beneath her, and she whined, then snarled and snapped at him.

It took him a few minutes of contortions to rip off his shirt. His pants and boots he just stepped out of.

He circled three times and lay with his head on his forepaws with his eyes half closed, trying to say by body language he was no threat. Neither of them moved for two hours.

The sour smell of fear was so strong he thought she probably couldn't smell his desire. He didn't even let his ears flick when she inched towards the meat, but he couldn't help jerking in shock when she became a girl again and yanked on the door. She flickered back to a wolf so fast he didn't actually see it happen. Again, she was a girl, then a wolf, then a girl. The changes happened so fast they dizzied him.

As a girl, she sobbed and pulled at the bars, her terrified gaze locked on him. A shiver traveled her, and she screamed as she fell to the floor, panting hard. This transition he saw. It took about thirty seconds like his did. He realized he'd backed away and now crouched beside the couch.

She'd so amazed him, he hadn't realized he'd moved. He didn't know any wolf that could break the call of the full moon. Hold it off, sure, but once the wolf was out, it wouldn't go back until the full moon set.

On her stomach, she crawled into the corner and stared at him from golden eyes. She was a beautiful shade of silvery-gray except for one white sock on her rear, left leg and a few wisps on the tip of her tail.

Small and delicate, she had a puppyish-air with feet and ears too big for her frame. His wolf wanted to rub against her and nip her neck. He closed his eyes and breathed deeply of her scent. Every flick of his tail or twitch of his ear made her snarl.

He resumed his human shape the instant the moon lost its hold on him. The sun hadn't quite risen, but the moon had set. To spare her embarrassment, he dressed with his back turned and then sat cross-legged before her.

"See, I'm not crazy. I know you're wondering if I did this to you somehow, but I swear I didn't. I'm not sure who did, but I think it was that boy in the woods. He was a wolf I'd been tracking because he'd gone feral and was trying to make a mate. I came across you and knew what you would become."

She remained motionless before him.

"You're lucky I did," he continued. "Feral wolves are dangerous. You should eat. Denying the wolf within can make us crazy. The wolf can take over and force us. A feral wolf will kill and eat a person. You can smell me and know I'm telling the truth. A liar will sweat and smell nervous. I'll know if you tell the truth too. I'm going to ask you to keep us secret, and if you lie, I'll know. If you won't keep our secret, we'll try to keep you away from humans, but if that doesn't work, you'll be killed."

She whined and backed further into the corner. Her claws rattled against the tile floor, and she stamped her feet but couldn't stop her trembling. Her fear hurt him and infuriated his wolf. He had to breathe hard a second to calm himself before he did anything stupid.

"I know it sounds harsh, but it's the only way for

us to be safe. But you can return to your life once you know how to be a wolf. I'd like you to come with me to my home, but you don't have to. I'd really feel much better if you'd eat. There are no drugs in it if you're worried about that. You should be able to smell tampering if you try.

"God, this must be so scary and confusing. I was born a wolf, and I'm almost a hundred and fifty-years-old. We live a long time. The healing thing is true. So is the silver thing. Never try to wear silver jewelry and metal will remain when you change so make sure to never wear tight necklaces.

She sneezed, licked her lips, and the roof of her mouth as if she'd eaten peanut butter, then shook her head hard.

"Fillings fell out? It's nothing to worry about. All your teeth will be perfect. You're perfect," he said softly.

She snarled and stalked to the steaks on the floor, grabbed one, and scuttled backward growling. A thick meaty smell rose into the air and made his stomach rumble. His wolf was hungry too. She grabbed the steak awkwardly with her forepaws and ate ravenously.

He wasn't sure how aware she was. Sometimes, the newly turned didn't understand human speech while in wolf form. On rare occasions, wolves lost humans speech completely while in wolf form and never understood it while a wolf. On even rarer ones, the human stayed trapped in wolf form. It was much more common to choose to be the wolf and let your humanness go.

He wasn't worried about her being trapped, and she seemed to understand him. She finished both steaks and lay on her stomach, resting her head on her paws.

He glanced at his watch. The soft light of sunrise would be gilding the trees. He wished he could take her for a run and let her enjoy being the wolf, but he didn't have time.

"See if you can change back."

She continued to lick her paws as if she hadn't heard him.

"Kelly," he said sharply, and she jerked and hunkered, growling.

"Try to change back so we can talk."

She straightened from her hunker and paced before the bars a moment before turning her back on him.

"Do you want privacy?"

Her ears flickered, but she didn't move.

"I'll be back in five minutes."

At the top of the stairs, he paused and glanced back, but she hadn't moved. He raided his refrigerator and ate three pounds of cold cuts before his wolf was sated. He took a quick shower, he stank of rut to himself, and threw on clean jeans, a blue t-shirt, and a plaid flannel. When he returned downstairs, Kelly whirled from the sink, clutching her ripped shirt closed. Water dripped from her chin and sparkled in her hair.

"Will you keep this secret?"

Her gaze flicked around the room, and she nodded.

"Do you forgive me? I'm sorry I had to do this, I really am."

He couldn't help his small smile when she cocked her head and took a deep sniff.

"See? I'm telling the truth. Your nose will be bringing you lots of new information, and you'll hear and see better. It can be confusing and hard to manage at first. I'm here to help you."

"I want to go home." She clutched the bars with both hands and stared at him hopefully.

"You can, but you'll have to lie."

"My scar is gone. My mother is bound to notice."

"Which is why you shouldn't go back. Lying is hard. Come with me, and you can be yourself. In a year or two, you could come back—"

"They'd never forgive me. If I go, I can never come back. I have to go home," she finished. Panic laced her voice.

"What will you tell them?"

"That I fell and knocked myself out."

"You don't have a mark on you." He held up his hand as she opened her mouth. "I'm not trying to force you. We could make a mark. You'll heal fast, so it will need to be done right before you get home and maybe again if they bring you to a doctor. Can you see how hard lying will be?"

"Please, let me go home."

He unlocked the door and stepped back. "I'll

drop you off. Run through the woods towards the Carston's place—"

She rubbed her wrist, then clutched her ripped shirt closed again. "That's nowhere near where I fell."

"I know. Say you were headed for the reservoir, that I asked you to take a long ride and when you crossed the road, the horse spooked at a motorcycle. You hit your head and fell, and got lost trying to take a shortcut through the woods and waited for daylight. There was blood on the saddle, so make a small scratch in your hair with a stick so it will be hard to examine, and roll around in the leaves to get some dirt and twigs in your hair. I'm going to be at your house, and I'll come whenever I can, but they might make me go now."

Tears sprang to her eyes. He longed to hug her but didn't dare.

"I want to hug you, but our wolves are too close to the surface. No touching for us, okay?"

"You'll let me go?"

"Everything I've said is true." He gestured to the door. "I'll sneak you back. Are you willing to lie to them?"

"I'll lie. I promise."

Her terror hurt. He didn't know if it was becoming a wolf or fear of him, but she reeked of fear. The smell of fear was so strong he had no idea if she lied or not, but he figured her fear would keep her silent, at least at first, and he could ask again when she was calmer.

"I believe you. You don't need to be so scared. Call me whenever you want, and if you change your mind, I'll take you away. You should meet the pack. If you let yourself, you'd enjoy your wolf. Running through the woods in the starlight is magical."

Magical." She snorted derisively. Then her eyes widened, and she peered around as if she expected monsters to leap out at her. "Are there vampires too?"

"A few. None around here though. They prefer big cities, and they're nothing like the books say. I'll tell you about them sometime, but we should get going."

She lay quietly on the floor of his truck. The sharp scent of terror eased. She was still afraid, but no longer terrified. He dropped her off and watched her run into the woods. His wolf raged within him, and he struggled to hold it back. The wolf wanted to go with its mate.

A younger wolf wouldn't have been able to hold back, and for once he was glad he was so much older than she. He drove slowly to her house, having to stop twice to force his wolf back down. He didn't know if seeing her would be worse or settle the wolf but he had no choice. It would be suspicious as hell if he didn't show to search.

Nine

Kelly cast a terrified glance behind her, but Mark hadn't followed. Half-rotting leaves left their pungent scent in the air as she slid to her knees and began crying. She glanced behind her again, but no one was there.

"He won't kill me," she whined continuously as she rolled in the leaves.

Still crying, she pushed herself to her feet and ran. She stopped after taking a few strides and dropped on all fours to the forest floor. The heady aroma of moist earth and live trees called to her. She felt as if she could run forever— she longed to run forever.

"Oh, God, how did he do this?"

She lifted a trembling hand to her face and examined her normal looking hand a moment before fumbling with her jeans to lower them and examine her now scar-free leg. The skin felt soft and smooth under her hand, and she smelt her own piss and fear on her clothing.

This must be a dream, she told herself desperately, but she felt clear headed. The rough bark of the tree felt real on her hands and lips.

She shrieked, "This can't be real!" and scratched at the tree until her fingers bled. Sobs convulsed her on the ground. Her hard pants brought her scents she'd never smelled before, and her skin felt sensitive as if she could taste the wind on it. Trembling badly, she rose and wiped her face on her torn shirt.

"He won't kill me. He let me go." The sound of her own voice terrified her. It sounded louder and richer, she could almost hear thoughts in it.

"He'll kill them though."

She scrambled to her feet and began running again. She only remembered she needed a wound when she reached the Carston's backyard. Her hands shook so hard she dropped the twig she picked up three times before she could scratch herself hard enough to produce blood.

She'd cut deeper than she'd intended, not yet used to her new strength. Blood dribbled down her neck, the smell making her hungry. Nausea roiled her stomach and doubled her over to vomit. In the house, a dog began barking. She forced herself to bang on the door.

"Dear God, Kelly! Are you okay?" Mrs. Carston asked as she threw open the door.

A small brown dog bounded out, and Kelly shrieked and cowered.

"Get back, pest. Henry!" Mrs. Carston called as

she put her arm around Kelly and kicked the dog away with her foot. Kelly was crying and clinging to her. So many scents and sensations crashed over her, it left her dizzy and weak.

She turned to peer over her shoulder as Mrs. Carston led her inside and saw no one. He would be busy, this was her chance, but she'd believed it when he'd said he'd kill to keep his secret.

"Henry!" Mrs. Carston called again and grabbed a towel hanging from the stove that she wet and placed against Kelly's head. "Hold that right there, sweetie." She ran to the phone and began dialing.

"Please call my mother."

"I am, sweetie. You need an ambulance –" she cut off mid-word as her husband, Henry, ran into the room. She handed him the phone and crouched before Kelly to gently dab at the blood on her face.

Henry spoke into the phone, telling whoever was on the other end to send an ambulance and giving his address. He dialed again when he hung up.

"Kelly is here," he said and gave her a kind smile. "She's hurt, but I think she'll be okay."

"Can I talk to my mother, please?"

"Sure, sweetie." Mrs. Carston patted her knee and held out her hand for the phone.

Kelly grabbed the phone in her trembling hands and could barely speak past the lump in her throat. "Mom, please come get me."

"Kelly, thank God. Are you okay?"

"No. Please come get me." The little brown dog

jumped on her knee, and she screamed and tried to back away, knocking the chair to the floor and dropping the phone. "Please, Mom," she called and began to sob.

Mrs. Carston grabbed the phone and the dog.

"Sorry, our dog scared her," Mrs. Carston said.

Kelly collapsed against the table crying. "I thought he would eat me. I thought he would eat me. I hate them. I hate them. Oh God." She cried and moaned not really knowing what she was saying until someone put a cold, wet towel on her face. When she looked up, a policeman leaned over her.

"That's right, catch your breath. You took quite a hit, young lady. Can you tell me what happened?"

Kelly rubbed her face on her dirty shirt, avoiding their stares. "I fell from my horse. From Marigold, she isn't my horse."

It's okay, sweetie, you're safe now." Mrs. Carston glared at the officer and hugged Kelly. She smelled of peach shampoo and garlic with a hint of tomato and cigars. Kelly breathed deeper and shuddered hard.

It shouldn't be possible to smell these scents so clearly.

"How did you end up over here?" the officer asked.

"Marigold spooked crossing the road to the rez. A motorcycle passed us, and I fell. I think I passed out because I don't remember her leaving, but she was gone when I opened my eyes."

The officer tipped her head to the side and frowned at the blood in her hair. "This looks fresh."

"I fell again outside. Please, can I go home?"

"Yes." The officer offered his hand to help her rise. Henry handed his wife a blanket that she wrapped around Kelly's shoulders.

"She's shaking. She needs a doctor," Mrs. Carston said.

"We'll take care of her. I'll be back to speak with you." The officer led Kelly from the house to his squad car. She wrinkled her nose at the odors emanating from the back seat but slid in.

"So, what happened when you got up?" the officer asked as he started the car.

Kelly pulled the blanket to her face and breathed deep, hiding her face in the lavender scented folds. "I ran home, taking the shortcut, but it got dark out, and there were dogs." Her breath caught, and her trembling escalated. "I was afraid they would find me, so I hid. I hate them," she said and began to cry again.

She was what she hated. She wanted to beg the officer for help, but Mark hadn't been lying, not about anything. He would kill her if she told, she was sure of it. She swallowed hard, trying not to vomit.

"Are you going to be sick," the officer asked as he pulled his car over. He didn't wait for an answer, yanking her door open so she could scramble out and vomit on the side of the road. He helped her back into the car and covered her with the blanket.

Back in the front seat, he spoke on the radio, but she didn't understand his codes.

"Looks like lots of volunteers are still here," he said as they turned onto her street.

Cars lined the road and people milled about her front yard. "Go right inside. No one will stop you, and I'll clear them out."

She nodded woodenly. Her face flamed from her embarrassment. Half her school was there. A news van almost blocked her driveway. The woman reporter shouted after her, but the officer blocked her advance. Kelly's parents waited on the porch and rushed to her when she stepped from the back seat.

She started crying and glanced around. Mark stood alone at the back of the crowd. His worried gaze followed her, lingering on her parents. Kelly licked her lips and yanked her mother inside the house, ignoring the paramedic who reached for her.

"I had an accident is all," she said loudly, hoping Mark would hear her and believe she was going to keep their secret.

"We're going to the hospital," her mother said.

"She got lost trying to find her way back. She wasn't riding here but by the reservoir," the officer said loudly. "Thank you all for coming, and I'm sure we're all glad she made it home." The crowd began breaking up, talking excitedly amongst themselves.

The officer kept them from approaching. Another officer joined him.

"Let's leave them in peace," he said and tried to

shoo the news van away. "It was a traumatic experience, and Kelly should get her head wound checked."

Kelly's face burned as the reporter continued to yell questions.

Her mother glared at the reporter and headed to the ambulance, dragging Kelly with her.

"I don't need a doctor. Please, Mom, can we just go inside?"

"Honey, you're covered with blood. We're getting you checked out."

Mark pushed through the crowd and rose his hand as if he was going to lift her hair. She flinched away, and he dropped his hand.

"Jeez, Kelly," he said in a mix of exasperation and worry.

Her mother glared at him. "I want that horse off my property by the time I get back."

"Mom, it wasn't Marigold's fault," Kelly said as Mark said, "Yes ma'am."

"I'm sorry, Kelly. I really am," he added and she knew he meant it.

"She's a nice horse, Mom. It was my fault for crossing the road without looking."

"You're all over blood," her mother said, and her glare deepened when she pulled the blanket away to examine her daughter, revealing her ripped shirt.

"Mark didn't do anything wrong," Kelly said quickly when her mother turned her hard glare on him.

Mark held up his hands and made a placating

gesture. "I'll remove Marigold."

"And stay away from my daughter."

"Mom," Kelly hissed as the people around them began to mutter. "You're making a scene." She climbed into the ambulance, hoping her mother would follow and forget Mark.

The paramedic prodded at her head. "Head wounds bleed a lot. Looks like you banged it more than twice."

"I did. Dogs scare me, and I heard one and panicked and ran myself into a tree. It started to bleed again."

"Well, you don't appear concussed"— he continued to shine a light in her eyes— "they might want a scan to be sure though. Are you dizzy or nauseous?"

"I threw up, but it was from the Carston's dog."

Her father took her hand. "That little thing?" he said in a teasing voice, but his eyes were sad and worried.

"I heard dogs last night, Dad. God, I was so scared." She began to cry again and huddled into her father's embrace. He stroked the unmated side of her head. Her mother held her hand and didn't want to release it when they reached the hospital.

Kelly refused to put on the robe, but let the doctor check her wound. He pronounced her well enough to go home and prescribed Tylenol and a hot shower.

Kelly was relieved no one remained in their yard when they returned.

"I'm never going to live this down," she muttered, making her father laugh.

"Don't worry about it. It'll blow over soon. We're just glad you're okay. I'll admit I worried about dogs too when I saw the blood on your saddle."

"I worried about Mark." Her mother glanced over her shoulder at her. "If he hurt you, or threatened you, we can protect you from him."

Kelly closed her eyes and leaned her head back on the seat. "Mark didn't do a thing to me. It isn't his fault his horse spooked. Animals have instincts. It's my fault for not being more careful."

She knew she should beg for Marigold to be allowed to stay, but she didn't want to see Mark again either.

Her mother said nothing. She exited the car and strode into the house.

"You'll be fine, kiddo," her father said as he opened her door. "She's upset but not with you. We were really worried."

"I'm sorry, Dad," Kelly said sincerely.

She rubbed her eyes as tears began to trickle down her cheeks.

"It isn't your fault dogs scare you. Go shower and take a nap, and I'll make pancakes for dinner when I get in from the barn."

She smiled wanly at him and headed for the door. At the foot of the stairs, she hesitated and glanced around. The hair on her arms rose. A hint of wolf came to her on the breeze. She knew she could follow the hint to the source. Somewhere close, Mark waited. She shuddered and ran upstairs to shower. She wanted nothing to do with him.

Ten

Kell," her sister said as she hugged her. She stepped back and gently ruffled her hair. "I was worried, and they wouldn't talk to me. You seem normal." Her sister quirked an eyebrow and examined her with her lips pursed and head cocked as if she expected something different. "Are you okay?"

"Fine. Embarrassed." Kelly sniffed, then hugged her sister again to sniff her neck. She smelled odd, chemically and dirty as if she hadn't showered in a week. Male scents lingered on her skin and hair. A heavy floral odor couldn't cover the smell of male musk. Kelly pushed away and tried to smile.

Stacy picked up a book from the shelf beside her and smoothed the cover.

Kelly's pulse began to pound when she spied the werewolf.

Her sister gave her an indecipherable glance and held out the book.

"I always believed there was more to this world,

that magic, witches and vampires exsisted. I needed there to be more... I wished I could be more. It's why I started using, it opens your mind but it's so deadly. Never do it, Kell. There has to be a better way."

Tense silence settled between them and Kelly hoped it was just her who felt the weirdness. Her sister couldn't know, she told herself firmly and tried to look bored.

Stacy fussed with the book then glanced at Kelly again and scowled. "But these are just stories, and I'm stuck in this shithole town." She slapped the book closed and threw it on the seat beside her. "I'm getting out of here one way or another though."

Kelly offered her a sickly smile. Her glance flitted to the non-fiction section where she knew Mark lurked. She'd smelt him when she'd come in, but he hadn't approached.

"I bet you were embaressed," her sister said, drawing her attention back. She bit her lip and leaned closer. "You know, you can tell me anything. I'm in your corner no matter what. If something, um, bad happened to you, and you don't want our parents to find out, I can help you."

"There's nothing to tell. Nothing happened except Marigold threw me, and I cried like a baby all night afraid the dog I'd heard would find me."

Stacy tapped her lips with a finger a moment before giving her an insincere smile and saying, "Where's your shadow today?"

Kelly started guilty, and her gaze again went to

the non-fiction shelves.

Stacy turned and pursed her lips. "She doesn't need to spy."

"Abby isn't here." She took her sister's hand and pulled her to the periodical alcove where she sat in one of the hard swivel seats before the magazine racks.

Stacy thumped into a chair beside her and picked up a magazine from the table. Her eyes narrowed as she flipped the pages. "God, they must never eat a thing."

"You're just as skinny as they are," Kelly said.

She rummaged in her bookbag and handed her sister the envelope with her lunch money. Just thinking of food made her stomach growl, and her sister laughed.

"Go home and get something to eat, and thanks for this." She stuffed the envelope in her purple purse, then glanced at the gaudy silver watch on her wrist. She wrinkled her brow and stood. "I got to run. Jason hooked me up with a photographer. Wait until you see my headshots. He's awesome." She kissed Kelly's cheek, ruffled her hair again, and gracefully sauntered out in her four-inch stilettos.

Kelly tensed and peered around when Mark approached, but no one seemed to be looking.

"How are you doing," he asked as he slid into the seat Stacy had just vacated. He wrinkled his nose and squirmed a second before relaxing and crossing one leg.

"Good, I guess. I didn't tell."

He patted her hand. "I know. I'm not worried about that. We need to talk though. You have nineteen days left to decide what you're going to do. You'll need to be out of sight before dusk and can't go back until after dawn."

A flush burned Kelly's cheeks as she stared at her clasped hands. "I can come to your house?"

"Yes. Or I could tie you in the woods, or you could come to our ranch to live and be yourself all the time. It must be hard to keep the wolf locked down. If it gets to be too much, tell me. But never change without a spotter or in a securely locked room."

"It hasn't been hard to hold her back." His words had surprised her. She hadn't realized the wolf could appear when it wanted or that she could stop it.

Mark gave her a small half-smile. "We all talk like that as if the wolf is a separate entity, but it isn't. It gets easier if you accept what you are and all your wolf's needs."

"I hate vegetables now."

He threw his head back and laughed, and she was struck again by how handsome he was.

"That wears off once you and the wolf merge. You'll like raw meats best, but you still need vegetables. Try stews or using the blood from really rare meat as a gravy."

She wrinkled her nose, and he laughed again.

"You'll get used to it. Don't let yourself grow hungry. I can hear your stomach rumbling. Wolves hate being hungry; it makes us cranky. If you get too hungry, your wolf will make you eat."

"Humans?" The thought sent hot and cold chills over her.

"Sometimes, although we usually go for domestic animals first."

"Eww," she said and wrinkled her nose.

"Exactly. So, don't get hungry." He handed her a wad of folded bills. "Meat is expensive, and your parents will notice if theirs all disappears, so buy a few steaks and keep them deep in the freezer for snacking on. We can eat day-old meat with no problem. You'll be able to smell if food is too spoiled to eat it, so you can leave food under your bed or wherever. If you find yourself with the urge to hunt, call me right away. The urge is perfectly normal, but that's when you're the most dangerous."

"Will I have time to call?"

"As long as it isn't the full moon or you haven't been denying your wolf's urges. Give in to all the wolf's urges you can, and it's easier to hold her back when you really need to. Another reason to not let yourself get hungry. If you need anything at all, call me."

She stared down at the money she held. "This is too much. I can't accept money from a stranger.

"We aren't strangers. I'm your friend. Hopefully, your pack one day, and the money is nothing. If you can't get to a store to buy meat, just tell me, and I'll get meat to you."

"Thank you." She meant it.

He was being kind, and he didn't need to be. It

would be easier to kill her than babysit her.

He sighed hard and rubbed his eyes as if he was tired.

"Don't thank me. I know you hate this. I wish I could change it for you."

"I'll come to your house on the full moon."

"Where will you tell your parents you are? I don't want to get arrested."

"Abby's. I'll have to tell her not to call me, but they won't suspect."

He reached into his pocket and handed her a key, closing her fingers around it. "This is the key to my back door. Use it anytime." He cleared his throat and released her hand. "Call me first if you've got your period and it's the full moon."

"What happens then?"

"I stay far away from you. You'll have to lock yourself in and might need to wait in the cage until someone else can release you. You've heard of cat's in heat, right?"

She flushed so hard she thought she might faint.

He grinned at her but was flushed too. "It's an instinct. I'm an unmated wolf, and so are you. An unmated male wolf won't be able to resist you, so you need to make yourself safe from us and us safe from you. You could trap one of us. Once we mate, that's it. We can't choose another. It's considered a crime to trap a male wolf that way. Not that you'll be locked up, but the other wolves will despise you. Males will try to avoid you if they think there's a chance you can be menstruating on a full moon.

Accidents do happen though, so be careful."

"Okay."

"Do you have any questions for me?"

She hesitated before asking, "You're following me everywhere?"

"Most places. And I'll keep following until I'm sure you're under control."

Fear made her palms sweat.

He ran a hand through her hair, then jerked it back as if burned. "You don't need to be afraid of me. I'd never hurt you. This is for your protection, to make sure you don't hurt anyone."

She nodded slowly. He'd meant it. He was trying to help her. She offered him a tentative smile; his return smile was blinding.

"I better go," she said and scrambled to her feet. "My mom will be here soon to pick me up."

"Call if you need anything," he said.

She nodded but grimaced. She couldn't call him; she had no phone. Her mother was too worried she'd use it get into trouble. She didn't have internet access either for the same reason. She could hardly call him from her house phone. She giggled as she imagined her mother overhearing that conversation, 'Mark, I've got my period, so stay out of the house tonight.' Her giggle died, and worry grew.

How was she going to pull this off? Her mother watched her like a hawk. Abby would cover for her but would ask questions too. Where the hell could she say she was?

Eleven

One Month Later

*D*id you have any trouble getting away? Mark asked as he opened the door to let her in.

She crouched on his floorboards and shrugged.

Mark clenched the steering wheel tighter to keep from running his hands through her hair like he wanted to.

The wolf within him wanted to sniff her neck and rub against her, but it was happy to be this close. Watching from a distance this last month had been torture. He'd taken every opportunity he could to get within smelling distance to ease his wolf, but there hadn't been many opportunities.

"My parents think I'm at Abby's, and Abby thinks I have a bad headache and went to bed early."

He handed her a ball cap and a denim jacket. "Tuck your hair up and put this on."

She stuffed her hair beneath the cap and shrugged on the coat. The sour odor of fear rose. Sweat beaded her brow, and she chewed her lower lip.

"Kelly, you're going to be fine. Let the change take you quick, eat the steaks, then sleep. I rigged you a den of sorts. I'll leave you alone if you want privacy." He hesitated then asked, "Does your transformation hurt?"

"No. It tingles like a stretchy feeling." Her eyes widened, and she stared at him nervously. "Does it hurt you? Will it hurt?"

"It doesn't hurt me. I like the feeling, but some of us don't. For some, it takes much longer, and it's very unpleasant. I have a good friend who is scared to death every time it happens. There isn't reason to fear it though if you respect it."

He smiled slightly and glanced at her as he drove. She stared at him doubtfully.

"You're imagining Hollywood style changes? Blood and bone exploding from your body into a wolf?"

"That never happens?"

"It happens." He shuddered and licked his lips, sorry he'd brought it up. "Don't fight the change on a full moon."

"It kills you?"

"Not the first time. My mother—" he had to swallow hard past the lump in his throat— "my mother forced her wolf back. She didn't want to be her wolf and mate with my father, but she knew the wolf would force her. God, she tried everything to rid herself of him. I think she'd have tried to kill him if she hadn't killed herself. It was such a waste… He'd have died first if he knew what would happen."

"What happened?"

"She held her wolf back almost an entire night, one of the strongest feats of willpower I'd ever seen or heard of, and on the second full moon, a month later when she tried again, it burst free so violently it killed her."

"I'm so sorry. Why didn't she just leave him?"

"She did. But wolves mate for life. She couldn't resist him on a full moon. Her wolf was to in charge."

"He raped her?"

Mark winced. Kelly sounded horrified and sick.

"Yes. But my father had a wolf too. You'll see how hard it is to hold your wolf back when she really wants something. I always blamed him when I should've blamed our alpha. But I was a boy when it happened and had no real understanding of a wolf's needs. Is all I saw was my mother crying and how much she hated my father."

He slammed his hand on the steering wheel and cursed, angry with himself for allowing the memories to upset him and her, but he really didn't want her to try to suppress the wolf and kill herself.

"Sorry, I shouldn't have told you. It doesn't happen often because most shifters can't resist the change long enough to have the wolf get that desperate."

"You were desperate to change last month. I could have killed you," she said horrified.

"That was nothing. I could go longer than that.

My mother could have too if she hadn't denied every wolf urge for months. Hell, for years. For my entire life, she denied her wolf. She killed herself and two good men." He waved his hand in the air as if brushing off the memories. "Let's not talk about this. You don't need details. Just believe me when I say denying your wolf is dangerous."

"I'll be careful," she said in a small voice.

He groaned; he'd frightened her with his stories.

They rode the rest of the way in silence. In his basement, she eyed the cage doubtfully and sniffed the air.

"It smells different."

"I've had parties here."

She didn't want to enter, and he didn't blame her. His wolf hated to be caged too.

"Want me to stay?"

"No. Thanks, but no."

"I could come back after you change to keep you company."

She took a hesitant step forward, then turned to him. Her eyes glittered with unshed tears.

"I'm afraid."

"I know, but I promise it won't happen like that." He was cursing himself for telling her those stories before a change. He should have waited until she'd shifted again. "No one will bother you. Take off your clothes and make yourself comfortable. I removed the sound insulation from the window so you can see the sky, so try not to howl too much. Let the moonlight take you away and enjoy the wolf."

"You won't come in?"

"Not if you don't want me too."

She straightened her shoulders and strode forward. He closed and locked the cage before she could change her mind

"If you want me, hit this red buzzer." He pointed to the buzzer he'd installed above the door yesterday. "I placed it high so you can't hit it accidentally if you're just frisking around. If you get too loud, I'll have to come back and tranq you, so try hard not to."

"Tranquilizers work on us?"

"Yes, but not for long and they make us sick and our wolves really irritable. It isn't a great solution. If your wolf needs to be loud, we'll go to the woods next month so she can howl all she'd like."

He paused at the top of the stairs and glanced back. "You got this, kid."

She nodded and offered him a weak smile, but the scent of her fear followed him from the room.

Twelve

"God, I hope he isn't a pervert and watching on a hidden camera," Kelly muttered as she stripped off her clothes.

She gratefully wrapped herself in the blanket he'd left and paced nervously. Her stomach rumbled at the smell of the charred meat, but she couldn't eat it. Nerves made her queasy. She washed her face and hands, then filled the sink with cold water and waited.

"I should have asked for a book or something. This is boring." Sunset hadn't yet turned the sky orange. The sun still shone brightly. She finally hit the buzzer.

Mark ran down the stairs shirtless. She pulled her eyes away before he caught her admiring the muscles rippling under his skin. Broad shouldered with narrow hips, he was model beautiful. She blushed and ducked her head, hoping he couldn't smell her attraction. No way would a man be interested in a skinny girl like her. She'd just embarrass them both if she developed a crush.

"Everything okay?" he asked.

"I'm bored. Can I watch tv or something?"

He handed her the remote. "We could play cards, or talk if you want."

He rummaged in a box on top of a small poker table and waved a deck of cards at her triumphantly. "I'll teach you to play poker."

He dealt her a hand and slid it beneath the bottom bar of the cage.

"How often can we shift?" she asked as she examined her cards.

"Depends. I can shift about three times in an hour. Shifts to close together take longer, and I don't like how that feels, so I stop. I could probably make myself shift more but haven't had a need to. Werewolves always eat more than humans, our metabolisms are much faster, something to do with cell regeneration. Shifting burns through calories, so make sure you have enough meat if you're going to be shifting."

"Are we contagious in both forms?" She laid two cards on the tile and slid them beneath the bottom bar of the cage. "Hit me."

He grinned and dealt her two cards. "No, only the wolf is contagious. We're stronger and faster though, and our human bite will hurt more because our teeth are much stronger and sharper."

"I don't plan on biting anyone," she said as she examined her new cards, careful to keep her expression smooth.

"I smell your excitement. You have a good hand."

"Hey," she said in outrage.

"What am I holding?"

"I have no idea."

"Then I'm in for a—" he glanced around and jumped up to grab a bag of pretzels from the coffee table— "two pretzels." He emptied the bag and slid her half the pretzels.

The room darkened as the sun set, and her wolf's anticipation danced beneath her skin. Pins and needles grew progressively worse as if small electric shocks zapped her, but it was the wolf's longing that finally made her put her cards down.

"We can finish another time," he said as he rose and dusted pretzel crumbs from his jeans.

"You were tromping me anyway because you cheat."

She smiled after him as he ran up the stairs, closed her eyes and let her wolf take her. Her body expanded as if she inhaled and drew in energy from the setting sun. Every nerve felt vibrant and alive. Tingles traveled her in waves from her head and toes meeting in her stomach and bursting to life, and she became the wolf.

This time it didn't scare her. She stretched and rolled and sniffed the air. The meat smelled delicious, and she grabbed a bite-size chunk. He'd cut it for her. She could smell him on the food. She smelled him on everything, a delicious aroma she wanted to roll in.

The cold water tasted of chlorine at first but slid down her throat with a burst of flavors. She snapped at the droplets, then chased her tail in dizzying circles. If she were human, she would've laughed.

She explored the cage with her nose and found the dog chew he'd hidden in the corner beneath the bedding. She gnawed it a while. The rubber nubs felt good on her teeth and gums, but it didn't satisfy like steak bones did. She nosed the empty plate and flopped to the floor, bored again.

She dozed off and when she woke dawn lit the room in pale gray. The return to human form felt like a yawn, her muscles tensed, stretched, and released and she flowed into her human shape. She had to pee but didn't want to use the bucket or newspapers he'd left.

Just to see if she could, she called her wolf out. It came eagerly to her call, breaking from her skin with the same pins-and-needles tingling. She jumped around the cage a minute and got caught up in her play, only remembering she was human as she peed in the corner. Humiliated, she grabbed for her human form and sat shivering on the floor.

"Jesus." She stood on shaky legs and mopped up the mess she'd made with the newspapers, then dressed and hit the button.

"Next month we need paper towels and cleaners," she said in embarrassment. She hesitated then blurted. "I didn't mean to do it. I didn't even realize I would until I did."

"It's nothing to worry about. You're a brand-new

wolf."

"I remembered to be quiet," she said proudly.

"You did great. Want some breakfast or a shower?"

"Yes, please. I can't go to Abby's until ten or so. Can we get steak bones next time?"

"Sure," he said and gestured her to the stairs. "See, that wasn't so bad, was it?"

"Nope." She grinned at him, then caught a whiff of her urine and shivered.

Thirteen

The scent of gun smoke wafted in the air. Distance muffled the men practicing on the far range to muffled talk and laughter interspersed with gunfire. Mark took a deep breath and held it. He loved that smoky metallic smell. The man beside him drew back and loosed. The arrow smacked into the target with a sharp thwap of sound.

"Nice shooting," Mark said, meaning it.

He lifted his bow and released, intentionally aiming low and to the right. The arrow released with a soft whiff of sound more felt than heard. He growled a bit when it hit three inches from where he'd intended.

The man beside him slapped his shoulder and offered advice.

Mark let it roll off his ears as white noise and shot again, this time hitting exactly where he'd meant to. He continued shooting, avoiding the bull's eye, getting just close enough to be considered a respectable shot.

"See ya Saturday at the shoot," the man called as he packed up his kit to head out.

Mark gathered his gear and returned to the counter to buy another box of ammunition.

"Want to get a drink at Moe's?" the man behind him in line asked the men grouped before the counter.

Mark waited until other men agreed before saying yes.

Moe's was crowded and noisy like usual when they arrived. He spotted Jessie's friend and nodded hello but didn't approach. He hadn't called Jessie again and didn't plan to.

The men he came in with laughed and joked, flirting with the barmaid and pointing out the single girls they would pick up if they weren't married. One of the married men left with a prostitute, and Mark wrinkled his nose.

The talk grew livelier as the beer flowed. The crowd and noise felt suffocating. Good-natured teasing following Mark as he left the bar to approach a pretty brunette who drank alone at a corner table. She appeared older than him with laugh lines around her eyes and mouth, and he could smell the dye in her hair, but she had a sweet smile, and he didn't want to date her just make it clear to Jessie's friend that he'd moved on.

He exchanged numbers with the woman, not meaning to call; he no longer needed an alibi, but as an excuse to leave. He was in his truck three minutes when his phone rang.

He glanced at the number and winced, but answered.

"Hey," he said.

"We're over then?" Jessie asked without preamble.

"Were we ever a thing? I like you, but we were never serious." He felt like a shit; she'd been serious, and he knew it.

She sniffled, probably thinking he couldn't hear.

"Sorry, Jess. I didn't mean to give you the wrong impression. You're a really nice girl and if I were looking to settle down…."

"No. I'm sorry. You're right. You don't owe me anything. It just surprised me when I heard you were with a girl at Moe's."

"I wasn't really with her. I just met her."

"Then we're okay?" she asked hopefully.

"Because I like you, I'm not going to lead you on. I won't be calling," he said softly and as kindly as he could.

She was quiet, and he wondered what she thought.

"Okay. I'm sorry it didn't work out for you. See ya around."

"Bye, Jess," he said, but she'd already hung up.

The tears in her voice made him feel even worse.

"Get a grip. She's the crazy one. We went on three dates."

He slipped his phone back into his pocket and

rested his head on the steering wheel. Rejection hurt, and he wished he could make her feel better, but calling would just raise her hopes and what would he say? *It's not you, it's because I'm a werewolf and you aren't.* That wasn't the truth anyway. He wouldn't want her even if she was a wolf. He wanted Kelly.

"Fuck," he muttered and slipped his cell back in his pocket.

He'd been planning to leave his truck here and run through the woods to Kelly's but Jessie's friend would spot it for sure and maybe ask around to see who he'd snuck off with and someone might realize he'd left alone.

He drove home and changed, putting on a sweat suit and jogged back. Cool night air refreshed him. As always, the trees welcomed him with their leafy embrace. He stripped, left his clothes beneath a low-limbed pine, shifted, and slunk into the field beside her house. He peered beneath the fence as her father left the barn and headed home.

"Abby called looking for Kelly," Kelly's mother yelled angrily as soon as her father opened the door. The door closed, muffling the sound of her yelling. The yelling escalated until he could clearly hear her calling Kelly a lying whore.

His ears went back, and his teeth showed in a soundless snarl. Silent on the dewy grass, he crept forward and stood on his hind legs to stare in the window.

Kelly stood in the doorway of her living room

with a red face and her hands clenched while her mother shook a finger in her face and her father glared. He watched until she ran upstairs.

Her parents entered the living room, still arguing, and he could no longer make out what they said. They'd stopped yelling, but the tone remained angry. He wanted to rush inside and take her away from this, but it wasn't their fault. He'd be worried too if his daughter snuck out.

They needed a better excuse, or at least Abby's active participation. He dropped to all four paws and loped away.

He had to wait until Thursday to speak with her. The delay aggravated and worried him. She knew he was waiting in the library for her. The entire time she spoke with her sister she glanced at him and yanked her eyes away.

"Is something wrong?" she asked anxiously as soon as he joined her when her sister left.

"I was thinking, what if you tell Abby you met a boy and he lives across the lake."

"She'd want to meet him."

"Could you put her off awhile?"

"Yes, but not too long."

"I could get someone from home to pretend to be the boy."

She wrinkled her nose and flushed.

"You don't have to like him, just show him to Abby."

"I guess…" she said it so doubtfully he laughed, pleased that she didn't like the idea of meeting another wolf.

"But where will I tell her I'm going? She'll never believe I spend nights with a boy I just met."

"Pick something Abby hates to do."

"So, I met a boy, and we go night fishing?" she quirked a brow at him. "And for that, I sneak out of the house?"

"Hmm, I see your point. Okay, tell her you go on real dates, movies, and whatnot, but he lives even further away. Like he just moved or something so you can't be back until real late and to not disturb either of your parents you sleep in the barn, but the boy doesn't know you have to sneak out."

"That could work. It better be a real cute boy though, at least as cute as you."

He grinned at her but she was staring into the distance with a thoughtful expression and her lips pursed. "I could tell her I'm visiting my sister. She'd believe that and would cover for me, and never want to see Stacy."

"Even better." He relaxed his tense shoulders, glad he wouldn't need to introduce her to anyone else. "You better give me your phone number. I promise I won't call unless it's important."

"You can't call my house, and I don't have a phone."

"Really?" He thought all teenagers owned cell phones.

"My parents won't let me have one."

"I could get you one."

"Where would I keep it? No, they'd freak if they

found it. I'm trying to be a good daughter. I hate lying to them."

"I know you do." He wanted to hug her and offer comfort, but already the librarian was giving them the stink eye. "We can't meet here every week either. If you need to speak to me, and can't use your house phone, put something red in your window. If I need to speak with you, I'll leave a soda can in the street by your mailbox, and we can meet on the path behind the lower barn."

"I'll have to lie forever," she said sadly. Tears filled her eyes, and she covered her face with her hands. "I'll have to disappear, won't I? I won't age like them; they'll notice."

"Not for years, and a lot can happen in that time. Try not to let it worry you."

She sniffled and wiped her arm on her sleeve, giving the librarian a guilty glance.

"You better go. Ms. Holt is giving us the evil eye."

"You're okay?"

"Yeah."

She wasn't, but he left her there.

"Abby bought it," Kelly said as she climbed into his truck the night of the next full moon.

"Your parents don't mind you sleeping over her house on a school night?"

"We're on vacation from school still. I don't go back until January second. I'll have to claim I'm working on a school project or something next month."

She sounded miserable, and Mark gave her a sympathetic smile she didn't see, too busy staring at the hands twining in her lap.

This time she left her clothes in his bathroom and sat at his kitchen table wearing a towel to play cards.

When sunset filled the kitchen with tones of rose and golds, she folded her hand and sighed hard.

"Ready?" he asked softly.

"I don't mind the change. I like the wolf, she's fun, but I hate lying."

"I know, and I'm sorry you have too."

"I can change way more than three times in an hour."

He rose an eyebrow.

"I locked my door and put a roast under my bed. I was careful, but I wanted to try it."

"How many times in how long?"

"Six in a half hour but I could have done more. My dad came home, and I didn't want him to come in to say goodnight and catch me. It was easy, and my wolf didn't push me to do anything. I would like to run though."

"When can you get away for a few hours?"

She shrugged.

"I'll take you into the woods, and you can run, but you'll need a few hours and maybe a backup plan in case the wolf won't let you go for a bit."

"Saturday," she said eagerly. "I'll tell Abby I

met a boy and to cover for me if I don't get to her house by eight. She can tell her mom I changed my mind about sleeping over. But my wolf will let me go."

"I'll stay human unless you try to run from me. If that happens, I'll have to hold you. I won't be trying to hurt you, but I might. I'll keep a leash and collar with me, and if your wolf feels like she's going to roll you, bite it, and I'll tie you."

She nodded seriously after every word he said.

"Kelly, I like you a lot, and my wolf loves you. Make sure you're not menstruating. I'd hate to take advantage like that."

Her face flushed crimson, and she scrambled to her feet. "I better go downstairs."

She hurried to the door, avoiding his gaze. At the bottom stair, she stopped and turned back. "Give me a few minutes, then come down to lock me in. I want you to stay, but if your wolf scares me, please go. I'm really afraid of dogs. I know you aren't one but…"

"I can do that." His heart beat hard, thudding against his chest, and he wondered if she could smell his excitement. He waited ten minutes, and when he went downstairs, she waited in the cage with her tail tucked around her feet.

"You're beautiful," he said, and she sneezed, making him laugh.

He turned the key in the lock, and she ducked her head, laying on her stomach to hide her face with her tail. One golden eye stared at him. He turned and let his pants fall to the floor following them down to kneel and let his wolf out. It came joyously, faster than it ever had, knowing she waited.

His wolf wanted to paw at the fence. It wanted to brush against her and sniff her neck. It wanted to play. Ears flicking and nose going, she backed away when he approached. He crouched with his ass in the air and tail wagging. She mimicked him, then barked and raced in circles.

She wanted to play too. The gate rattled slightly when she pawed it. A low whine built to a growl and she scratched hard at the tile. He flopped on his side and stuck his snout through the hole. She stopped scratching to sniff him. The meat he'd left her caught her attention, and she whirled and pounced. Blood and drool splattered as she wrestled happily with the bone.

He whined. He really wanted to lick her face and paws. The guilty expression she gave him made him sneeze in wolfish laughter. She dragged her bone to the door and tried to share it, but the decorative filigree was too small to fit more than an edge through. He licked it politely and nudged it back.

When she finished eating, she returned to the gate and stretched out beside him with just the cast-iron keeping them apart. Her body heat warmed him, and he drowsed beside her perfectly content. The door rattling woke him. She was trying to lick his face. He stood and stretched, enjoying the feel of his muscles straining, then darted the length of the room and back. She followed on the other side of the fence.

Eight feet wasn't enough room to run, so he jumped over the furniture and twisted and bounded. She watched him with her tail wagging. Her small space didn't allow for much movement, but she rolled and pounced until he returned to the gate and lay back down. The metal pinched his muzzle, but he stuck his nose through anyway to lick at her. Wolf hair caught in the decorations as she rubbed hard against the fence the length of his body before settling to the floor with a low whine.

He was glad the fence was between them, it would be too easy to seduce her, and she was too young to make that decision. Moonlight filtered through the small window, beckoning him to come outside, and he wondered if it called to her too. Some wolves didn't feel the need for the trees and forests as much as others. And some never left it, unable to bear humans or civilization.

He dozed again and woke her when he stood. Her gaze followed him up the stairs, and she whined when he became human again. He didn't look back.

He took a shower before returning to let her out.

She waited wrapped in the towel and flushing.

"And that's why we don't touch," he said softly as he unlocked the door.

Her flush deepened, and she ran up the stairs.

Fourteen

"Get in here right now, young lady!"

Kelly started and jumped to her feet. She'd neither smelt nor heard her father's approach. She pressed a hand to her wildly beating heart and glance to the window where his angry face glared at her.

"You scared me."

"Get inside." His head disappeared back into the attic.

Kelly dusted the snow from her jeans and took one last glance around at the snow-covered fields before swinging into the window. She landed lightly before her father. He stood with his hands on his hips and scowled at her, his eyes flicking from the window to her.

I probably should have climbed down not swung in, she thought and bit her lip hard. Mark was out there watching, she smelt him all the time, waiting to make sure she didn't tell their secret and she was pretty sure even an accidental exposure would get them killed.

"I was just sitting there, Dad."

His frown deepened.

"I'm sorry. I won't do it again, but what's the big deal?"

Shock left her motionless when tears filled his eyes, and he hugged her tight. He kissed the top of her head before drawing away to say gruffly, "When Stacy was just a bit younger than you are now, she began dressing all in black. Do you remember that?"

Kelly smiled in remembrance. "Her goth phase."

"Your mother and I thought that too. We told each other it was only a phase, she'd grow out of it, but it wasn't a phase. It was a warning sign, and we didn't heed it. I'll be damned if I make the same mistake again. So, what's going on with you that you need to sit on the roof in the snow in just your sweatshirt?"

He pursed his lips, then grabbed her, surprising her again. He ran his hand over her jean's pockets removing her folded brush and a pencil stub, then patted her down before leaning close to sniff her breath. He opened the brush and examined it a moment before handing it and the pencil back.

"I told you, I was just sitting," she said indignantly.

"Normal people don't sit on their roofs." He strode to the window and leaned out.

Kelly followed and peered anxiously over his shoulder. "You don't need to climb out there. I promise you, I was just sitting. You're smothering me, Dad. Normal fathers don't pat their children down. You can't keep treating me like a criminal."

"Then stop lying."

She threw her hands in the air and headed for the stairs. "I was just sitting!"

He grabbed her arm and yanked her to a stop. "It isn't just this, Kelly. You're acting odd and don't pretend you don't know what I'm talking about. You pick at your food, then sneak down to the kitchen at night and gorge. You start at the barest noise and run around like a maniac. Your mother watched you sniff the living room furniture for five minutes. Your mom and I are worried."

She couldn't help her guilty flush or nervous sweat that she was glad he couldn't smell like she could. He released her to close the window and leaned against the wall, rubbing his hands together as if they were cold. Kelly's anger left her. He looked old to her, old and tired. And he smelled worried and a bit afraid.

"I'm fine," she said and gave him her best smile.

He rose both hands to rub his face hard.

"I'm not Stacy. We should help her, Dad, not abandon her."

He dropped his hands and glared. "Don't you think I tried? Why do you think your mom and I are so worried about you? Stacy was a hard lesson. I get you can't change who people are, but you can guide your children, and we failed with her. We were too lenient, too forgiving. We made excuses when we should've cracked down, and by doing so, we lost a daughter. And whether you believe it or not, that hurts. My Stacy died."

"She's alive, and you can have her back!"

Her father snorted and thumped onto an old chest beside the window where he rested his elbows on his knees.

"I begged her to get help. Every week I went and offered to take her to rehab, but she likes the evil thing she'd become. She doesn't want to change it."

"She isn't evil."

"She's as bad as a person can be."

"You sound like you don't love her anymore."

"I don't. I don't want her back. She disgusts me. It kills me that your mother still has hope."

Tears sprang to Kelly's eyes, and she held her trembling hands to her cheeks.

"You think I'm harsh, that I'm abandoning her because I disapprove of her lifestyle and that's true, I do disapprove, but Stacy only shows you a part of herself. She hides who she really is because you're a soft touch and she knows she can use you. I should make you go to her house and see how she lives, in the filth with the human trash. They walk around naked and fuck like animals."

He covered his face with his hands and spoke low, only her wolf hearing let her hear him clearly. "I went every week and begged her to come home. She was just seventeen and ran away from every place we sent her for help. The counselors, the doctor, and police all said she had to hit rock bottom before she would accept our help, but where is the bottom for her?"

He straightened and clenched his fists at his side.

"I could take the drinking and the drugs. I told myself Stacy had a disease and it wasn't her fault. Lies, stealing, all part of her disease. But the sickness is in her soul, and maybe I could have beat it out of her when she was young if I had seen it."

He jumped to his feet and punched the wall behind him, making Kelly flinch. Her wolf wanted to run, and she had to force her gaze from the window.

"I fucking saw it, but I didn't act until it was too late, and I hate myself for that, so you'll have to excuse my harshness, but I'm not going to put up with any more fucking lies from you. I'll be damned if I drive downtown and my other daughter smiles at me, wearing too much makeup and clothes that reveal her body, and offers me a blowjob for five dollars. And she fucking laughed and waggled her tits at me while her scumbag friends watched and egged her on. Stacy is a fucking animal, a barely literate, lying whore who loves how she is."

He strode forward and slapped her cheek. She stared at him in shock and stumbled back as he rose his hand again. Her wolf surged, and she fell to her knees, trying to contain it. She missed his next words as he dragged her up and shook her hard, too busy holding back the animal that wanted to burst from her skin and flee.

"Stop," she said through her sobs as she held her hands to her face to block his blows.

Breathing hard, he thrust her away.

"No more fucking lies. No sneaking around. Are you drinking or smoking on the roof?"

"I swear, I wasn't doing either. Please, Daddy, you've got to believe me."

"Like when you told us you were going to Abby's last week?"

A red flush burned across her cheeks. "I'm sorry. I should have asked to go to that concert but—"

He slapped her again, so hard her neck snapped backward.

"Enough with the lies! I want to get you help, but I need to know what kind of help you need. Or are you like her? Do you just like lying for the sake of lying? Is sneaking out fun for you? You feel like you're getting one over on the old man?"

She stared at him not knowing what to say. To tell him the truth would mean their deaths. She was certain the wolves would silence any threat, and the truth might not change how he felt. Stacy had a disease, and he hated her. His voice dripped with hatred when he said her name. The thought of her father saying her name in the same tone made her stomach hurt.

"I'll never do it again," she finally said.

He turned away without a word.

"Daddy, please," she called after him and sank

to her knees to sob.

Outside a wolf howled and she shivered. Mark was warning her. Cramps doubled her over. Her wolf scratched at her insides. She wanted so bad to let her free and run through the moonlit night, to feel the snow and cold wind on her fur, to gulp red meat that still steamed— she forced the longings back and rose to her knees. She'd let the wolf out in her bedroom.

Somewhere downstairs glass broke, and she ran, her heart thudding in her chest and her breath stifled by the lump in her throat. But it wasn't Mark breaking in to kill them, it was her father ransacking her room.

"What did you do!" her mother yelled as she ran from her bedroom.

"Nothing."

"You're turning into quite the liar, aren't you?" Her mother gave her a disgusted sneer and pushed past her to begin rifling her drawers.

Kelly sank to the floor, clutching her knees and crying as they ripped apart her world. Her insides quivered, and she thought she might be sick. Pencils and pens clattered to the floor followed by the desk drawers her father yanked out and checked for secret compartments before dropping them to the growing pile in the center of her room. Her mother shouted at her while she wrenched her clothing from the drawers and hangers and searched it.

"We won't let you grow up to be a whore like your sister. Just tell us the truth. Or are you so evil already you'd rather see us like this?"

Kelly rose her hands to her ears and rocked on the floor, whining softly. She didn't know how much longer she could hold her wolf back but to release it would be their deaths. She'd smelled Mark's sincerity when he warned her. To tell would mean death.

"I'm not on drugs or smoking! Please, can't you just trust me? I love you, please…."

Her mother glared at her and began ripping open her teddy bears. She turned and bolted.

"Get back here right now! her father bellowed after her, but she couldn't.

The wolf was coming. She barely made it to the tree line before the change ripped through her. She lay panting in the snow, trapped in her clothes, dizzy and sick. She wanted to run to make sure she was far enough her father wouldn't find her but couldn't catch her breath enough to get her feet under her.

"I'm here," Mark said softly, and terror rose her ruff. "Relax and let the wolf—"

He took a quick step back when she rolled onto her back to expose her stomach. Her own fear blocked his scent from her. The sharp smell of urine laced the snowy air. Her entire body trembled but the wolf knew she had to submit and she relaxed and stretched her neck out, praying he'd be quick and not play with her as the other wolf had.

"Kelly…" He gathered her close and ran through the snow, holding her tightly to his chest.

"Don't be so afraid. Your wolf will release you. Let her out. Stop fighting her, and it won't hurt."

She'd have laughed if she could. He had no idea why she was afraid. The thought calmed her. He hadn't come to kill her— this time.

He settled with his back to an enormous oak and held her tightly until her breathing calmed.

"I want to release you, but I don't want you to run away. You can run around me but don't leave my sight."

He removed her clothes before letting her go. She shook hard and rolled in the snow. Clean and cold, it felt better than she'd thought it could, and she rolled and snapped at the flakes she kicked up. She got so caught up she forgot he watched her. Smells called to her and she wanted to follow each of them. Half-rotted limbs cracked with satisfying crunches and leaves fluttered enticingly. She swatted and bit and chased her tail until his low laughter reminded her of his presence.

Fear grabbed her hard, and she dropped to her stomach. Her human self was embarrassed by her whining and tail-tucked submissive posture, but she couldn't stop it.

"You don't need to be afraid of me," he said as he stroked her fur. "I'm here to be your friend and help you learn to be a wolf." He pursed his lips and stared at her thoughtfully. "I promise if you turn feral, I'll do my very best to stop you and bring you far from humans, and if you can't be stopped, I swear on my soul it won't be me who kills you. You can trust me, Kelly."

He picked her up again and cuddled her close, rubbing his face against hers. Her trembling slowed, and she relaxed in his arms, accepting the comfort he offered. He released her when she squirmed and seemed to understand she wanted privacy to dress when she grabbed her jeans in her teeth.

Arms crossed, he faced the tree and spoke without turning to look at her. "You'll need to eat. Raw meat would be best."

The winter air felt bracing on her bare skin. She'd have liked to roll in the snow in her human form, but the thought of being naked before him caused a hot blush to burn her cheeks. She scrambled into her clothes.

"I'm decent."

He turned to face her.

"I heard the yelling and was worried. Are you okay?"

"No. My parents know I lie about going to Abby's. I can't sneak out again. They won't forgive me."

"Come with me." His intense stare traveled her hopefully, and he clenched his hands behind his back.

"I don't want to. Can't you leave me alone? I have good control. You see when you lock me up I don't fight you. I'll stay in my room; I promise."

"Kelly— what if your wolf gets hungry? What if you can't control her. She needs the forest. If you keep denying her, it will get harder and harder to stop her. She could break free and hurt people."

"I know, but I'll be careful. Let me stay in my room and I'll meet you here in the woods when I can, and we can run. If you'll bring me meat, I swear I can keep her in the room. I wouldn't risk my parents. Please, let me try. You can wait outside, and you'll hear if I try to break down my door. Please, Mark. I don't want them to hate me."

He reached a hand to her but dropped it before touching her.

"Okay. We'll try it your way. Kelly, I— want you to be happy." He winced and spun away speaking over his shoulder. "You've been gone three hours. They're sure to be furious."

She began running back home. "If you let me stay home, they'll forgive me."

"This isn't what I wanted for you," he called after her.

She didn't answer or look back. Sharp bangs perked her ears as she approached her house. Her father was nailing something and hitting harder than necessary. She glanced back but couldn't see Mark. She knew he was close though, and this time the thought didn't scare her but reassured her. He would stop her from hurting them if they scared her so badly her wolf emerged. She straightened her shoulders and opened the front door. The alarm dinged, and the banging stopped.

"It's me," she called.

Her mother stopped on the top step. "Where did you go?"

"For a run in the woods."

"You're a liar." She strode two steps down and rose her voice. "It's freezing outside and you don't even have a coat. Where the hell did you go!" she was shrieking by the end and breathing so hard Kelly worried she'd have a stroke.

"I was outside in the woods." Kelly stepped forward and examine the living room with dismay. They'd searched that too.

"This is ridiculous. Are you going to search the entire farm?"

Her mother ran at her and slapped her face. Then she clenched her hands and stepped back, lifting her shaking hands to her cheeks. She nodded to a bag beside the door. "You're going to rehab."

"I'm not on drugs!"

"We'll see. You won't be able to hide it there." The anger left her mother's face, leaving her looking sad and hurt. "Let us help you. Please, Kelly, let us help you."

Kelly snatched the bag and stood trembling in the doorway. "Fine. How long will this take?"

"As long as it needs to."

Her father came down the stairs shrugging on his coat and still clutching the hammer. Without a word, he strode to the truck. No one said anything for the hour and a half drive. She recognized the clinic as one Stacy had been brought to.

"Mom…"

"I love you, honey. Please get well. Don't let whatever is riding you take you away from us. Your father and I will get you any help you need."

Tears streamed down her mother's face. Her father kissed her cheek and pushed her through the door where a woman wearing a nurse's uniform waited. "They'll call us when you can come home. I love you." His voice broke, and he clamped his lips hard before spinning away.

She stared after them angry and confused, not knowing what she should do or say. She understood why they doubted her, but it still hurt. She turned back to the nurse who waited patiently. Her wolf didn't want to enter. Frozen in the doorway, she watched her parents drive away and spied Mark's truck. Her tense shoulders relaxed. He would get her out if her wolf couldn't take it. She let the door close behind her.

Fifteen

Mark climbed onto the two-story roof by leaping from a nearby tree. He caught the edge of the roof to swing himself up, then dropped to his stomach. No one inside seemed to notice the soft sounds he made. Outside, low clouds darkened the sky. It would rain soon. No one walked the street, and he'd smelled no one outside when he'd checked the perimeter.

She'd gone inside willingly with her head up and shoulders straight, which was the only thing that let him drive past and not rush in to throw her over his shoulder and take her away. But he needed to speak with her.

A light flicked on in the house across from him, and a second later a television threw muted colors against the curtains. Voices traveled through the walls below him but too low for him to make out what they said. He knew where she was though. She'd stood in front of a window on the second floor for twenty minutes, staring out into the night.

He'd watched anxiously for her to place something, anything, in the window, but she hadn't. On his hands and knees, he crawled across the roof and examined the yard carefully with his nose, ears, and eyes before lowering himself off the roof with his hands. He swung his legs and released to slide down the wall and catch the thin lip of the window with his fingertips. Muscles strained in his shoulder as he gripped with just his fingertips and lifted himself to brace his feet on the window trim.

He didn't have to tap. Kelly was already running to the window, peering over her shoulder at the closed door.

"Let me in," he growled.

She placed both hands flat on the glass and smiled at him. "I can't, the window is alarmed." She glanced at the door again and spoke in a bare whisper. "They did blood tests."

"Won't show a thing."

Her shoulders eased, and her smile brightened. "They'll let me out in a few days. I'm nothing like the rest of the kids here."

He growled again when she shivered and rubbed her arms.

"I hate leaving you here." The promised rain began to fall in a slow drizzle. He shivered irritably as it slid down his neck.

"I hate being here, but it's a few days, and then my parents will believe me. I need to act more normal."

"They need to not be so quick to condemn you."

She shrugged and looked miserable. "I do act weird. Who can blame them."

He placed his palm against the window, and she smiled and rested her hand against his. He could feel the heat of her through the glass, and he growled again. His breath fogged the window, and he awkwardly wiped it with his sleeve.

"I'll be right outside. If you need me, put something in the window, but if you have to run just jump through this glass. I'll hear it and be waiting for you. Do you have enough food here?"

"For a day or two." She grimaced and wrinkled her nose. "They try to make us eat healthy. Dinner was veggie burgers and carrot strips with jello for dessert. We did get cookies and brownies before bed though. I can take it a few days."

"Don't let the wolf get hungry. She'll be frightened locked in here."

Kelly rubbed her arms again. "I know. She doesn't like this at all. You help though." She closed her eyes and pressed her cheek to the glass.

He growled again and pressed as close as he could. She whirled to the door and took a step back.

"Someone's coming," she hissed and ran to her bed.

He used his sleeve to wipe his handprint from the glass and let himself fall just as her door began to open.

The next day, he left his truck parked three blocks

away and slipped through his open window as his
wolf. He wore a thick, brown dog collar with tags,
one of which offered a large reward for his safe
return. Richard would be pissed, and he'd never live
it down if he had to be rescued from a pound, but he
needed to make sure Kelly was okay.

A few people glanced at him as he trotted down
the sidewalk, but no one approached or called to
him. He jumped the low fence in the neighbor's
yard and crawled beneath the chain-link that
separated the house from the clinic. A half-full
industrial garbage bin blocked the small driveway
from the road. He could use it to hide behind, and it
made a great cover if he was caught here.

The sounds of arguing pricked his ears, and he
stood on his hind legs to peer through a dirty
window. From this close, he could hear them
clearly. Teenagers sat in a circle on a worn wood
floor and passed a stick with a white flag on it to
each other as a tired looking woman, wearing a
brown sweater and tan slacks, took notes. She
smiled at the kids and made encouraging gestures,
clearly a counselor.

Mark's gaze measured the kids for a possible
threat. His golden eyes narrowed on a plump black
girl who hit the girl beside her when she took the
stick. The counselor rose, grabbed the stick from the
girl, and began lecturing them.

Wet grass brushed Mark's stomach as he
crawled to the next window to peer in the window
at a classroom. The next window was a doctor's

office, the next a small infirmary. He passed two more offices before he found his girl. She sat before a wide, wooden desk, which had seen better days, speaking to an older man in a blue sports coat who sat leaning back with one leg crossed, revealing blue striped socks and brown loafers.

Mark tapped once on the glass and hunkered to his stomach.

"— Because I like being outside," Kelly was saying.

Mark heard her chair scrap and glanced up, wagging his tail when she stared out the window. She laughed and slapped her hands over her mouth.

"What's so funny," the doctor asked in a kind voice.

"I'm trying to convince you I'm normal, but I'm not. I hate being in closed rooms like this. Can we open the window?"

"Sure."

She opened the window and leaned out to take a deep breath.

"I'm okay," she whispered in the barest breath of sound.

He breathed deeply of her scent and whined softly. She gave him an exasperated glance and returned to her chair.

"It isn't unusual to like the outdoors," the doctor said.

"My parents think it is. They never let me just sit outside or run in the woods alone."

"And do you want to run?"

"I want to join the track team. But really, I just like the solitude of the woods. They think I like it to do drugs or smoke, but that isn't it. I try to be a good daughter. I love them, but they're stifling me."

"They're worried."

"I know—"

A knock on the door interrupted them.

"Excuse me," the woman who poked her head in the door said. "Angelica is having an issue. If I could interrupt and borrow the doctor for a minute?"

"Sure. I'm good," Kelly said.

"You are good," the doctor said as he rose. "We'll talk more, but I can see you're a good kid. You can return to your art class or go to the library."

Mark risked another peek. Kelly stood in the doorway. She glanced back at the window and gave him a grimacing smile before stepping into the hallway and shutting the door.

He ran back to the garbage and jumped into the bin. It took some searching, but he finally found a bone. It had been boiled so long it hardly smelled at all, but it would do as a prop. He returned to the doctor's still open window and laid down to wait, but she didn't return that day. The doctor met with children all afternoon and seemed kind and genuinely interested in helping them, which relieved Mark.

When dusk arrived, he crossed the street and found an angle where he could see her window and still be unnoticed from the street. Crouched beneath a ratty tarp over an old car he stared at her lighted window. Rain began to fall, thick drops that bounced from the asphalt before forming puddles. He was soaked in minutes, but glad it wasn't snowing to reveal his pawprints.

He lay on his stomach and half-closed his eyes. The rain continued, turning to sleet. When a gray dawn broke, he loped back to his truck, through the still sleeting rain, and jumped through the open window onto his wet seat. He glanced around, then lay flat to resume his human shape and struggled into his jeans.

Once dressed, he drove to a nearby coffee shop, bought himself breakfast, and returned to park on the street where she'd be able to see him. The streets came alive around him, people heading out for the day and shops opening. His nose twitched at the smell of fresh meat. A deli down the street was busy with early morning sandwiches. He hoped from his truck and waited his turn, buying two, foot-long, meat-lover sandwiches and two pounds of roast beef, which should sate his werewolf metabolism.

Back in his truck, he sipped his cold coffee and opened his laptop to browse the news. The pack could always use money, and there might be someone worth killing.

Sixteen

ell, Kelly, your parents will be glad to know they're worrying for nothing," the doctor said three days later as he tapped the stack of reports on his desk. "I appreciate their concerns though. You might not be doing drugs or even smoking, but you're doing something they won't approve of if you're sneaking out all night to do it."

"I went to see my sister."

"Ahh." The doctor leaned back and tented his fingers on the desk before him.

Kelly turned to stare from the window.

"I see. Did Stacy ask you to come?"

"No. but I needed to see her. I didn't understand. I still don't understand."

"Understand what?"

"Why she changed so much and why they stopped loving her."

"Did she change?"

Kelly frowned and leaned her forehead on the cold glass.

"I'm going to be speaking with your parents, and I recommend you see a counselor together. Stacy has disrupted all your lives, and you need to deal with that. I understand you still love her, and that isn't a bad thing, but sneaking away to see her isn't the answer."

"I won't do it again."

"We have to accept people are who they are, and sometimes, when we really see who they are, we can't love them even when we want to."

Kelly peered over her shoulder at him. "You think Stacy is bad too? Unlovable?"

"Right now, she is. She could change. People grow and learn, but right now your sister likes who she is and isn't trying to change it. Some people, people like her, like how she is too. Stacy is loved. She isn't alone. She has friends of a sort but not the type of person I would befriend, and if you're honest with yourself, I think you see that too."

"She loves me."

"Does she?"

Kelly turned back to the window. Her breath misted the glass, and she wiped it with her sleeve. Mark glanced at her, then turned back to his computer screen. He sat out there every day all day, and she thought he might even be there all night.

The doctor rose and opened the door. "Go pack. It was a pleasure to meet you, and if you ever need help, we're a phone call away." He laid a hand on her shoulder as she passed. "Think about what love is."

Kelly sat in the metal chair outside the doctor's office for almost two hours before her parents exited.

"Call us if you need us," the doctor said and shook all three of their hands.

When they got in the truck, her father laid his arm along the seat and turned to her. "I'm sorry, but you should have told us you were going to see her. From now on, we're going to trust each other. We'll believe you when you say you're going somewhere, and you'll ask to go places. If you need to see your sister, we can work something out, but you're not to sneak off to see her."

"She can't go see her alone," her mother said worriedly and grabbed her father's arm. She released his arm to turn awkwardly in the seat to grab Kelly's hand. "Never go to see her alone. Stacy would think it hilarious to drug your drink or something. And she'd hurt you to get back at us. Promise me, you won't go alone. We can hire someone, a chaperone or something."

"I won't go alone, and I'll be careful around her if she shows up."

"Does she show up?" her father asked unhappily.

"Sometimes she comes to my school or the mall."

"Kell, we can't lock you up to keep you safe, and I know you don't want to see this side of your sister, but your mother isn't wrong. Stacy would hurt you if there were something in it for her. You do need to be careful around her. Frankly, I hope she gets arrested again soon. She's a menace to all good people."

"I'll be careful," Kelly repeated.

A small smile flitted across her face. She didn't need a chaperone, she already had one. Right now, he was two cars away, pretending to be asleep in the front seat of his truck with a newspaper against his face and a cowboy hat pulled low.

Her mother squeezed her hand and straightened in her seat. "She needs a cell phone, honey, and then she can call for help if Stacy or anyone else bothers her." Her mother pursed her lips, but her eyes twinkled when she said, "And this isn't a bribe for good behavior. We expect you to keep it on you when you leave the house and answer our calls."

Kelly grinned, and her father laughed as he started the truck. "We have a way to go, but we're getting there. I can't tell you how relieved I am you aren't sick."

Kelly stared down at the hands twining in her lap, avoiding her father's eyes in the rear-view mirror, her relief turning to dread. She was sicker than they could imagine.

Seventeen

Mark squatted on his haunches to catch his breath. September sunshine filtered through the trees and highlighted Kelly's gray fur. She peered over her shoulder, her tongue lolling in doggie pants as she lowered her muzzle to the trickling stream and slurped.

"I'm not sure this a great idea," Mark said. "I'm willing to help you make the track team next year, but don't runners wear shorts?"

She wrinkled her nose at him and sneezed. He sighed and hitched her bag higher on his back. They'd barely gone half a mile when they heard someone else crashing through the brush on the lower end of the trail. The path they ran curved up and around the mountain. Little more than a deer trail, he'd never seen or smelled anyone else on it. She whined and nudged his arm. He let her pack fall to the ground and ran off the trail. Whoever ran up the trail wasn't in great shape. He huffed and puffed so hard it didn't take wolf hearing to hear him.

Mark easily caught up, running lightly through the trees. His eyes narrowed at the boy jogging the path and holding his side.

He soundlessly followed the boy to Kelly who'd dressed and jogged in place on the path.

"Jason," she said, sounding surprised.

"Abby told me you run up here. It sure is a good workout," Jason gasped out. He rested with both hands on his knees, taking deep breaths.

Kelly giggled. "You're sure outa shape for a football player."

Jason straightened and grinned. "Maybe you'll run with me and get me into shape?"

Pink bloomed in Kelly's cheeks, and Mark bit back his growl, glad he was downwind so she wouldn't smell his angry sweat.

"Want to come to the after-game party with me, Friday?"

"I have to ask my parents."

"Sure. Call me and let me know." He waved at the path. "How much farther do you go?"

"We can head back."

They headed back at a slow jog. Mark kept downwind.

"I'm surprised you still like the forest what with the leg and all."

"I carry mace now," Kelly said in a tight voice.

Jason grabbed her arm. "Sorry, didn't mean to upset you. I heard rumors, and it sounded pretty gruesome."

"It was, but the scar is almost gone now. Look, I

don't like talking about it."

"Sure, sure, I understand. I wouldn't want to either." He released her and bumped his hip to hers. "Race you to the bottom."

Mark tromped on his jealousy and forced his wolf back as she giggled and ran after the boy.

"I'm such a hypocrite," he said to his reflection as he shaved. He washed his face with steaming hot water, then felt his cheeks for stubble. "She's a sixteen-year-old girl, of course she wants to date sixteen-year-old boys. What did I expect her to do, tell him to bugger off that she loves a two-hundred-year-old werewolf?" He threw his razor into the sink and stalked from the room.

"You need to get laid and leave her the fuck alone." He began to dress, putting on jeans and a black t-shirt.

Moe's was noisy and crowded. He took a seat at the bar and glanced around, eyeing the women who flirted and laughed in small groups throughout the room. He spotted Jessie, but she hadn't seen him yet. She sat with her friends, the same crowd as a year ago, and sipped a fruity drink. It shocked him to realize he'd been here almost a year already. Time had flown by, and he'd accomplished nothing.

Well, not nothing, he thought and had to bite back his growl. Kelly was comfortable now with her wolf. So comfortable she didn't really need him. He was tempted to approach Jessie, but that would be stupid, and she deserved more. He turned his back on her and eyed the working girls lining the bar.

The hair on his arms rose as a familiar scent wafted to him over the perfume and alcohol infusing the air. His gaze narrowed on a skinny brunette. She wore so much makeup it was hard to judge her age, but he knew she was nineteen, three years older than her sister. Too young to be in here and way too young to be working.

He stepped closer and sniffed. She smelled sour and sickly, but the family resemblance was plain to his nose and his eyes. He hoped Kelly never looked this hard.

Stacy turned to him and smiled without showing her teeth. Half-inch-long red manicured nails tapped on the beer bottle she held, then rose to trace her cleavage. Disgusted, he turned away, and she must have felt it because she muttered, "Fag," loud enough to make her friend giggle.

He headed to the other end of the bar and ordered a jack and coke.

"She's a might aggressive," the woman beside him said and nodded to Stacy.

Mark peered over his shoulder in time to see Stacy rub her hand along a man's crotch. She slipped from the barstool and pressed against him a moment before leading him from the bar. His skin rippled, and he took a deep drink. Someday, his

Kelly would look like that. She'd begun getting curves that he tried not to notice.

"Some men like that though," the woman continued and laid her hand on his knee.

"I'm not looking for a girlfriend." He leaned real close and sniffed her neck. A whiff of soap and nervous excitement wafted to him. He grabbed her hand as she withdrew it, and the pulse in her neck jumped. He stared down at the hand he held.

"Newly divorced?"

Her eyes widened, and she jerked away.

"No, I don't know you or your ex, but your finger has a tan line."

She laughed and waved her free hand before her flushed cheeks. "My ex was a prick and all, but I'm not looking to cause trouble by sleeping with one of his friends."

"He cheat on you?"

She snorted, picked up her wine glass, and sipped before she answered.

"So often it amazes me it took me three years to notice. Why do men do that? Why marry if you want to screw around?"

"No idea."

She frowned at the other end of the bar. He followed her gaze to another prostitute leaving on the arm of a short, chubby man.

"They make it look so easy."

He laughed, the laugh deepening when she looked offended.

"Sorry, but it is easy when you don't give a shit

who you're fucking. Their feelings don't get hurt when they get turned down, they don't care if the man likes them or will respect them in the morning, and they only want to see him again if he'll pay."

She downed her drink in one long gulp and stood. "I don't care if I see you again and don't care if you'll respect me. It might hurt a bit if you turn me down though as I'm offering for free and all."

He laughed again and pulled her close for a kiss.

She tasted like the wine she'd drunk, but her mouth was soft and warm. His wolf didn't like her one bit but didn't care that he kissed her. His conscience twinged but he told himself to shut up and deepened the kiss.

"Oh my," she said breathlessly when they parted. "Maybe I do care if I see you again."

"I'll be honest. I'm horny and hard and not looking for a girlfriend, but if you just want one night, I'm all yours."

Her eyes widened and traveled his body, stopping on the erection in his jeans before returning to his face.

"My place?" she asked breathlessly.

He grinned and kissed her again, letting her take his hand and lead him from the room.

Jessie stared with hurt eyes and his guilt deepened. It was clear they were leaving to fuck and that had to hurt when he'd turned her down for weeks. He averted his gaze and stared at the ass of the woman who held his hand and realized he didn't even know her name.

He didn't ask.

Outside, at her car, he kissed her hard and ran his hand over her breasts, tempted to just lift her skirt and fuck her right there. It would only take him minutes, but she would be left feeling dirty and used.

"I'll follow you," he said as he drew away. "You can change your mind," he added.

"I don't live far."

In his truck, he glared at his backpack, which smelled like Kelly, and followed his date. She smelled even more aroused when she let him in the house. He went through the motions of seduction, kissing her breasts and caressing her, but all he wanted was relief.

She was into it though, panting and squirming. He fingered her until she came, then flipped her over to slam inside her. Tight and wet she enveloped him and grunted as he thrust. It didn't take him long to come. And once his hips stopped jerking he felt sick.

Neither said a word as he dressed.

"Sorry," he said at the door without looking back.

Back in his house, he threw away his clothes and showered until he couldn't smell her on his skin. Relieving his body hadn't helped, it made him feel worse. He fixed himself a rare steak, but the hunger he felt wasn't for food or sex. Cramps twisted his stomach, and he ran to his bathroom where he vomited.

He took another shower then flopped on his bed to stare at the ceiling.

"This is going to suck. How do I make her love me?"

The blank ceiling gave him no answers.

"She sure as shit isn't going to love a guy who fucks strangers in bars."

Nausea roiled his stomach again, and he bit back his groan. When he finally fell asleep, he dreamed of Kelly terrified and whimpering in the cage in his basement.

Pale and shaken, he rose from his bed to pad naked to his kitchen. He made himself ham and eggs and took his plate to his back porch to eat it, not caring if the neighbors saw him. When he finished, he went inside to call Richard.

"She isn't coming to the ranch. I told her she could stay locked in her room."

"Jesus, Mark."

He was glad they spoke on the phone to hide his guilty flush. He'd been letting her stay alone for months now. "It'll be fine. You never saw a wolf with such good control. At the first hint of a problem, I'll get her out."

"You can't stay there indefinitely."

"Why not?"

Richard sighed hard. "Fine stay. We'll figure something out. There must be some kind of job—"

"I don't need a job. I don't need this house or any house. I'm going off the grid."

"Don't do that. No, hear me out," Richard said

as Mark began to argue. "Keep the house and the truck. The pack can afford it. Arny has a good lead in Mexico. You'll need a house; somewhere safe she can go if it gets to be too much, and we both know it will. She won't be able to hold back her wolf forever."

"She lets it out to run with me."

"When did this start?

Mark could see Richard's tight expression by his tone. He closed his eyes as if that would hide it and said, "May. She told her parents she was going to join the track team, and they're okay with her running in the woods."

"How old is she now?"

"Sixteen and four months."

"And you're absolutely positive her wolf is no danger?"

"She's handling it."

"Then come home."

"I can't," he said in a strangled voice.

Richard sighed again.

"Fine, stay there then, but keep the house and live like a civilized person. She doesn't need a homeless stalker." He was silent a minute before he said, "Come home for a visit. Rainy and Leah are organizing a meet to give the youngsters a bigger selection for mates. Come home for that."

"No."

"Well, can you come if we go to Mexico?"

"Yes, I think so. She should be okay for a week or so."

"What's that mean? Is she stable, or isn't she?"

"It means she's a teenage girl who lies to her parents and has hardly any friends. She worries all the time, and I won't leave her alone. You know how hard it can be for the kids, and she has no one else. So, yes, she's stable for a teenager, but she *is* a teenager."

"Right. You're right."

Mark could picture Richard squeezing his nose and smiled.

"Stay with her," Richard said. "Would it help if we sent some mated pairs there?"

"I don't know. She's terrified of wolves. Let me ask first. And thanks, Richard."

"You're pack."

Mark closed his phone and rested his head on his folded arms. It was a relief to know his pack had his back. He straightened and called Arny. He *was* pack, and they needed him too.

"Richard says you found a lead?"

"More than a lead. I'm casing now. We want to hit them when they're cash heavy."

"How much are we talking about?"

"Three million or so in the main house and another two spread over his top three dealers."

Casualties?"

"Twelve we need to take care of for sure and another eighteen maybes. I'm looking into it now. Six civilians live in the main house and men and women come and go at irregular intervals with the three dealers. The main house will be an easy roll, its cleaning up the rest that'll be tricky.

"Count me in."

"Great. I'll send you the maps and shit I'm working on, and you can help with the plan. Can you stay?"

"No. Sorry, but she needs me."

"I get that. It's going to take a while, but I'm sure they'll reorganize and try this again."

"Then we'll hit them again. They'll eventually get the point that someone really disapproves of child slavery."

"These are some seriously bad hombres. They'd pimp their own mothers for a buck. I hate leaving these drug labs going, but I don't have enough information to justify hitting the eighteen, but I don't want to leave them free if they'll retaliate by killing the help. I need more time."

"Be sure."

"You know I will be. Catch you later, bro."

Arny hung up, and Mark gazed thoughtfully into the distance. Five million was a decent score for the year. He'd be able to buy her anything she wanted with his share. He winced and stretched his tight muscles. She might hate how he really made his living. Yet another hard truth to tell her. Truths she needed to hear. She was going to hate the sex talk, and he fucking hated having to tell her as if it didn't matter to him if she took human lovers. He growled and threw his phone across the room. Plastic shattered around him.

He stomped the remainder until it was

unrecognizable then gathered the shards and headed out to buy a new one.

"We need to talk," he said the next day as he ran beside her.

She slowed and glanced over her shoulder, golden eyes alight. Unable to resist, he ran a hand along her flank, and she wagged her tail.

"There's some things you need to know about werewolves."

She slowed even more.

"Werewolves and humans can breed, but it's very dangerous. A male human can impregnate an unmated female werewolf but to carry the fetus to term your body needs to manufacture the correct organs. For mated werewolves, that happens when they bond. For unmated female wolves, it will happen if you become pregnant. At first, it will feel a bit crampy, but by the first full moon, it will hurt so bad you won't be able to move. If the full moon comes too soon after conception, the fetus will abort. If you make it through the full moon, it becomes much less painful, but the chance of miscarriage remains very high.

"Female werewolves don't carry many babies to term. The change aborts them unless they can change slowly enough. You, with your quick changes, will have an especially hard time. Even old wolves with good control who do everything right can abort. A werewolf pregnancy lasts seven months. The fetus will grow quicker but be smaller than a human child. Female werewolves experience all the same symptoms of a human woman plus they need to pacify their wolves. A pregnant werewolf will usually want to be alone deep in the woods with just her mate. Even other wolves will upset her except for the pack alpha and his mate.

"You'll like Leah. Nature makes her scent soothing. She smells like home and safety like Richard does. But she's also a very nice person. She has a young son so understands how hard it is—"

Kelly leaped up and grabbed the bag off his shoulder. He turned away so she could dress.

"Why are you telling me this now? No don't turn," she said, and he walked further away to give her privacy.

"That's another thing you need to get used to. We see each other naked all the time and it doesn't mean anything."

"Stop changing the subject."

"I'm telling you this because you're a young girl with a boyfriend."

"He isn't my boyfriend."

Mark snorted.

"Fine, whatever. Can male werewolves impregnate human women?"

"No. We can only breed with our mates, and it usually takes a long time."

"How old is Leah?"

"Ninety-six. She's been Richard's mate for eighty years, and this is their first child."

"Wow."

"Yeah. We have a thirteen-year-old boy born from a female werewolf and a human man, and he's the only one I know of, and it almost killed his mother. The only reason it didn't is modern medicine. Pregnant wolves crave meat, but human fetuses can't survive on an all meat diet. Vitamins help, but she had to gag down the vegetables she needed and keep them down. It wasn't fun for her."

"But if I get pregnant and change to fast I'll lose the baby?"

"It isn't a form of birth control.

She flushed and looked away.

"I don't mean it in a moral sense, but you're a wolf. That fetus will smell like a wolf child to you, and your wolf will be sad she lost it. It's one of the leading causes female wolves go feral. The wolf's pain is so severe the human recedes to comfort them, and it can take years to recover. So, use birth control and if you think you're pregnant, call me, or Leah, or Richard."

She settled cross-legged at his feet. "Why do we need to keep ourselves secret? Being a wolf doesn't seem that horrible."

"For you, it isn't, and I thank God for that, but lots of us have problems controlling our wolf until we're older."

"You mean you kill people?"

"Some have, but we're careful and keep a close watch on our young wolves. I have a friend who was like you, a girl bitten who had no idea. When she changed for the first time, her wolf rolled her, and she killed and ate her entire family. Not their entire bodies mind, they rotted before she could finish them off, but she snacked on them all. When Richard found her, she thought she was a wolf. It took four years for her to change back and when she did, guilt almost killed her."

"But it wasn't her fault."

"Would that make you feel better if you ate your mother?"

She paled.

"She didn't mean to hurt anyone, and if she hadn't been trapped in the house, she would have run away. Instead, she fought, and like a wolf ate what she killed. It isn't something you get over."

"Have you killed anyone?"

"Yes, but not by mistake. I knew what I was doing."

"Humans, I mean."

"Yes."

When she recoiled, he smiled slightly and squatted before her. "Soldiers kill. Your dad was in the service. Is he a murderer?"

"He didn't kill anyone."

"You know what I mean."

"So, you're saying you've killed in a war?"

"I'm saying, I've killed my enemies. I've never killed for sport. And I've never killed in anger or in a fight if I could escape and doing so wouldn't put another at risk. There's lots of bad people out there. I wouldn't spare one if he attacked me."

She nodded slowly. "But with modern medicine maybe we could give our healing and improved senses to humans."

"Maybe someday. There are werewolf scientists who study us, but right now we can't do that. Ninety-six percent of those bitten die. It's a crazy chance to take to try to change a loved one, and we do it all the time. You'll be tempted to bite a friend or your parents, but your bite is poisonous. Most of us wait until our loved ones are dying and then try, and that could be why so many don't make it but how could you live with yourself if you killed someone you loved?"

"But we could tell the real scientists, and they could help us."

"You really think we'd be accepted and not hunted? How much do you think a man would pay to capture you and force you to conceive his child or make you bite people?"

He sat and pulled her into his lap, and it didn't occur to him until after he did it was a dangerous thing to do but he felt no overwhelming sexual attraction just a need to comfort her.

She cried in his arms a few minutes before pushing away.

"I've got to get back."

She took three running steps, then spun back. "Thank you." She gestured vaguely about her. "For all of this. You must have better things to do than babysit me."

"Once your pack, you'll understand. Come meet

us. Let us be your family."

A pained expression crossed her face.

"I can't."

He let her run down the hill alone.

Eighteen

bby sprawled across Kelly's bed with her feet in the air and eyed Kelly critically. "You should wear a dress or a skirt."

"Not going to happen."

"No one will see the scar. It isn't like we'll pull up the skirt or anything, and you've got great legs." She sat and rummaged in her bag, emerging with a red bra. "Tada! For you. At least wear a nice top." She waggled the bra at Kelly. "See push-up to make more of what you lack. Not that they're tiny, but this will make them impressive."

Kelly giggled and grabbed the bra. She turned her back to change and adjust herself.

Abby clapped and laughed when she turned back around. "Perfect. He'll drool." She hopped from the bed to sort through Kelly's closet, frowning at the shirts inside.

"You have like nothing to wear. Doesn't your mother realize you aren't ten anymore? We should go shopping."

"I have no money."

"Because you give it all to Stacy." Abby frowned at her, then sighed and looked sad. "She's taking advantage of you."

"My problem."

"Well, it's my problem too if you look like a dork. Wear one of my shirts."

Kelly rolled her eyes and snatched a tank-top from her drawer. Light pink with a lacy edge she pulled it on and glared. "I'll wear this with my white button-down shirt open.

"Guess it will have to do," Abby said doubtfully. She sat at Kelly's desk and began putting on makeup. "Save some money though. We'll need killer prom dresses." She yanked Kelly to the desk. "Close your eyes.

"Light!"

"I know." Abby fussed a few minutes before sitting back. "Wallaha. You look beautiful."

Kelly stared at herself doubtfully.

"You need some jewelry. How about these?" Abby rummaged in the box full of jewelry she'd brought and offered a pair of dangling silver earrings.

"No thanks. My holes keep getting infected, so I let them close. I'll borrow your pink beads though."

Abby adjusted the sparkling glass beads and stepped back. "Perfect." She grinned broadly. "I still can't believe you landed Jason Marson."

"Me either." Both girls laughed as they headed out the door.

"Be home by twelve and no drinking," her mother called after them.

"I'm actually surprised she's letting you go," Abby whispered.

"Me too," Kelly said, and Abby laughed ruefully.

Noise assaulted her ears as they pulled up to the football stadium. The press of bodies and mix of smells nauseated her. She sat beside Abby on the worn wooden bleachers and tried to take shallow breaths through her mouth. School was nothing like this. School smelled of dusty books and boredom with the occasional whiff of male rut or female excitement. She avoided the cafeteria and science labs, but even they didn't have this overpowering stench.

The wooden bleachers smelled of urine and spilled beer. An underlying odor of dog feces permeated everything as if everyone had tromped through dog shit and wiped their feet on the seats. The smell of dog poop was so strong from the metal garbage cans on the edges of the bleachers, she could almost see it as a haze in the air. This field was a popular place for dog walkers who picked up their dog's excrement but didn't bring it home, instead, using the garbage cans here where it sat for weeks, cooking in the cans before they were emptied after a game.

The people smelled of sweat and excitement.

The air smelled of sex and rotten food, the combination making her gag.

"Don't be so nervous," Abby whispered.

She accepted the covered cup from her boyfriend, Matt, and winked at Kelly as she sipped.

The strong smell of brandy tickled Kelly's nose. She rose.

"I need a bathroom; be right back."

She pushed through the crowd and headed to the bathrooms, but they smelled worse. Her eyes began to water, and she lurched away not knowing where to go.

"It's okay. Take a few deep breaths," Mark said.

She jerked around, shocked to see him there.

"It'll get easier. Concentrate on each smell." He breathed deeply and closed his eyes. "The man behind us at the gate handing out tickets ate taco's recently, and he smokes a pipe and has a cat. The girl with the red shirt and blue pants had sex and used condoms, cherry flavored ones, I think," he whispered.

Kelly slapped her hand over her mouth and giggled.

His brown eyes laughed into hers.

"The boy leaning on the fence just smoked a joint and peed on himself. He also stepped in dog shit recently, within the last four days, I think." He cocked his head, and his smile widened. "And he's hungry. I can hear his stomach rumbling.

"Take your time and sort out the scents and sounds. I admit the hot dogs smell off, but if you don't try to smell them all at once, it isn't so bad."

She giggled again.

"Are you okay now?"

"Thanks."

"I'm here for you."

She nodded and ran back to Abby. When she glanced back, he'd disappeared. She searched for his dark red t-shirt but didn't spot him and felt a pang of disappointment that he'd left.

"Well?" her mother called when she came in.

"It went okay, I guess. We won, anyway."

"Were they drinking afterward?"

"Some of them. We mostly danced." A blush heated her cheeks. She had mostly danced, but she'd kissed him too.

Her mother rose from the couch and gave her a quick hug. "I guess we should talk about birth control."

"We can if you want, but I don't plan on having sex with him. It was one date."

Her mother laughed and hugged her again.

"Still, it's my job to prepare you so you aren't taken by surprise. When you like someone a lot, and they kiss you, it can be hard to stop. So, it's best to be prepared. That doesn't mean sleep with whoever you want to, but plan ahead and be smart."

"I'm a virgin."

Her mother blushed and turned away.

"I believe you, but you'll be grown before we

know it, and you'll fall in love, and I want you to be ready."

Kelly didn't know what was worse, the sex talk from Mark or her mother. Both she and her mother were blushing by the time her mother was convinced she'd explained biology to her daughter.

"We're going to a movie Friday if that's okay?"

"It is. I like him. He seems like a nice boy. I remember he came to look for you."

Kelly's blush deepened. Her mother's smile fled, and she cleared her throat.

"What really happened that night, Kelly."

"Exactly what I said happened. I've never been so scared in my life. Believe me, if I could have come home, I would have."

"I believe you were scared." She hesitated then blurted. "I also always sort of thought something bad happened to you. Did a man— did Mark Miller hurt you?"

Shocked, Kelly jumped to her feet.

"No. Why would you say that? He's always been nice to me."

"I saw how he looked at you. It's silly, he has a girlfriend, but you disappeared after speaking to him and came home crying with a ripped shirt…"

"He has a girlfriend?" She wanted to smack herself for saying anything. Her mother's eyes narrowed and her lips pursed.

"Do you see him?" her mother asked.

"Sometimes. Around town and stuff. He waves or says hi. I saw him at the game for a few minutes," she added in case someone mentioned it to her mother.

"He's too old for you."

"Mom. He's never been anything except nice. We were the mean ones kicking him out. It wasn't Marigold's fault either."

"I know." Her mother patted her hand. "I sort of feel bad for that. He was really worried. I'd thought he'd be sick when you showed up. I hate to say it, but I thought he looked nervous and was worried you got away from him. I almost accused him right then."

"Jeez, Mom, that would've been so embarrassing. Marigold spooked, and I fell. I should've said where I was riding, but I didn't think it a big deal. My head hurt from the branch, and I got lost and then scared of the damn dogs. I shouldn't have tried to take that shortcut. No one hurt me," she finished in a softer voice.

"You were so scared." Tears filled her mother's eyes.

"I was. I was terrified the dogs would smell my blood and attack me. All night I cried, afraid to move."

Her mother stroked her hair and kissed her brow. "Well, it's over now. I'm sorry I sent Mister Miller away."

"I miss Marigold."

"Your dad and I were talking about getting you a horse of your own but with college coming up so fast…"

"It's fine, Mom. Flit is good company. He's fun to walk."

"He's been a good pet." Her mother rose and headed to the stairs. "Good night, sweetheart," she called.

Nineteen

Kelly ran upstairs and showered, the words, 'he has a girlfriend' ringing in her head.

Mark answered on the first ring. "What's wrong?"

"Nothing."

"It's one thirty in the morning. What's wrong?"

"Do you have a girlfriend?"

"No."

"Liar. My mother says you do."

"Kelly, what's this about?'

"I shouldn't have called."

She stabbed the off button and almost threw the phone from her. The alarm clocked mocked her with the blinking time, so she slapped it to the floor.

Yes, the wolf inside her said, and she grabbed her pillow to rip it to pieces. Her phone dinged telling her she had a text message. She didn't want to look, she knew it would be from him, but she couldn't stop herself.

'CALL ME RIGHT BACK OR I'M COMING

TO GET YOU,' he'd written in all caps.

She snarled and called him back.

"You're upset and I'm sorry, but I don't know why. Are you in control? Should I come get you?"

"I'm fine."

He sighed, sounding irritated.

"This won't work if you lie. I don't need to smell you to know that's a lie," he said.

"I'm angry you lied, or are you saying my mom lied?'

"I didn't lie. I don't have a girlfriend. What are you really asking?"

She said nothing. *What right do I have to question him about anything?* Suddenly, she was hugely embarrassed and glad she hadn't confronted him in person.

"Kelly, if you're asking if I have a mate, then the answer is no. Your mother didn't lie. She saw me with a girlfriend, but I haven't seen her in a year now, and we weren't that serious then. If you're asking if I have human lovers, then the answer is yes. I've had human lovers. I have none currently, and I'm not looking for one."

"Do you love them?' her voice sounded strangled to her own ears, and she didn't know why it mattered to her.

"No. Well, one, but she died a long time ago."

"How come you didn't make her one of us?"

"You know why. Plus, she didn't want too."

"You told her?"

"Yeah. We lived together for ten years. She

knew everything—"

"You hypocrite."

"Kelly?"

"You can tell, but I can't?"

"It isn't like that, and if you fall in love, we won't stop you. We aren't monsters. We love too, you know."

"So, I can tell my parents?"

"Jesus, look, can we talk about this in person?"

"Just answer the question."

"I shouldn't have to. You and I both know what your parents would do if you told them. They would seek help for you. Do you think anything we said would stop them from trying to help you?"

"So, you'd kill them to keep them quiet."

"What's this about?"

"Would you kill them to keep them quiet?" She practically spat the words she was so angry.

"Not me personally, but it would probably be done. We would try to reason with them first, and maybe lock them up, but yes, to protect the pack, I'd kill almost anyone."

"Don't come near me again."

"Kelly…"

"I mean it. Stay away. I'm no danger, but you are. You've seen me run. My wolf is happy. Leave us alone."

"Please, Kelly, what happened? I thought we were friends."

"And as a friend, I'm asking you to go."

"I can't," he said in a strangled voice.

"Then don't let me see you." She threw her phone across the room and cried herself to sleep.

Twenty

Mark stared at the phone in his hand for five minutes before gently setting it on the table. His wolf cowered within him, a feeling he'd never felt before. He needed fresh air and mountains.

Twice he almost swerved off the road, tears blurring his vision. He left his truck in the bar parking lot and ran into the woods. Just inside the trees, he stripped and left his clothes laying where they fell. On quiet paws, he ran into the woods but the night held no charm for him. He sat and howled his despair at the quarter moon.

For a day and a night he ran, trying to outrun his pain. He attacked his dinner with animal ferocity and human cunning, ripping the rabbit in half with one swipe of his claws. He finally returned, the wolf needed to check on her, to find his truck towed.

That night he stood outside the movie theater and

watched while she kissed Jason and held his hand. Fury clenched his hands so tightly his nails gouged into his palms. He wanted to kill that human boy, and if he thought it wouldn't make her unforgivably mad, he would.

He envisioned Jason's neck ripped out and smiled.

Yes, his wolf said and scrabbled to get loose, a sensation like claws ripping from the inside out.

He turned away and breathed deeply, trying to calm his jittering insides. Killing someone Kelly loved wouldn't make her love him. For the first time, he admired his father's restraint. To not kill the wolf his mother loved must have been hard. He'd always considered his father a weak man, and maybe he was, but he'd tried his best to make his mate happy. His mother had never tried, blaming his father for the ruin of her life, but his father had a wolf too.

Mark banged his head on the steering wheel. Rehashing his parents failed marriage wouldn't help him. Except he could learn from his father's mistakes. His father should have left his mother and gone far away so his wolf couldn't roll him and rape her.

"I'll go," he whispered and turned the key. Then he remembered he was supposed to ask her about other wolves coming to guard her. But she had no choice now. She needed a guardian until she was fully grown with a stable life. He turned his truck off and was considering his options of informing her when someone rapped on his window.

To his surprise, Stacy stood there. She pursed her lips and tapped again.

He rolled the window down.

"Spying on my sister?"

"Don't be stupid."

"Not even going to pretend you don't know who I am?" She lifted a plucked eyebrow and smirked.

"I know exactly what you are."

"And I know what you are."

The way she said it rose the hair on the back of his neck. She stared at him a moment then licked her lips and looked away.

"I know you give her money." She turned back and gave him a coy smile while twirling her hair around one finger. "I'm not that much older than she is."

"You make me sick."

"And you'll make my dad sick. What do you think he'll do when I tell him you're stalking his precious angel?"

"Whatever." He began rolling his window up.

She grabbed it with her red nails. "Okay. I was trying to be friendly, but we can play hardball."

He hesitated to roll the window, not because of her threats, but because he didn't want to hurt her. Kelly would be furious.

She smirked again. "I've got pictures"— she waggled her cell phone at him—"you and Kelly talking at the game, at the library, in the mall. You turn up wherever she is."

"So?" he smacked her fingers hard.

She yelped and jumped back. "Fucker."

He started his truck.

"Wouldn't it be easier to pay me than go to jail for rape?" she called after him.

Heads turned in the parking lot, but most stared at Stacy in disgust. He wished he'd thought to record her attempts at blackmail but her showing up decided him, he needed to talk to Kelly once more before he left.

He waited before the turnoff for Kelly's house, growing angrier the later it got. Her movie had ended at nine forty-five, and it was a quarter to eleven. He slammed his truck into gear and headed to the theater. Then he had a better idea and pulled over. It only took him a minute to sign into her phone account and click the find-my-phone button.

He passed the turnoff for the dirt road and had to turn around. The deserted road gave him pause. She'd obviously wanted to be private with Jason but what if he'd brought her here without her permission. As stupid as the idea was, he couldn't let it go. He had to know she was safe.

"We're just checking on her, we aren't spying," he said to his wolf, knowing he lied, as he exited his truck. His wolf neither knew nor cared why they were going to her, it was just glad they were.

Twenty-One

Jason kissed her again, his hand sliding beneath her shirt. She returned his kiss but pushed his hand away. His kiss felt nice, but his hand made her uncomfortable, and he smelled funny. She slid farther away from him and broke from the kiss.

"I should be getting home."

"It isn't even eleven." He grinned and leaned closer.

She let him kiss her, not enjoying the attention anymore but not knowing how to stop him without making him mad.

He kissed her mouth then her neck, his hand beneath her shirt pinching her nipple. It made her feel sick. When he pressed her hand to his erection, she jerked away.

"What's wrong?"

"Just take me home."

"Aww, don't be like that. We were having a good time."

"I'm tired. Please, just take me home."

He pulled away, frowning at her, and she almost cried.

"I've got twenty bucks."

She frowned at him, puzzled now.

"Your sister only charges ten."

A wave of heat passed over her, making her feel dizzy.

"Five for a blowjob. I'll give you ten for one," Jason continued eagerly.

She slapped his face harder than she'd meant to.

He jerked back, fingering his red cheek. "What the hell?"

"I'm not a whore!"

"So, you're a tease?"

"What the hell are you talking about?"

He dropped his hand and smirked at her. "You were plenty into it a second ago."

"A second ago I thought you liked me."

"I really don't have more cash on me," he said in a cajoling voice and lightly tugged her hair.

"You—" So angry she couldn't think of a bad enough word to call him, she reached for the door handle.

"Oh, come on," he called after her and laughed.

He got out on his side and leaned over the roof.

"I'll take you home. It was a just a misunderstanding. You can't really blame me, can you? You were kissing me back."

She stopped and spun. "Is that why you asked me out? You thought I was easy?"

He shrugged and smiled.

"I could maybe scrounge up more money," he said and winked.

"Are you kidding me? You think I'm holding out for ten more dollars? Did it ever occur to you I'm holding out 'cause I'm not ready? This was our second date for crying out loud. Two dates and I'm supposed to drop my pants?"

"Well, you could keep them on, but it's more fun if they're off."

"You're fucking unbelievable."

He narrowed his eyes and straightened.

"What's that supposed to mean?"

"What's what supposed to mean? You're a pig!" She whirled to storm away, having no idea where she would go but needing to be away from him before she beat the smug smile from his face.

"And you're a whore. If you say one word about this—" he squeaked, and metal banged.

She whirled back in time see Mark hit him again. He held Jason with one hand around his throat. Jason pawed at his arm and gasped for breath.

"Let him go, right now!" she yelled.

Tears of shame burned her eyes. She was mortified that Mark had heard the entire fight. Maybe he'd even seen her let Jason paw her. Her flush felt like fire on her cheeks. She jumped to the roof in one leap and grabbed Mark's hand as it descended.

"Let him go," she yelled louder.

Lights turned on in a car twenty feet up the road.

Mark shook Jason hard and threw him into the car. He stared at her, panting with anger.

"Fucker," Jason gasped out.

Mark slapped his face and leaned close. "Get in your fucking car and never go near her again. I hear a fucking word of this, I'll fucking kill you. You'll tell everyone she's a nice girl. Bad mouth her in any way and you'll be fucking sorry." He punched Jason in the stomach, and she grabbed his hands and dragged him away.

"Go. He means it," she called over her shoulder.

Muttering curses, Jason got into his car and peeled out. More lights flicked on, and hands rubbed misted windows.

Kelly dragged Mark to the woods.

"I can't believe you came here to spy on me," she snapped as she pushed him away.

"Good thing I did too."

"Oh please, I could've handled him."

He smiled and ran a hand over her hair. The tenderness in his eyes angered her more.

"This isn't any of your business!"

"I know. I'm sorry." He looked sad and turned away. "I came to tell you someone else will be watching you. I'll text you the number, and they'll be staying in my house. Call if you need help."

"You're going away?" Her stomach dropped, leaving her feeling hollow and alone and sorry she'd yelled at him.

"Do you want me to stay?" He glanced from the road to her, and a new wave of embarrassment scorched her.

The flush deepened as she realized he could smell her nervous sweat just like he could smell everywhere Jason's popcorn scented hand had been.

"Just go," she said tiredly.

He stared a minute, his eyes glittering in the starlight.

"Let me bring you home at least."

"I can manage."

"I know. I just— I—"

He pressed his hands hard to his face. "I hate that you're so angry with me."

"I'm not angry. I'm embarrassed and confused, and I need some time to figure out what I'm doing."

He tossed her his keys and began taking off his clothes. "Take it. Leave it anywhere. It doesn't matter. I'm going to Mexico for a while. If you need me, call, and I'll come. You want to be a normal girl, I get that, but you can't be, and I'm so sorry. I only meant to be your friend, and instead, I'm the bringer of everything bad to your life. The pack wants you. You're never alone. Don't let your parents change who you are. I love who you are."

Before she could form a reply, he'd dropped to his knees, fur sprouted, his muscles writhed and bent, and he bounded away.

Her cold, clammy hands gripped the steering wheel, and she didn't remember the drive home.

"What happened," her mother jumped to her

feet, dropping her book, and Kelly burst into tears.

"He called me a whore. He tried to pay me twenty dollars to have sex. Thinks it was a lot." She fell to her knees crying as if her heart would break.

"Who?" Her mother peered out the window before she knelt beside Kelly. "Mr. Miller?"

Kelly cried harder.

Her mother shot to her feet as her father ran down the stairs. "That goddamned bastard, I knew he wanted you." She ran for the phone.

Kelly scrambled to her feet.

"Not Mark, Jason. Mark saw me walking home, and when I wouldn't get in his car, he gave it to me. Told me to keep it, he was going out of town."

"Jason," her father said. Did he hurt you?"

She began to cry again, and her mother hugged her while trying to make the phone cord stretch.

"Who are you going to call? Don't be stupid. You'll just embarrass me." She pushed away and ran up the stairs.

"What's going on," her father called after her.

She slammed her door and screamed in anger. She didn't want to hear them. Her mother told her father Jason thought she was a whore like Stacy as she kicked off her high-heeled boots. Boots Abby had made her buy to impress Jason, and threw on her sneakers and a sweatshirt, then ran back downstairs.

"I'm going for a run."

"Take your phone," her mother said.

"No." She slammed the door and ran for the

woods.

"Let her go," her father said and pulled her mother back into the house.

Kelly didn't look back.

Twenty-Two

*A*rny greeted him at the airport with a hard hug. His dyed black hair hung in a thick ponytail past his shoulders, and he wore a heavy bronzer over his tan. He looked like a native.

"We could go for a run," Arny offered as he guided the Jeep 4x4 down the dirt road. Dust billowed up behind them in thick clouds.

"Later. Tell me the plan."

"Same as always. We go in as humans and out as wolves. We'll be living in the hills and leaving the same way. They'll have no way to track us."

"Gear?"

"That's going to be our first hit."

"When do we go?"

"Soon as Richard gives us the okay."

"Who's here now?"

"Everyone except Richard and Leah. He wants her to stay home for JJ. She wants to leave him with Audrey."

"So, they'll be here tomorrow?"

Arny laughed. "You know she won't let him come alone.

"He shouldn't come either."

"He's the Alpha."

They were quiet the rest of the way to their camp. Mostly because they left the jeep at a campground and ran the last fifteen miles as wolves. His pack greeted him with hugs and neck biting depending on the form they were in. Twenty-two males, ranging in age from nineteen to three hundred, and two females, gathered around a fresh deer carcass.

Mark helped himself, letting the talk and whines roll over him, letting himself be his wolf.

Mexico was bright in his wolf senses, rotting vegetation soft beneath his paws, the animal scents new and interesting. Nose to the ground, he followed a scent and explored before returning at dawn to settle beside the others to sleep, enjoying their closeness. For the first time in months, he relaxed, completely at home with his pack. A distant part of him worried for Kelly, but he knew that was a dumb worry. She had her wolf under control. A bigger part of him missed her, but he'd have to get used to it.

He woke when Leah settled beside him and licked his neck. He rolled onto his back and waved his feet in the air. She snapped at him playfully and wrestled him until she grasped his neck again and began licking the fur beneath his jaw. He let her presence sooth him and dozed off again while she groomed him.

"Okay, everyone human up except Star and Allen," Richard called.

Mark stood and stretched, shaking out his fur and fluffing his tail before resuming his human shape. He didn't bother to dress. There was no point in getting his clothes dirty until tomorrow when they attacked.

Supplies were limited to what they could carry in the small packs that fit a wolf's back, and he'd only brought one change of clothes and a pair of boots along with the detonator caps for the C-4.

Star had brought disposable clothing for everyone, including ski masks and gloves. The first to arrive on the scene, as always, she'd taken a pet-friendly hotel room where everyone left their real clothes, filled their small rucksacks, and headed out.

They needed no supplies, neither food nor camping gear. Mark thought even bringing guns was a waste of time, but he agreed the explosives were a must to break into the safes.

Star was their resident hacker, and she was great at it. Without her help, it would take them ten times as long to track the money and the criminal activity. She and Arny worked as a team, correlating information to send to Richard while her husband, Allen, ran surveillance.

"Arny is going to be leading the first strike team, and they're going out tonight," Richard said.

Mark quirked an eyebrow in surprise.

"He'll be taking ten of you. Grab our gear, and

the money, and burn everything else. If you haven't already, check the board to make sure you can scent who we're after."

Mark rose and headed to the only 'furniture' in the camp, a straight limb with pictures, most mug shots with rap sheets attached, and scraps of fabric stapled to it. He sniffed each fabric and examined every picture until he was certain he could match the scent with the face. Richard handed out assignments and then joined him at the board.

"Fuckers got it coming to them."

"And then some," Mark agreed.

He went to dress, pulling on the brand-new khakis from a Walmart in Saint Lewis that Star had brought them and a black t-shirt, but leaving off the ski mask. He put on the cheap boots he brought by the dozen, knowing he'd leave them behind when the job was done, and stamped his feet. Beside him, Leah did the same. She flashed him a quick grin, and he gave her a hug.

Arny handed him a tube of camouflage paint and hugged Leah while Mark applied it. Mark sat and waited for the others to get ready, eyeing Richard thoughtfully. Leah was a beautiful woman with thick, curly, black hair and full red lips. Her eyes were a bright blue, striking in her tanned face and she had all the right curves on her trim, athletic body. He wouldn't want Arny to hug Kelly like that or admire Kelly's curves or the color of her eyes. Not that he felt lust for Leah, but he did admire her beauty.

It had never occurred to him that Richard might resent his wolves touching his wife. Not that he appeared to mind it now but he was keeping his distance, and it worried him. Leah settled beside him and took his hand.

"Give her time. When she's full grown, you can pursue her without guilt."

"If she doesn't fall in love with someone else."

"A human?" Leah curled her lip and lifted an eyebrow.

"It could happen."

"I guess, but the bond between wolves isn't even close." She nodded her head towards her husband. "Why do you think he stays away from me on missions?"

"I was just wondering about that."

"No, you were worrying so hard I could smell it. Richard stays away to spare my blushes. Like we can smell your worry, my arousal would be hard to miss. At home, we can run off and be private, but here, we need to stick together for safety, and it's easier on me if he doesn't touch me."

"You don't like us to smell you?"

"I don't care at all, but it makes it harder to concentrate if I'm mooning over him. And with your mate, if I smell he's worried or worked up it worries me too. So, I hug you guys and play and groom, and I feel relaxed, and you feel relaxed, and so he feels relaxed."

"But doesn't he get jealous?"

"Of pack? Never. We're family. Would you get

jealous if your brother hugged your mother?"

"I wish Kelly were pack."

"Ahh, she found a boyfriend?"

"A little snot I could break in one hand."

"So, you ran."

"What else was I supposed to do?"

She patted his hand. "You did the right thing. It is too soon for her to mate. But very soon it won't be. What's a year or two to us? When she's a woman, you can seduce her. Send her candy and give her flowers, take her on romantic dates like humans do and let her fall in love."

Much lighter of heart, he laughed, falling back in the brush and taking Leah with him. Her breasts brushed his chest, and her hair drifted over his face. It didn't arouse him in the least. Wolf biology saw to that. Leah's scent was homey, not erotic.

"She is a human, isn't she. I should woo her like one."

"There's hope for you, my friend."

Leah kissed him on the cheek, then jumped to her feet. "Let's go kill us some bad guys."

Still chuckling, he rose to follow her.

A wolf howled to Mark's left. The long, drawn-out sound seemed to linger in the thick air. It would rain any minute. A silvery haze sparkled in the air giving the trees and buildings soft edges and glittered on the points of barbed wire surrounding the compound.

Mark ran forward and jumped, pulling himself up and over the barbed wire fence in one move. He dropped the eight feet to the ground and ran across the quiet compound. A flicker of movement caught his eye, but it was only Arny racing for position.

Mark reached his target and grabbed the man by the throat before the man knew he was there. He squeezed and twisted with one hand, grabbing the man's gun in the other. The man dropped the gun to claw at the hand on his throat with both hands. Mark smacked him with the gun and let him fall. This man wasn't on the kill list.

Mark slung the gun over his shoulder and braced his hands on the doorframe so he could kick hard. The metal door buckled in two kicks. A gun sounded to his right, and a man yelled inside the building. Glass shattered, and a man screamed as another, longer, peel of gunfire sounded. He raced into the room and took a shot to the shoulder. Blood sprayed in a glittering arc, and he hunched, still running for the shooter.

The man scrambled backward and shot again but missed. He frantically yanked the hammer back. This shot connected low and forced a grunt from Mark. Mark grabbed the gun hand and twisted. The bone broke with a satisfying snap, and the man screeched. This scent he recognized. The screech cut off abruptly when Mark ripped his throat out with his bare hand.

He left the corpse twitching on the ground and kicked open the next door. Leah stood over a man cowering on the floor.

"Not it," she called and ran back through the doorway and through the opposite door.

Two men opened fire on him, so he ducked back and grabbed a filing cabinet beside the front door and rushed them holding it. A second later he had two more guns and left the men beneath the cabinet cradling their broken hands.

Loud voices in the next room warned him his team was already inside. Gunsmoke and the coppery odor of blood mixed with the sour odor of fear made scenting confusing.

"It's me," he called as he came through the door.

"I got this," Richard said. "Go change and load up."

The five men kneeling on the floor, holding their hands in the air, glared at him. One said something in Spanish, which Mark didn't understand. Richard replied in the same language.

Leah passed him in the hallway and frowned at the blood oozing from his shoulder.

"Go change."

"Yes, boss." He gave her a sloppy salute and a smacking kiss on the nose.

She laughed and pushed him away. He jogged down the short corridor and entered a room with one dead man and two pack members. Jeff and Hugh were already sorting the guns and flak jackets. He stripped and let the change take him. The dull pain of his wounds vanished as he shook and stretched.

Arny entered and threw Jeff a pack custom-made to fit a wolf's back. The men stuffed guns, ammunition, and armor into the packs. Arny tightened the straps of one pack on Mark, and they ran from the room.

"Clear," Arny called.

"On five," Richard called back.

Mark stood in the doorway beside Leah when a whoomph of hot air fluttered his fur. He raced to the west with her trailing. She carried a bag that probably weighed more than she did. They reached Richard right as an enormous fireball burst from the picture window in front. Men ran out of the building as something inside exploded. The pack hadn't been there ten minutes yet.

Mark followed his pack back into the forest where half of them assumed their wolf forms and stood still to get the packs tightened on before racing through the dense underbrush. The five in human form followed slower. Mark had shed his backpack and was eating another fresh deer by the time those five reached camp.

Arny passed out the gear they'd stolen and handed Mark the clothes he'd worn to the compound.

"I fucking hate dirty cops," Leah said as she accepted a hunk of fresh meat from Arny. "We should've killed them all."

"Only capital crimes get a death sentence. We aren't savages," Richard said.

Mark glanced at him and snorted with laughter.

Blood dribbled down Richard's naked chest as he ripped off a gob of raw meat from the leg bone he held.

A musky scent emanated from Leah.

Richard held out his hand." My wife and I need some alone time. Get some rest. We leave in four hours."

The two headed into the brush. Richards cock was already hard and bobbed with every step he took. Mark looked away to hide his jealous gaze. He didn't want Leah, but he did want a mate who would live and fight with him.

Arny slapped his shoulder. "We could go to Buenos Aires after this. The women there are hot. We could find one to share and run on the beach afterward."

"Thanks, but no. I'm going home when we're done here."

"Good, the ranch will be good for you, and Audrey misses you."

"No, home to Kelly."

"Ahh. She's the one, huh?"

"Yes."

"Well good luck, bro. I wouldn't want one, but I hope it works out for you."

"When you smell the right one, you will."

"Hasn't happened yet." Arny shrugged and lay back in the bracken, cradling his head in his arms. "It's pretty here. Except for all the bugs." He flicked a spider the size of a half dollar from his bare arm.

"I'd miss the snow," Mark said.

"Me too but this might be nice for a year or so."

They stared up at the sky in companionable silence.

"I'll come home to welcome her into the pack."

"God, I hope so." Mark closed his eyes to picture her face.

Arny slapped another bug and curled up.

"This place gives me the willies," Mark muttered as he flicked another spider from Arny's leg.

Arny laughed and stretched, "Pansy," he said as he popped a hairy spider in his mouth.

Mark made gagging noises and drifted to sleep with a smile on his face.

Twenty-Three

"What's got into you? You've been moping around for a month now."

Kelly glanced up from her History book but didn't answer. Chin resting on her hands, she breathed in deeply, inhaling the scent of fresh meat from the bowl before her mother on the counter. Her stomach rumbled, and she glared irritably.

"Don't let him get to you. I'm tempted to call his mother"— her mother waved her meat-covered hand as Kelly half-rose—"I won't, but I should. The nerve of him."

"All the kids think I'm a whore like her."

Her mother made an unhappy sound. "Don't worry about it. One more year and you go away to college. No one will know your sister or care. Have you thought about where you'd like to go?"

Hot tears slid down Kelly's cheek and dampened the page before her.

"Oh, honey," her mother said softly.

She left the counter and took a step forward,

holding out her meat covered hands.

Kelly jumped to her feet and ran out the door. With all her soul, she wished Mark would be waiting in the trees. Her breath hitched in her throat, and she thought she might vomit. She'd wanted to lick her mother's hands. She could imagine the horrified expression, and what if she hadn't been able to stop. Retching and gagging, she fell to her knees and crawled to the tall grass edging the stone wall.

"I need you, Mark," she muttered and started crying. "Why did you leave me when I need you." She cried herself to sleep in the grass. Something hit her face, waking her. The sky was just beginning to darken. She hadn't slept long. Her father called her from the field.

"I'm here." She stood and walked slowly to him.

"Don't run off like that; you'll catch a cold." He wrapped a blanket around her shoulders. "Your mother is worried and so am I. Abby called and wants to know if you're okay. She's worried too. Don't close us out, honey. Should we call that nice doctor so we can talk?"

"No. There's nothing to talk about."

"I can't imagine how hard it is to have a sister like Stacy."

Kelly jerked away. "Stop! I'm sick of her. She has nothing to do with me. Nothing!"

Her father put an arm around her shoulders and kissed her brow. Immediately, she felt bad. It wasn't Stacy that had gotten her so upset. But how could she explain? If Mark were here, maybe it wouldn't bother her so much to be so ridiculed at school. She sighed and gave her father a quick hug. Together they entered the house and sat at the kitchen table. Her stomach rumbled, but she couldn't eat the meatballs.

"Let her go," her father said when her mother urged her to eat.

She ran to her room and cried herself to sleep.

Twenty-Four

$\mathcal{R}$ichard sat beside Mark and handed him the satellite phone.

"Call Ben. You're driving us all crazy."

"I haven't done a thing," Mark protested.

"You're going to get yourself killed." Richard's eyes narrowed, and he lowered his voice. "Are you trying to get yourself killed?"

A hot flush burned across Mark's cheeks. "No," he mumbled.

"Well, slow the hell down then. Find another way to spend all that angry energy. You get shot once more and I'm leaving you in camp. Call and check on her, and stop moping."

The flush on Mark's cheeks darkened. He was being reckless, rushing in and attacking savagely. So far he'd been shot twelve times, taken three knife wounds, and broken his leg in a fall. No one else had been shot once. Richard had been the soul of patience but being careless put the pack at risk. He vowed to himself to slow down and pay attention, rushing wouldn't get him home quicker, it'd just get him embarrassed.

Anna answered, sounding as if he'd woken her.

Mark smacked himself on the forehead. "Sorry, I forgot about the time difference."

Richard snorted.

Mark glared and turned away. "Is Ben there?"

"No. He's trailing Kelly." Soft fumbling sounds followed for a second, then Anna said," Actually, it's after midnight, he'll be sleeping now outside her house. Is something wrong? How's everything there?"

"We're all good. Why is he spending the nights?"

"She's been running really early and really late."

Mark scowled, not liking the defensive tone. "What happened?"

"I'm not sure." Anna sighed hard. "She comes home crying and… she asked for you."

Shocked, Mark held the phone away to stare at it a moment before saying, "Asked for me? She talks with you?"

"No. Kelly ran from her house and was talking to herself. She cried herself to sleep. I woke her before her dad could startle her, but Ben and I are a bit worried, what with her being such a new wolf and all, so we're watching her around the clock."

I'm coming home."

"No you're not," Richard said and plucked the phone from his hand. "Anna, can you and Ben handle this?"

"Yes."

"Great. We'll be home in a few weeks."

Richard turned off the phone. "Stay," he said, using the voice that meant or else. Mark glowered but remained seated when Richard rose to replace the phone in his pack. He spoke quietly with Leah a moment before returning to sit beside Mark.

"You're going to stay and do your job and leave her alone." He held up his hand when Mark opened his mouth. "It's just a few weeks. She's in no danger. Let her cope on her own for a while, and maybe she'll realize she needs a pack."

"No." Mark rose.

Richard grabbed his arm. "You will not go."

The two men stared at each other. Never before had Mark tried to pit his strength of will against Richard's

"Calm down," Leah said as she laid her hand on his arm. "We want what's best for her, and you, and the best thing is for her to realize wolves are pack animals."

"Anna said she was crying for me… How is ignoring her best?"

"Don't be stupid," Richard said in exasperation. "What are you going to do? She doesn't want to see you, or have you forgotten that?"

"If Leah were crying and called for you, wouldn't you go check on her?"

Richard pursed his lips.

"Anna is checking on her," Leah said and hugged him.

Mark absently returned the hug but continued to glare at Richard.

"Call and speak to Ben tomorrow," Richard said.

Mark growled.

"Get some sleep. We leave early in the morning."

The command in Richard's voice was clear. He was trying to force Mark to obey. It took an act of will to stand his ground. His wolf wanted him to slink away. Mark growled again and pushed Leah away.

"Both of you knock it off." She stepped between them and held her hands out. "What are you going to do? Fight Richard? Don't be silly."

"Let me go." Mark half-crouched, his eyes never leaving Richard. Only one of them would walk away if they fought. Mark had never contemplated fighting Richard before; he was like a father to him. Richard had killed his old pack leader and taken over his pack mere days after Mark's father had died and Richard had raised him. He was happy in the pack, but he knew he was a strong shifter. He could be an alpha if he were willing to fight for it, and he'd fight anyone to get to Kelly.

It must have shown on his face because Leah said, "Let him go."

Richard turned his glare on his wife. "No."

"Richard, let him go. You'll win but at what cost? He needs her. Let him go."

Leah and Richard stared at each other a moment.

"Fine. Go. I'm sick of this argument." Richard grabbed Mark and shook him hard. "Kelly needs a pack, not just you."

Mark said nothing and didn't try to pull away.

"Richard…" Leah grabbed his arm and tried to yank him off.

Richard sighed, then shoved Mark hard. Mark stumbled back a step, and they glared at each other again. Mark's gaze flicked to Leah who looked scared now, and he slowly sank to his knees.

Richard's glare deepened.

Leah whined the barest of sounds, and Richard pulled her close, his face relaxing.

"Go. You're right. If Leah called for me, I'd fight anyone to go to her too. But, Mark, Kelly does need a pack, and Leah is right, time alone will show her that. Try to talk her into meeting us."

Richard pulled Mark to his feet and hugged him. After a moment Mark hugged him back. Leah made an odd noise sounding both scared and excited, and Mark turned to her. The rest of the pack had gathered, and he'd been so caught up in Richard he hadn't noticed.

"I'm sorry, Richard, but I have to," Mark said.

Richard nodded. His gaze traveled the pack, and he stepped forward. "Mark isn't the only one of you who could become alpha. I chose strong wolves; it's what makes us a strong pack. We're also civilized. I like to think we're a family and like family, we'll disagree and fight, but make no mistake, this is my pack."

Mark knelt with the rest of the wolves, the power of Richard's voice pushing him to his knees. He could fight the power, but it would be a fight, and while Richard might leave him alive, he'd then be packless, and he did love his pack.

"I'm sorry," he said again.

Richard offered him a hand to rise. "Go. Make sure she's safe and talk her into meeting us."

Mark kissed his cheek then hugged Leah hard, burying his face in her hair. "I'm sorry, he whispered.

"Don't be. I'd fight to reach him too. We love you."

"I love you too." He released Leah and called his wolf. Without a backward glance, he ran.

Twenty-Five

The titters and whispers when she walked to class grew daily. Half her friends avoided her now.

She thumped into an empty seat beside Abby at the lunch table and picked at her food.

The girls at her table straightened as a group of boys approached. Kelly glanced up and away as Jason leered at her and whispered to Mike Walters who walked with him.

"You coming to the game this week?" Jason asked her and smirked. His buddies high-fived him and Mike, and they all laughed.

Kelly frowned at him, not sure what he was implying. She hadn't attended any games except her track meets since that one she'd gone to with him. Still laughing, the boy's left the cafeteria.

"Don't go to the game," Abby whispered. Her cheeks turned bright red, and she avoided eye contact, examining each leaf of lettuce in her salad.

"What? I never go? Why would they ask?"

Whatever Abby was worried about made her sweat smell sour.

"Stacy goes," Abby blurted and pushed her salad away. "She charges them twenty bucks a piece in the boy's bathroom. Has her own stall and everything."

Bile rose in Kelly's throat, and she peered around the room at the people staring and laughing behind their hands.

"They all know?"

"I'm so sorry, Kell."

"When did you find out?"

Abby's flush deepened, and she ducked her head.

"Matt told me after the first game. I didn't know how to tell you."

"It's fine. Not your fault." Kelly rose and dumped her uneaten food into the trash. She was glad Abby didn't attempt to follow her, and no one was in the girl's bathroom to see her crying.

Later that night, she cried again in her room until her head hurt. She skipped the next three days of school and stayed in her room, claiming she was sick. She only went the next day because her mother threatened to take her to the doctors.

She managed to avoid her friends until lunchtime. Abby watched her with worried eyes, and she felt the hugest hypocrite. She was the worst friend, and Abby deserved better. Her friends pretended not to notice the smirks and stares, but they all knew what her classmates thought of her.

She tried to act normal, but it all felt so pointless. Why suffer like this and make her friends suffer when she would run away soon anyway? It got harder and harder to tear her eyes from the classroom window and the beckoning trees and concentrate. The first snow of the year fell in fat flakes, and she longed to run with Mark by her side. Tears trickled from the corners of her eyes, and she angrily dashed them away.

At the bell, she rose and plodded to the cafeteria where she sat without speaking or eating, trying to ignore the muffled laughter as her classmates passed her.

After lunch, Abby trailed her to her locker.

"Are you mad at me?"

"God, no. I just suck as a friend."

"You're my best friend," Abby said, then frowned and leaned closer. Before she could speak, Mike Walters, the school's star pitcher, laid his hand on the locker between them.

"Hey, Kell, want to go to the game with me next week?"

"No thanks, I'm busy."

He grinned and tapped his back pocket. "I got plenty of cash."

"Go fuck yourself! She said no," Abby snapped and yanked at his arm.

"Oh, I get it, you like the girls. How much would a three-way cost? I'm totally down for that."

"Don't be such a dick—"

"I got this," Kelly said, cutting Abby off. "Tell

your friends I'm not interested. I'll never be interested. You're too mean for me to date. I can't help who my sister is but you choose to be an asshole."

"You're too good for me, huh?"

"Damn straight she is," Abby said.

"No one asked you, Flabigal." His sneer widened when Abby stepped back as if she'd been slapped.

"Why do you smell like Steven Wright's cologne?" Kelly leaned closer and sniffed him. "I saw you two coming out of the boy's locker earlier. You two getting hot and heavy in there? Well, I'm not willing to be your cover girl. Come out of that closet. Gay pride— whoo-ha." Kelly waved her hands in the air and made cheering motions.

"Skank." Mike turned on his heel and stormed off, his face white and furious.

Abby pressed her hands to her mouth, stifling a nervous giggle, and stared after him. "Mike and Steve?"

Kelly shrugged.

"Were you guessing or did you really see something?"

Kelly pressed her lips together and shook her head. The scents were clear to her. She was certain Steven and Mike were lovers, but she couldn't prove it. She didn't want to prove it. She just wanted to be left alone.

"It doesn't matter. I love you, Abby, and because I do, I'm going to do you a favor. Don't talk to me any more. You think they're mean now, think how bad it's going to get when I don't knuckle under."

"Don't be stupid. I would never turn my back on you."

"I know; that's why I'm turning my back on you. Don't call me anymore." Kelly left her staring after her, and it broke her heart, but it was kinder this way.

"See, doc, I know what love is," Kelly said as the main door closed behind her.

She walked home. Her mother glanced up and frowned when she came in.

"The school called."

"Yeah, I skipped like four classes. Abby and I aren't friends anymore. Don't try to fix it, Mom, it's better this way. They're mean to her, and you know she'll stick up for me. I'd really like to switch schools. If you won't let me switch, I'm dropping out."

Her mother rose slowly to her feet. "I understand teasing can be hard to bear, but you can't drop out."

"Teasing? Is that teasing? It feels like sexual harassment to me, but if I complain, it's my word against theirs, and what about my friends being called names and picked on? How would you like it if your best friend was humiliated because of you? I can hold my own, it wouldn't even really bother me if weren't for my friends catching flack, but I can't bear her being hurt, Mom, I really can't."

"You really think changing schools will help?"

"It couldn't hurt. They can say whatever they like and it will just be to me. And Abby can have a good senior year and go to prom and dances without me dragging her down." She started to cry and angrily scrubbed her face with the hem of her sweatshirt.

"Fine, I'll talk to your father and see what we can do, but it isn't like we get to choose schools, you know.

"Then homeschool me. I'm not going back." She dropped her book bag and ran out the door. She knew her mother was staring at her anxiously, but she didn't slow or look back.

That night she lay in bed listening to her parents argue. The tiniest effort let her ears elongate. She twitched them and ran her hands over their soft silkiness. It was like turning the volume up to ten. The indistinct murmurs clarified.

She walked to her mirror as they argued over sending her to a new school. Her reflection made her shriek.

"What!" her father called as she yelled, "Nothing! Just a spider and it's dead now!" She lifted a trembling hand to her protruding ears. The bones of her skull had flattened and curved, leaving hairless ledges on which her ears sat.

"That's freak show ugly," she whispered to her reflection.

She concentrated, imagining her wolf pushing only her muzzle through her skin and her muzzle formed. She snapped at her reflection then let herself become her wolf totally. Scents dialed up by a hundred percent and her paws felt every broken stitch in the threadbare carpet she stood on. Her clothes dangled from her body, and she was glad nobody could see how silly she looked. She was so caught up in her reflection she forgot she was listening for her parents until a board creak in the hallway. She shifted back and yanked up her pajama bottoms right as her father knocked.

"It's open," she called while smoothing her hair and checking to make sure she hadn't left any dangling wolf parts. The idea made her giggle.

Her father smiled and relaxed. "What's so funny?"

"These pajamas. I think I've had them since I was ten. Maybe I can get a part-time job or something?"

"We can afford new pajamas."

"I know, but why not? Lots of kids do."

"One thing at a time. I'm not saying no but let's work out school first. I wish we could afford to send you to a private school but we can't. We could homeschool you, but do you really want to sit in here all day?"

"As opposed to being offer fivers for blowjobs?"

Her father winced. "I can talk to the principle and their parents."

"Do you think that would help? I don't. I think it would make it worse."

"I sort of agree, but how about if we talk to your

friends and their parents?"

Kelly pursed her lips doubtfully.

"Your mom and I understand how upsetting it is to have your friends hurt, but if we talked to them, and asked them to ignore you in school, and explained why… I mean if Abby turned her back on you, you'd be crushed, but if she came to you with her mom and you saw how important it was to her?"

"The last thing I want to do is hurt Abby's feelings."

"What about your feelings, honey? Have you considered how much your feelings will be hurt if your friends turn away from you?"

"No. I don't know what to do, Dad."

"Me either," he said worriedly. "Stay home tomorrow and give us some time to figure this out. Nothing is insurmountable if everyone tries and compromises."

She turned to the window and leaned her head on the glass. "Can I go for a run? The snow looks so pretty, and it's so peaceful outside."

"Wear a coat and be back in an hour."

She grinned at him over her shoulder. "I'll wear a coat, but give me two hours. I want to sit on the hill awhile and watch the stars."

He smiled and kissed the top of her head. "Two hours and bring the mace. It makes me feel better when you're out alone at night. Who knows who else thinks this is a good night for a run."

Twenty-Six

Mark crept backward when she opened the door. It had taken him days to get to her. He'd run straight north and crossed the border on foot. Not by plan, by instinct. He'd run for a day before it occurred to him driving would be much faster but by then he was deep in the jungle, and it seemed quicker to keep running.

He'd left so quickly he hadn't brought any clothes with him, and he'd had to rob a house so he could catch a bus. The hours spent on the greyhound felt like painfilled years.

His wolf clawed for release, cramping his muscles, making him moan and sweat. The other passengers had given him a wide berth, probably thinking he was crazy in his ill-fitting clothes, clutching his head and telling himself to stop it.

But he was here now, and his wolf relaxed as soon as he shifted and smelled her.

She waved and closed the door, then began jogging through the snow. Mark followed, keeping downwind and two hundred yards between them. She stepped off the path and into the trees to strip and then ran hard. Trees, shrubs, and the need to be quiet slowed him, but he knew where she was going.

Snow drifted onto his back as he crawled on his stomach to the edge of the clearing at the top of the hill. His tongue lolled in a wolfy grin. She rolled on her back, chased her tail, and kicked up gouts of snow and rotting leaves that she snapped at. She finally slowed her silly play and sat panting, staring up at the sky.

Her howl started low but built until she cried to the night. He wanted to run to her and howl with her, but she didn't wish to see him. He would respect her wishes and keep out of sight despite his fierce need to be with her.

Her howl was sad and lonely. If she'd been in human form, she'd be crying. He left her crying to the moon and ran back to Ben's truck. He had promises to keep.

The lock on Jason's front door gave with a dull crunch. Somewhere in the house, a television played softly.

Mark ran up the stairs and crouched to sniff door handles. Jason sat in bed holding a laptop. He glanced at the door when it opened and didn't have time to do more than look shocked before Mark grabbed him. Mark punched him hard in the stomach and rolled him in his sheet while he wheezed.

The sheet kept Jason's thrashings and kicks contained and muffled his whimpers. Mark hit him again and threw him over his shoulder to run back down the stairs.

"Make a goddamned sound, and I'll slit your fucking throat," he said when he stood on Jason's front porch.

He carried his silent captive a quarter mile through the woods and dropped him. Snow dampened his black fatigues as he squatted on his haunches. Jason thrashed free of the sheet and yelped, jerking away from him. Mark removed his black face mask.

Jason's wide-eyed gaze locked on the blade in Mark's hand.

"I fucking warned you," Mark said in an even tone.

"It wasn't me."

Mark punched him in the face, knocking him to the ground.

Jason cried out and clutched the sheet around him.

"I wasn't fucking kidding. I told you I'd fucking kill you."

"I swear to God, man, it wasn't me." Jason scrabbled backward on his hands and knees when Mark lifted his fist again.

"The way I see it, I can save myself a lot of time and trouble by wasting your ass. You're a fucking blight on humanity. Why pick on her? You know she isn't a whore." He nudged him with his foot.

"That was a question."

Jason's gaze skittered from the knife to Mark's furious expression and back. "I'm not. I didn't say anything."

Mark tapped the knife against his hand absently and pursed his lips. "Okay. I'll give you one more chance. You have three days to make this better. If Kelly comes home crying again, I'll have no mercy for you."

Jason sat shivering in his sheet and nodding.

"You're going to stop this shitty rumor you started. You're going to apologize so sincerely that Kelly believes you're really sorry, and you're going to pray you never see me again."

Mark kicked him lightly and turned to go.

"Where am I?"

"At your fucking grave if you piss me off again," Mark said without turning. "If you're asking how to get home, it's straight ahead. Try not to freeze to death."

"You won't get away with this. I know who you are!" Jason called after him.

Mark turned and sauntered back. "You really are stupid, aren't you? Instead of wasting your limited time before you freeze to death telling me the obvious, you should be running home. What you shouldn't be doing is pissing off a man who really wants to kill you." Mark punched him in the nose and smiled when bone crunched and blood sprayed.

He hit him again and smiled wider when Jason screamed.

"Tell whoever the fuck you want. As far as the world knows, I'm in fucking Brazil enjoying the tanned women and pristine white beaches and won't be back stateside for a week. So, go right ahead. Say I beat you up and threatened your life. Good luck proving it. And I'm sure the authorities will be thrilled with your soliciting a minor when you tell them why I did it." Mark picked him up with one hand and shook hard before dropping him at his feet.

He jogged away, not carrying if the dumb shit died in the snow. In a thick stand of trees, he stripped and stuffed his clothing into his pack and put the strap in his mouth. The cool winter air felt good on his skin. He stretched a few minutes before dropping to his knees to shift.

A quick tug on the strap tightened the pack enough to hold it on as he loped through the woods. He looked forward to sleeping within sight of his girl.

Twenty-Seven

Gravel crunched outside in the driveway louder than the car that pulled in. Kelly glanced anxiously at her mother and clasped her hands tighter before her. Her mother patted her on the shoulder as she hurried to the door. Before she got there, John opened the door and ushered Abby and her mother inside.

"Thanks for coming on such short notice," Alice said as she extended her hand. The two women shook hands, and everyone took seats around the pine table in the kitchen.

"This is stupid," Abby said. She leaned back in her seat and crossed her arms. "So what if he calls me fat or anything else?'

"I care. It hurts my feelings. It's mean to call you fat when you aren't."

"Well, suck it up. Boys can be jerks. You don't bail on a friend because one's an idiot."

"Girls." Alice held up her hand. "Kelly is worried, and it's a valid worry. You know we love you too, Abby. This isn't all about saving your feelings though, it's about her's too. Neither of you wants to hurt the other, and that's good, but for a little while we'll try things Kelly's way."

"But that's not fair. We didn't do anything wrong," Abby said and scowled at Alice.

"I've spoken to the principal—"

"Dad! I asked you not to." Kelly glared at her father.

"Well, I did it anyway. I explained the situation and asked him to rearrange your schedule. So, starting next term, you'll get out an hour and fifteen minutes earlier. I called in some favors and got you a part-time job. You'll work after school for three hours a day with Ms. Holt at the library. The pay is crap, but the experience will be good."

He laughed when Kelly jumped up to hug him.

"'Your mother and I will buy you a used car to get back and forth in, and you can use your mother's until we find one. Abby, I know this isn't fair to you, but it isn't a horrid change, is it? You can see each other after school if you want to. This will just separate you in classes, and Kelly will drive herself to school. This doesn't mean you aren't welcome here."

"I guess," Abby said sulkily. "I still think it's stupid. I really don't care if idiots don't like me."

Kelly glanced away guilty. "But I care. I don't want to worry about it. I just want to go to school and not worry about people picking on my friends. I hate being the cause of your unhappiness."

"If they see it bothers you, they'll just do it more. You know how that crowd is."

"I don't know what else to do." Kelly stared at Abby's angry face, and all she could think was she should have left with Mark, but her mother looked so worried and her father… she couldn't just leave and not say a word, it would kill them. This way was better. She smiled, and it felt like a million pounds floated off her shoulders.

"What," Abby said suspiciously.

"I'm just happy you agree," Kelly lied.

She wanted to go call Mark right then and tell him to come get her. Her heartbeat picked up and her palms sweat. It suddenly seemed so obvious to her. She didn't fit in here, and instead of trying to hold on, she should be trying to fade away.

She could break her ties here kindly, and then, when she left, she wouldn't have to disappear because no one would expect to see her. They wouldn't even miss her. She felt a pang of regret when she met Abby's angry eyes, but Abby would have a full life without her. She'd have friends and boyfriends and live her life without ever knowing Kelly's secret and Kelly could stop feeling bad for having secrets. She could stop worrying about losing control, she could be free.

"You're grinning like an idiot," Abby said.

Abby's mother squeezed Kelly's hand a moment before putting an arm around her daughter. "Kelly wants what's best for you."

"What about me? Who am I supposed to hang

out with?"

"Don't be so dramatic. You can still talk to her."

Abby stood and stomped to the door. "Well, I think you're a coward and this is utter bullshit, but fine, I won't talk to you at school." She slammed the door behind her.

Kelly winced, and her mother looked as if she would cry.

"It's fine, Mom. She's mad, but she'll get over it. She won't even miss me if she gets the part in the school play."

Abby's mother rose and gave Kelly a sad smile. "You're a good person, Kelly. I understand why you're doing this, but you don't have to. Abby is a good person too and strong."

"I have too because I love her," Kelly said.

"Christmas break starts in a few days and maybe this will all blow over," John said as he held the door.

"I hope so." Abby's mother nodded goodbye, gave Kelly a sad smile, and closed the door.

"Thanks for finding me a job, Dad. I was thinking I'd like to apply at the pet store or maybe a vet's office for the summer. I want to work with animals and be a forest ranger."

"When did you decide this?" he asked as he sat back down. Her mother rose and began setting the table for dinner.

"I've been thinking about it a while now. I'll need experience with animals and some law classes."

"Plenty of forests around here," her father said cheerfully.

"I want to work in Alaska."

"Alaska?" her mother frowned and thumped the platter of fried chicken on the table. "Why Alaska?"

"The snow and the sky."

"Okay, now let's not get ahead of ourselves. No need to worry, that's years away." Her father stood and kissed her mother's head. "One problem at a time and goals are good. I remember when I wanted to be a train conductor."

"You still do," her mother said tartly and handed him a bowl of salad.

"Someday we'll take that train—"

A knock on the door interrupted them and startled Kelly who hadn't heard or smelled anyone approaching. Their gravel drive usually gave plenty of warning.

"I got it," Kelly said. She sighed and headed for the door. Her father watched unhappily. He thought it was Abby too.

She halted in shock, then jerked the door open.

"What do you want—" A grin burst over her face. Mark was back. The grin widened until it threatened to split her cheekbones. Jason lifted a hand to his broken nose and glared.

"I came to say I'm sorry." His glare dimmed, and he glanced nervously over her shoulder.

"Then say it and get out of here," her father snapped.

"I really am sorry. For everything. You didn't

deserve it. I always thought you were really nice. I don't know why I was a such a di— idiot." He cleared his throat and shuffled his feet. "I'll make the guys back off. I felt bad when I heard what Mike said. He won't say it again."

"You leave me alone, and I'll leave you alone. It'll be like we never met."

"Okay. I wish I could take it back."

"Goodbye, Jason." She slammed the door and ran to her room. Practically flew up the stairs her heart felt so light. *Mark was back!*

"Poor Abby. We did all that for nothing," her mother called after her, laughing.

Not for nothing," Kelly thought as she scrambled for her phone. *I realized where I belong.*

Twenty-Eight

A dull buzz shook the pack against Mark's flank. He growled low in his throat, angry with himself for picking this spot to lay. He had no real cover. The stone wall behind her house hid his black fur good enough, but his naked flesh would show. He changed back to human anyway. That was Kelly's ringtone.

His pulse tripped and his palms sweat. Jason had just left. She might be really angry.

"Thank you," she said when he answered on the fourth ring.

"Am I unbanished," he asked softly.

"Yes." She laughed and took a deep breath. Yes. Yes, yes!" I wish I could meet you now."

Her happy greeting made his heart soar. She'd missed him.

"Me too." His voice cracked, and he had to clear his throat.

"I'm coming with you."

Tears sprang to his eyes, and his hand trembled

on the phone.

"My place is with the wolves. I know that now, but I need time."

"Whatever you want," he forced out over the lump in his throat.

"Are you okay? You sound funny."

"I'm overwhelmed. God, Kelly, this is such a relief."

A light lit on her back porch.

"I wish I could talk, but I'm naked in your backyard."

She giggled.

She sounded funny to him too, shy and breathless and her laugh had a different tone.

Her backdoor opened and pulled his thoughts away.

"Tomorrow," she whispered and hung up.

He slipped his phone back into his pack with his still trembling hands, called his wolf, and hunkered on his stomach to crawl west, dragging his pack.

The wolf wanted to go to her, to lick her face, and prance around her. He wanted that too. He wanted it so much he had to lay still panting in the snow for five minutes while he talked himself into leaving.

He dozed in the trees beside her house with his head on his pack. The sun rose, and his ears perked, but she didn't call.

He left his pack and crept back in time to see her leave for school. Frustration made him growl. To spend his nervous energy, he hunted and gorged himself. He was dozing again beside his pack when she called later that afternoon.

"I'm going for a run."

"I'm waiting." He threw his jeans on but didn't bother with boots or a shirt. Tree limbs and brush crackled, warning of her approach. She ran gracelessly through the trees. When she saw him, her eyes lit, and she ran into his arms. For a long minute, they embraced. He let himself run his hands through her hair and kiss her shoulder before pushing away.

There was no hiding his arousal this close. He stepped further away. She was aroused too. His heart sang, and his wolf practically purred. He held up a hand when she stepped closer.

"No. You're too young. I can wait for you. Werewolf mating is serious."

She shook her head, sending strands of long, dark hair flying about her face. Her eyes shone, and he couldn't tell if it were tears or animal shine.

"No touching until you're ready."

She nodded again and smiled so brightly he took a step forward without realizing it.

"Damn," he muttered and turned away.

"You want me?" she sounded amazed.

"More than—"

Her phone rang, startling both of them. She glanced at the screen and winced. "I have to take this, it's my father."

"Come home. Mom had a little accident, and I need to take her to the doctors."

Kelly began running back to her house, trailing the scent of fear. Mark followed.

"I'll be there in just a minute. How bad?" "Nothing to worry over. She cut her hand, and she'll need help with her clothing. If you can follow us to the hospital in her car, I can head back to finish the milking once the doctor sees her."

"Be right there." Kelly glanced over her shoulder and shrugged apologetically.

"I'll be here when you get back," Mark said. He wanted to say I love you, but didn't want to pressure her. So, he smiled and lifted his hand in farewell.

She called him hours later. "I can't get out tonight."

"I'll see you tomorrow then."

"Tomorrow," she said breathlessly and hung up.

He sat cross-legged staring at his phone.

"Oh, boy."

He sighed hard and laid back in the cold, wet leaves. Resisting her would be hard, impossible if she teased. She couldn't flirt with him like he was human. He needed to make it crystal clear werewolves mated for life.

A broad smile crossed his face. She wanted him. The thought aroused him. He dropped his hand to his stiffening cock and stroked it slowly then faster until he came. More relaxed now, he shifted to wolf form and curled up with his tail over his nose to sleep.

The next day he waited for her outside her school. He wanted to see for himself how the other kids treated her. She parked her mom's car and walked in alone, but she smiled slightly. He returned at the final bell and watched her leave, again alone. She didn't talk and laugh with the others, but no one teased her. She walked through her classmates like a ghost. Only a few gazed after her, and she didn't seem to care. He was too far to smell her but her posture was straight and her stride firm.

With a small shock, he realized she'd grown out of her puppyish uncertainty, and he wondered how he'd missed the change. She was still slim but no longer gawky. She strode down the sidewalk with confidence and not a trace of fear. She was no longer a gawky adolescent but a confident young woman.

At her car, a tall, thin boy called to her. "Kelly, wait up. Did you need the notes from History class?" Without waiting for her answer, he thrust a sheaf of papers in her hand, smiled, and darted away, rejoining another group of kids.

Kelly stared after him, frowning in puzzlement before shrugging and stuffing the papers in her bag. She turned back to the car and hesitated, her head lifting, and he knew she'd scented him. She turned and scanned the lot, a smile blooming on her face.

He held up one finger, and she glanced around and nodded.

The parking lot cleared and he approached, careful to keep the car between them.

"I just wanted to make sure you're okay here."

Her smile softened. "I am. You don't need to worry. I feel bad for Abby, but it's good to break it off with her slowly. She'll make a new best friend soon."

"I'm sorry about that."

"Not your fault. You've always been so nice to me." She stared down at her fingers tracing patterns on the hood of her car. "Why are you so nice to me?"

"You know why," he said softly.

Her breath caught.

"I was here tracking, but you keep me here. Did you meet the other wolves while I was gone?"

"No."

"Would you like to before they leave? They're still staying at my house."

She bit her lip and shook her head.

"I'm not ready yet. Soon though," she added and gave him a tremulous smile.

"Take all the time you need. There's no rush. You have your wolf under control." He reached to her and dropped his hand. "I'll wait as long as it takes."

She flushed, and he cleared his throat.

"Werewolves mate for life. Biology makes it so. If you choose a werewolf lover, he becomes your husband. And wolves don't have divorce. I—"

"Isn't this cozy," Stacy said interrupting them.

Mark whirled. He'd been so caught up in Kelly he'd neither heard nor smelled her sister's approach, and she smelled rank.

Kelly smiled crookedly at him and gave her sister a hug, wrinkling her nose, making Mark hide a smile behind his hand.

"Mark was just saying hello."

"Uh-huh." Stacy pursed her lips and winked at him before turning to her sister. "Do Mom and Dad know you meet him?"

"What do you want," Mark said, not liking her tone at all.

"I was worried about my sister. She hasn't been in school lately. And good thing I checked on her. Aren't you a little old to be hanging out at the high school?"

"I wasn't hanging out. I was jogging by and saw an old friend."

"Sure, you can go with that story." She tapped her cell phone and smirked.

Kelly fumbled in her bag and withdrew a wrinkled envelope. "I won't be getting any more lunch money though," she said when she handed the envelope to Stacy. "My schedule next semester skips lunch period."

Stacy clutched the envelope in one hand and ran her red nails along the flap. "You must have to eat sometime."

"She does," Mark said harshly, furious with Stacy for taking advantage like this.

"Don't you have somewhere to be? You said hello, now shoo." Stacy waved him away, grinning mockingly.

"Like I'm going to leave her alone with you."

"I'll be fine," Kelly said

So angry his hands shook, he turned and spun away. He couldn't contain his snarl. He wanted to kill her. *How dare she threatened Kelly*. Kelly didn't see the threat, but he did. He snarled again and began jogging. Before he lost control, he needed to be deep in the woods.

Stacy's mocking laugh followed him.

Kelly called him crying an hour later. "You have to stay away. She showed me pictures and threatened to go to Mom and Dad."

"Let her. They're just harmless pictures."

"When I go, they'll think you made me."

"Kell, they'll think that anyway," Mark said softly.

"She's going to say foul things, horrible lies. I can't let them hate me— or you."

"Okay, sweetheart, calm down. We've done nothing wrong. I can stay away. But don't give in to her blackmail. Tell your parents what she said. Tell them I'm long gone. I'll sell the house, and no one will see me around town."

Harsh sobs muffled by her hand on the phone tightened the muscles in his shoulder.

"I'll pay her off if you want. I'll do whatever you want."

"I can't ask you to live in the woods for years."

"I'm offering. It isn't a hardship. I like the woods. Werewolf, remember.

She laughed, choking on her tears.

"You have but to ask and I'll do it. Don't worry about what I want, what do you want?"

"I don't want to, but I think you better stay away. I'll call when I can run, but it won't be often. God, this is so unfair to you. You're going to get sick of waiting."

"Never."

Her breath caught in a hiccupping sob. "I got to go."

"I'll be waiting," he said to dial-tone.

He snarled and shifted to his wolf so he could rip at the trees with his sharp claws. Panting in rage, he ripped and shredded, but it didn't ease him. He wanted to rip and tear the flesh of his enemy, but she loved his enemy. He lifted his face to the sky and howled.

He'd been so close.

Twenty-Nine

Her mother took one look at her tearstained face and thumped into a kitchen chair, cradling her bandaged hand to her chest. "What happened?"

"Stacy."

Her mother's eyes narrowed, and she held up one finger then pushed herself to her feet to snatch the phone. "Come home," she said and hung up.

She turned to the stove to make tea. "Your father will be in, in a minute, and we can talk. She didn't hurt you, did she?"

"Not physically."

Kelly sat and folded her arms to rest her head on them to watch her mother prepare tea.

Her father ran in the door, bringing the fresh scent of cows with him. "What happened?"

"Stacy is trying to blackmail me."

"What?" He absently took the cup his wife handed him and sat beside Kelly.

"I've been giving her my lunch moncy, and she's

mad because there won't be any more, so she cooked up this lie to force me to give her my pay."

"What lie?"

"She's going to claim Mark Miller and I are lovers. It isn't true," she added hurriedly when her mother inhaled sharply.

"How does she plan to prove it?" Her mother left her teacup on the counter and grasped the back of her chair, leaning forward and glaring.

"Mom, I swear to you, Mark has never been anything except kind to me. Yes, I think he's hot, but I know he's too old for me. He's never been inappropriate. I hardly ever see him. I think he might have moved. But Stacy has pictures of us talking at a game and at my school then she took more of him at the movie theater and library, places I go, and told me what she would say to the police. Horrible things about him forcing me and threatening me, and she told me her boyfriend would swear Mark brought me to their house."

Kelly clamped her lips hard and took deep breaths through her nose. "She's going to get an innocent man sent to jail, and I'll be the laughingstock of my school."

"Well, if all she has is innocent pictures, and half with just him in them, and a drug dealers word, I wouldn't worry about him," her father said, sounding relieved.

"There's nothing going on?" her mother asked as she slid into her seat.

"No." The lie brought a blush to her cheeks, and

she began crying. "Why would she try to hurt me?"

"For money. Don't buckle to her. I can't believe you were giving her your lunch money," her mother finished angrily.

"She's my sister!"

"Then let her act like one. If she'd been sincere in her concern, I could understand it." Her mother patted her shoulder as she spoke. "Mark Miller is too old for you. It would be criminal for him to pursue you."

Her father chuckled and then rubbed his face when her mother glared.

"He is!" she insisted. "You're four years older than me, but I was an adult when we started dating."

Her father sat back in his chair and said, "I agree. But it isn't a problem. He isn't interested. He isn't even in town. His truck hasn't been moved for a month now. We need to do something about that, by the way, and someone new is living in his house. I'll stop by there and find out where he's gone and get someone to take his truck back."

"That's sketchy, just disappearing like that." her mother said as she rose to grab her teacup.

"It isn't our problem." Her father rose and kissed her forehead before heading to the door. "Stacy is our problem. I'll stop and talk to her too. Maybe we should press extortion charges." He glanced at Kelly's face and sighed hard. "No, I guess not. I'd hate for you to have to face her in court, but I can threaten too," he finished in satisfaction and slammed out the door.

"I'm sorry, Mom. I shouldn't have given her money. I just wanted to help her."

"I know, honey, but some people are unhelpable. It's weird though how she picked Mark. If he does come around, stay away from him. I saw how he looked at you too and tried to tell myself it was my imagination but he stared so intensely."

"Really?"

Her mother snorted and slapped her fingers. "Don't sound so interested. He's too old," she said firmly as she rose, *but she was laughing now*, Kelly noted in relief.

She grinned at her mother, making her laugh harder and shake her head.

She'd never notice Mark much at all until he'd taken her. Remembered fear made her shudder. She'd thought him crazy and then thought he'd drugged her making her hallucinate when the wolf pushed through her skin. Another shudder rippled her skin, this one of pleasure. She jumped to her feet and grabbed her bookbag before she did something inappropriate before her mother.

In her room, she closed the door and stripped to let her wolf out. On four paws, she stretched and then rolled on the carpet. *God, it would be so good to run,* she thought wistfully but turned from the window. It wouldn't do to have her father see her as the wolf. She sneezed with wolfish laughter and gamboled about her room a moment before transforming back.

"He loves me," she said to her naked reflection.

Eyes narrowed and lips pursed, she turned slowly before the mirror, examining her body. Her breasts were still growing. They stuck out pointy and firm from her chest covered by wide, pink nipples and she hoped they reached at least a c-cup before she was done.

The nipples stiffened, and her stomach muscles tightened when she ran a hand over them. She could smell her arousal but didn't know to ease it. She dropped her hand and spun away from her reflection then peered over her shoulder at her ass.

"Looks like an ass," she said doubtfully and examined it from a few angles.

Her muscles were toned and taut from running, and she liked the shape of her legs. She pulled her hair back to examine her face. She hadn't had acne since becoming a werewolf, and her teeth were bright white.

She wished she had blue eyes, or green ones like Abby's. *Abby had beautiful eyes*, she thought wistfully, sad she hardly ever saw her now, and released her hair, shaking her head so strands fell forward over her breasts.

I do have great hair. Wonder if that's a werewolf thing? Mark has great hair too.

Long and thick her hair curled slightly in loose waves. Red and blond highlights glinted in the dark brown tresses more red than blond now in winter, but summer would lighten it. She liked her face, she decided and grinned at her reflection.

Not as beautiful as him, but not bad, she finally

decided.

"He likes me," she said again and laughed, grabbing her pillow to hide the sound.

She dressed in sweats and ran downstairs when she smelled super leave the oven and grinned again. Her mother had made meatloaf, pink in the center like she liked it.

Thirty

Mark lived in the woods as his wolf only becoming human to speak with Kelly. School ended for the year, and she stopped running as often. Her summer job at a veterinarian's office kept her busy days, and she didn't like to make her parents worry by running at night.

He didn't care. He was just happy to share any time with her. She was studying hard, using that as an excuse to avoid all her friends and he worried she was lonely, but she never complained.

The days blurred into one with him. Wolves had no real sense of time. The phone he slept beside required charging, and sometimes he forgot for days at a time, only remembering when he became anxious by her absence.

One evening, as he waited alongside the path hoping she would show, he caught the scent of wolf. His hackles rose, and he growled low in his throat. A dark-brown wolf bounded out of the trees and leaped at him. Mark snarled and snapped. The other wolf grabbed his throat and shook him hard, and it dawned on Mark this was his friend, Arny.

Shaken, he released him and shifted.

"Kelly called. She was worried. Says you aren't answering the phone or becoming human when she shows up."

Mark glanced around guiltily. He had no idea where he'd left it.

"Come home, Mark. You're going to go feral and take her with you. Or you could come back to Mexico with me. I told you they'd reform and they did. The sick fucks took an entire small town this time. The local government is afraid, but we can wipe their sorry asses out and make good money doing it."

"I need to talk to her first." He was shocked to notice the trees about him had lost their leaves and the chill of winter hung in the air.

Arny handed him his phone and strode away, giving him privacy.

"Kell, it's me," he said hesitantly when she answered.

"Mark, I was getting really worried. Are you okay?"

"Fine. Maybe a hair too wolfy, but fine. I sort of lost track of time."

"Tomorrow is the full moon." She laughed lightly, but there was a hint of unease in it and another sound he couldn't put his finger on.

"Do you need to come out for it?'

"I got my period today."

He recognized her embarrassment, but the other sound had deepened too.

"I was thinking I should run with you tomorrow," she blurted.

"No. Yes. No—" Mark shook his head hard and chuckled ruefully. "Let me try that again. Yes, I want you, but no. Our first time will be as people who choose, not animals who can't help themselves."

"Are you…" She took a deep breath. "Am I asking too much? I know I have no right to hold you here like this. It's just I hate to disappoint my parents, and it will kill them if I disappear."

He hesitated, not knowing if she meant to join the pack or him. "I love you."

She began crying, and he winced and rubbed his teary eyes.

"You don't have to love me back, but you should know."

"You'll wait for me?" she asked breathlessly.

"Forever."

"Your friend Richard is worried and wants you to come home."

"If you need me here, then I'll stay here," Mark said.

"I love you."

His breath caught hard, and it took a moment for him to regain it. Before he could gather his wits, Kelly continued.

"Because I love you, I want you to go home. You need to be human more. I can see that. I hate to ask you to wait for me, but I need more time. Damn, Stacy for putting those thoughts in my parent's head. This would be so much easier if I could come to your house. You need a house."

"I know," he whispered. He cleared his throat and continued. "Arny has a job for me. It shouldn't take more than a month or so. I want to run with you again, but the job won't wait."

"Go do your job. I'll be here waiting for you when you get back."

"Kelly, think hard. You're so young, but I won't be able to hold back if you offer yourself. You won't be able to change your mind a year from now or twenty years from now." He was proud of himself for saying it when he wanted to go to her now while her wolf would make her choose him.

"I understand, and you're right. Maybe— when you come back, don't call me. Maybe it's just my wolf that wants you. She wants you so much it's hard to think straight. God, I know I have no right to ask this. It's selfish and mean to ask you to hang around and not see you, but I need to know you're near too."

"I don't mind," he lied glad she couldn't smell him.

"Give me until I graduate."

"You can take as long as you like."

"June twelfth."

"I'll be counting the days."

Her breath hitched, and she hung up.

"Hey, Arny, what's the date," he called.

Thirty-One

Mark glowered out of the small window beside his seat. He hated to fly but more than that he hated to leave her.

"I should have stayed and spent Christmas with her," he said.

"Yeah, that's romantic, raw rabbit under the pines." Arny didn't glance up from his magazine.

"I wish I could give her a gift." He peered over Arny's shoulder at the jeweler's ad

Arny snorted. "Yeah, we love jewelry."

Mark lightly punched his arm.

Arny slapped the magazine closed. "Your pathetic, you know that, right?" He lowered his voice. "She isn't a woman."

"I fucking know that."

"No, moron, I meant she isn't a girl. I saw her, and she's definitely a woman. Give her something she would really like."

"When did you see her?"

"When I came for you, I stopped to scope her

out. She already smells like you, or maybe you smell like her." Arny leaned closer and sniffed his neck. The man across the aisle from them stared. Arny pursed his lips, then grinned and kissed Mark's cheek. Mark rolled his eyes but threw an arm around Arny's shoulder. It wasn't the first time he'd pretended another male wolf was his lover. Wolves liked to touch and smell, and it was better to give humans normal explanations for abnormal behavior.

He closed his eyes and leaned his head back on the seat. "She loves horses and books."

Arny leaned away from him to open his laptop.

"She'll need a den, err, a big den to store her books," he said loud enough the man beside them could hear and winced apologetically at Mark. He tapped keys a few minutes and turned the screen to face him. "Maybe somewhere hereish, close to the university and near the hills and only an hour from your parents." He winked and leaned back in his seat, taking Mark's arm as Mark clicked the mouse.

"I sure hope she likes me," he batted his eyes so hard Mark laughed.

The man staring at them looked jealous now. He hastily turned away when Mark caught him staring and spoke to the quiet woman beside him. The woman gave him a dismissive glance barely taking her eyes from her book.

Mark felt a pang of sorrow for the man he looked so lonely. His sorrow deepened when the stewardess offered the woman a drink and Mark realized she was his wife. A mated wolf was never lonely like that. The wolf was happy to be with its mate.

Of course, it had drawbacks too, he mused as his wolf growled within him. The wolf missed its mate fiercely.

He clicked the screen and entered 'barn' under must have. He'd buy Kelly a great house near a school where she could run whenever she wished and ride and have her new family over all the time.

"So, did you tell her where we're going?"

"Not yet, but I'm sure she'll understand."

Arny sneezed, scenting the lie, and curled his lip.

Thirty-Two

Kelly strode to her car through swirling snowflakes. The snow hadn't yet built up on the road, but the weatherman warned to expect three inches. Her Ford Explorer was ancient, but it had four-wheel drive. A whiff of wolf jerked her head up as she opened the door. Surprised Mark would seek her out here, she threw her backpack into the car and turned into the wind to sniff.

The small hairs on the back of her neck rose. It wasn't Mark. A man walked towards her from the street, cutting through the snow-dusted dead grass.

"Kelly," he said, sounding thrilled.

Her hands shook as she yanked her door open again.

"Wait. I just wanted to introduce myself."

Her pounding heart slowed a little, but she kept the open door between them and sniffed hard, searching for a weapon.

"I just wanted to say hello," he said again and held up his empty hands. "No threat. Just a friend saying hi."

"We aren't friends." Her words sounded growly and angry to herself, and she was glad he was downwind, making it harder to smell her nervous sweat. That he'd shown up the day after she'd asked Mark to go terrified her. He'd either been stalking her or been sent, and Mark would never send him, which meant Richard had, maybe to kill her because she wouldn't join the pack and she was endangering Mark.

While she thought, he took another step closer.

"That's close enough," she snapped.

He cocked his head, his smile changing to a frown and he sniffed hard. "No need to be afraid of me."

"I'm not," she lied.

He smiled again, shook his head and took a step back. "Didn't Mark tell you new chaperons were coming?"

"Yes. But you aren't him. He gets me mated pairs who *never* speak to me."

"Yep. Mark sent for a mated pair to live here one year, and Richard asked my parents to come, so here I am."

Kelly's shoulders relaxed, and she flexed to ease the soreness in them.

"I'm Andre," he said and held out his hand.

Kelly growled.

He jerked his hand back with a hurt expression.

"Are you this unfriendly to everyone or just us?"

The question stumped her.

"Everyone, I guess," she said unhappily.

Andre glanced around the parking lot and pursed his lips. "It must suck not having any real friends." His eyes grew sad. "And your parents… I can't imagine how hard that must be." He took another step forward and offered her a bright smile. "You don't have to be alone though. We want to be your pack."

"Hey, Kell," a girl hollered, and she and Andre turned to look.

"Sue," Kelly said relieved to have a witness but surprised to be hailed. She quirked an eyebrow at Sue.

"Glad I caught you. Can I get a ride to the library?"

"Sure." Kelly smiled and hit the locks, opening the passenger side door.

She liked how the girls treated her now friendly but not pushy about it. She got invited to parties and to the mall even though she rarely went, and it sometimes hurt to see Sue and Abby giggling together, but she knew it was for the best.

"Who's your friend," Sue asked.

"Andre Ramirez," Andre said as he smiled at Sue and winked at Kelly.

"Got to go or I'll be late for work." Kelly jumped in the car and closed her door before Andre could say anything else.

Sue craned her neck to peer out the back

window. "Wow, he's a hottie. Where the hell did you meet him?"

"Jogging."

Sue nodded thoughtfully. "Maybe I should take up jogging." She giggled and straightened in her seat, then rummaged in her bookbag, removing a wrinkled pamphlet. "We're joining a tanning salon after Christmas. Most of us are going solo to the prom. If you want the group discount, tell Barb, she's in charge of our prom stuff. Her uncle can get our dresses for cost if we order from his catalog. And we're going to chip in on a car and rooms at the hotel after."

Kelly let Sue's prom babble wash over her as she contemplated Andre's presence. He was handsome, and she wondered if all wolves had that sexy, dangerous vibe about them. Two was too few to judge by, but Andre had the same muscular build, and deep tan Mark did. Andre's hair was darker and longer, almost girly really the way it curled around his shoulders but his cheeks were stubbled, and the overall effect was hot.

She giggled, and Sue crooked a brow.

"Think it's safe for me to go?"

Sue patted her knee. "They joke about Stacy, but not you. No one thinks you're like that. The boys wish you were—" she laughed at Kelly's offended snort— "it must truly suck to be her sister." Two red spots appeared on Sue's cheeks. "You know she comes to the games, right?"

"I know. That's why I don't. At least she stays

away from the track meets."

"I can't believe what she'll do for twenty bucks. Sorry, Kell," she added hurriedly and winced.

"You'd think her mouth would get tired," Kelly said as she pulled into the library parking lot.

Sue laughed and slapped a hand over her mouth. "She really is gross. You're so normal it's hard to believe you grew up together."

"She's the poster child for drugs will ruin your life." Kelly hopped from her car and headed inside.

"I'm sorry, I shouldn't talk about her."

"Don't worry about it. I try to pretend she isn't my sister. I'm sure at every game she causes a scene and the kids all gossip."

"They do but not about you." Sue bumped her with her shoulder. "I was going to tell you it was even safe to accept dates but then I saw your hottie. You go, girl." Giggling behind her hand, she headed to the research section.

Kelly passed through the swinging gate at the main desk and hung her coat on a hook in the employee's lounge beside the main office.

"More filing today, Kelly," Miss Holt said and pointed to a metal trolley full of books with her chin. A plastic bin, also full of returned books and movies, sat beside the trolley. "When you're done with that, if you have time, begin hanging the Christmas posters. One on each door and keep them face height."

"Yes, ma'am."

Kelly squatted beside the cart and began sorting

books by section. She liked this job and usually spent an hour studying here when she was finished before heading home. The library had faster internet than the ancient dial-up she still used at home.

Sue waved to her when she left but didn't stop to speak. Miss Holt's gimlet stare followed her out. The peace of the library soothed Kelly's nerves as she replaced books. Someone always brought up Stacy to her, but no one spoke to her here.

"At least they always apologize too," she muttered as she slipped a book back in place and returned for the last batch.

She slowed when she entered the main room. Andre had come here. A quick glance around didn't reveal him, but he'd come to the front desk.

"What are you doing?" Ms. Holt asked

Kelly jerked back, her face flaming. She hadn't realized she'd bent to sniff the counter.

"Thought I saw an ant." She leaned closer and used a fingertip to remove an imaginary spec that she pretended to examine. "Just lint." She brushed her hands on her jeans and gave the librarian a sickly smile.

"A young man needs help in the computer room. Log him on and show him our system."

"Yes, ma'am."

Kelly's heart began to pound. She knew it would be Andre. She wasn't convinced his reasons for coming were benign, but surely, he wouldn't attack her right in the library?

He glanced up and smiled when she entered.

He'd chosen a seat facing the door. Two chairs sat at each computer station. The wide desks were meant to be used in pairs for studying although today most used them singly. Extra swivel chairs lined the back wall. Of the twenty stations, seven were in use. Most patrons sat in the front rows to be closer to the printer. Andre sat alone in the back row beside the noisy heating vent.

"We got off to a bad start," he said and offered his hand. "I shouldn't have approached without calling first, but I'm not really supposed to approach you." He grinned sheepishly at her.

She ignored the offered hand. "This is my job."

"Sorry for that too, but I thought you might like to see pictures of the pack."

He smiled smugly and tapped the mouse bringing up a picture of a two-story log cabin with deep porches and wide windows. "I like Mark, we're friends and all, but you don't need to hang out with the geriatric crowd. This is the ranch." He rubbed a finger over his lower lip and looked thoughtful.

"How much has he told you?"

She shrugged uncomfortably and whispered, "He told me he has a pack, and I can't talk about any of this."

"Ahh, you're scared I'm here to silence you. Nope, no nefarious plans. We don't let our enemies know we're going to attack either. We just do, hard and fast." He tapped the keys again. "This is Richard and Leah, and of course, you know Mark."

Mark stood with his arm around a pretty, black-haired woman. Slim, with generous breasts, she laughed over her shoulder at a blond man with a Vandyke beard. All wore casual clothes, jeans, and t-shirts, and it was clear by their body language they were good friends. Everyone appeared to be in their early to mid-twenties although she knew they were much older. Andre flicked to a new picture.

"Me and my parents. My mom, Carlota, and father, Alfonso."

"They appear young too."

"Wolves stop aging around twenty-two or so. Our scientists are studying us to find out why, but they don't really know. If you sustain lots of serious injuries or stay the wolf too long, you age a bit too. They have theories though and would be happy to talk with you and test you, of course," he finished with a slight grimace.

He changed the picture again, this one to Alfonso and Mark both wearing Montana Fish Wildlife and Parks windbreakers. They stood on the bank of a fast running stream with their faces in profile. Her eye caught on the low rolling hills and steeper forested mountains in the background and a lump formed in her throat.

"It's beautiful there. Where is there?"

"He never told you?"

"I know it's Montana."

He tapped keys a minute and opened a map app. "The pack owns about half a million acres that border this national forest and another half reaching into Canada. Some pack mates have ranches that border that. Most of us live along this edge of the property closer to town. He clicked keys again. "That's Mark's house. Well, driveway. His house you can't see from the road." He changed the picture before she was through staring at the thickly forested swath of woods.

"This is where I grew up."

On the screen, a white farmhouse with a wraparound porch sat before a red barn. A corner of another barn showed on the left along with a split rail fence. A black and white border collie stood before a fence on the right. The dog stared at two horses grazing the short-cropped grass. A green truck with the Montana Fish Wildlife and Parks logo on the side panel sat in the driveway. It looked perfectly normal to Kelly.

"The local branch of park rangers is staffed exclusively by us. We do rotations between the US and Canada. My uncle owns a diner in town that some of us work at too, and we own a hardware store and bar that employs humans and wolves and then there's the Henderson Olson Wildlife Sanctuary." He changed the pictures as he spoke and left the screen showing a cute shop that sold fancy paper and offered printing services.

"My mom's shop," he said as he turned to her. "We can do whatever we like. All of the pack works for HOWLS; some in the building and some just on paper."

Kelly snorted with laughter.

Andre grinned at her. "Richard owns and runs it. He hires humans too and working there lets us legally claim earnings. We don't actually need to work, our stipend from the pack is enough to buy clothes, pay for food and an apartment, and anyone can stay with Richard and Leah, but we like to keep busy."

"You get paid for being pack?"

"Yes, we work for the pack too, though. It isn't charity."

"Kelly, did you need help?" Miss Holt asked from the doorway.

"No, ma'am. He just had a few questions."

"You can socialize after hours."

"Sorry. I was just asking library hours and when the best times to use the computers are. I'm studying law and need good access," Andre said.

Miss Holts mouth unclenched, and she nodded slightly.

Kelly rose and cleared her throat. "You should have no problem getting a computer if you come early," she said over her shoulder as she hurried to the door.

She stayed an extra fifteen minutes to finish hanging the posters but clocked out at her regular time. Miss Holt gave her a satisfied sniff as Kelly grabbed her jacket. Kelly was grateful to escape without another lecture on friends in the workplace.

Andre waited beside her car. "Whew, what a tyrant."

Kelly giggled.

"Can we go somewhere to talk?"

"Yes— I don't want to lie to my parents though."

"Tell them the truth, most of it anyway. I'm a student at the university you met in the library."

"You really are studying law?"

"I plan to. I'm only in my second year of college."

"Shouldn't you be there then?"

"Thanksgiving break, silly. I'll be attending Carleton next semester."

A flush heated Kelly's cheeks.

"Not just to be near you. This is one of the things we do for our stipend. If Richard says go, we go. Don't worry, he asked, he didn't order, but I jumped at the chance. There aren't a lot of us young wolves."

Her blush deepened. "I love Mark."

"You still need friends, right?"

"It would be awesome to have a friend," she said truthfully.

He grinned at her and offered his hand.

She shook it and smiled back.

"What's wrong with you?" Andre said as he stood to pull out her chair.

She smiled her thanks and thumped into the seat of the busy coffee shop. She loved Andre's old-fashioned manners. She liked everything about him. He was funny and sweet and understanding about her fear of dogs. He hadn't bothered her once about shifting while they jogged together, but he wasn't Mark. Her heart didn't beat hard when she saw him. As much as she liked him, she had no desire to kiss him. And her parents were bugging her to meet her boyfriend.

"My parents want to meet you."

"And that's a problem?" He lifted an eyebrow and leaned way back in his seat, reaching for the creamers on the shelf to his right without looking. While she frowned at him, he handed her the creamer and slid her the coffee he'd bought her.

He glanced down at his loose jeans and t-shirt doubtfully.

"I could change my clothes."

"Your clothes are fine. They'll like you, but I feel like I'm leading you on."

He threw his head back and laughed. "Oh my God, your face," he laughed harder, grabbing his stomach and rocking. Other patrons in the coffee shop stopped and stared at them.

Still snorting with laughter, he grabbed her hand and pulled her from the shop.

"We've been hanging out for two months now. I have no doubt you like me and am equally sure you don't find me attractive."

"I think you're cute," she assured him hastily, then made a face.

"No, I meant attractive." He wiggled his eyebrows at her and leered. "It's cool. I'm too late; you're in love already, but we can still be friends, and I'm willing to be the fake boyfriend."

"What about you?" Kelly asked.

"What about me?" He sighed hard and hugged her. "I'm attracted to you, yes, but that isn't your fault, and once you mate with Mark, I won't be anymore."

He chuckled and released her.

"That's so weird."

"We aren't human," he whispered. Then said louder. "I get dates and all the action I want."

"Eww."

He rolled his eyes. "What, I'm supposed to be a monk until I find a wife? That could take years. It could never happen."

She hugged him again, trying to ease the sadness in his eyes.

He returned her hug and rubbed his cheek on hers. "Take me home to meet your family."

Thirty-Three

Mark slunk on his stomach along her back fence. Fury and hurt made him clumsy. Her mother's delight was evident in her tinkling laugh and high voice. Mark's skin rippled, and he growled softly, fighting the urge to attack. Unable to stop himself, he slunk forward.

"—Your parents do?" Alice asked.

"My dad works from home doing research for a law firm. My mom doesn't work. She's looking for a job though and volunteers at the hospital."

"Kelly has told us so much about you, I feel like we know you already."

So, this was why she never called him, never looked for him, never ran on their mountain. She'd found a wolf she liked better. His ears flicked, and his jaws gaped in a soundless snarl. Andre was a mere pup.

Kill him the voice of his wolf whispered. *She's ours*, the voice screamed.

Mark growled again and gathered himself to

leap through the open window. He shook hard, trying to force his wolf back. If he'd been in human form, he'd have been sweating. Instead, he panted as he strained to control his wolf. He shouldn't have come and broken his word, she'd never forgive him for killing her parents. The wolf within him pleaded and fought, trying to gain dominance.

"We're just friends, Mom," Kelly said.

His wolf relaxed at her exasperated tone.

"I haven't won her over yet," Andre said.

"Well, stay for dinner. Her father and I are happy she's making friends. Tell me about your classes. Kelly has been applying to schools."

Mark bounded to his feet and sprinted for the woods. In the distance, a tractor rumbled, and the scent of silage lingered in the winter air. His heart hurt, and he wondered if wolves could have heart attacks.

Five months remained before he could speak to her again. On the edge of the woods, he wrestled with himself trying to force his wolf to relinquish his body. Pain skittered along his spine, and he bit back his shriek of agony as skin and bone reformed then resumed their wolf shape in waves across his torso.

"We will not force her," he gasped out and ruthlessly pushed the beast inside him back. Dirt and leaves stuck to his sweaty skin. He lay on his back staring into the blue, winter sky and panting.

"Let her still love me. Please, God, let her love me." He lay sweating in the dirt a few minutes before pulling himself to his feet and running naked through the woods. He'd left his phone and clothes behind but didn't dare go back for them until he was sure she wouldn't be at home.

Sleep eluded him that night, and he grew angrier by the minute. His alpha had betrayed him.

"Richard wouldn't do that," he yelled to the stars. *Maybe Andre had come on his own*, he thought, then had to push his wolf down again. *Andre could force her to mate, but she knew that*, he reminded himself. She'd treated him as a friend. He'd heard no fear in her voice.

His skin rippled and his stomach clenched hard. A sensation like pins-and-needles, as if he'd fallen asleep with his limbs tight beneath him and returning circulation hurt, cramped his arms and legs. It was harder to resist his wolf this time. He too was afraid Andre would force her. Only the fact that he'd known Andre since birth let him hold the wolf back. Andre was a good kid.

"He won't hurt her," he cried out and fell face first into the low brush.

He remained lying there until he was sure she'd have left for work, then let his wolf take him. The power and quickness of the change awed him.

This must be what her shifts feel like, he thought in a corner of his mind as he stretched and wriggled.

He darted through the trees, not caring how much noise he made, and resumed his human shape after taking a cursory look around. He pulled on his pants and boots before calling Richard.

"You sent Andre?" he asked without preamble the minute Richard answered.

"You just noticed now?"

Mark's hand clenched on his phone. "When did you send him?"

"He went with his parents the day you called me. Before you get your knickers in a twist, I didn't tell him to go meet her, but I'm glad he did. He tells me she's lonely, and I'm thinking of sending a few more.

"Don't you fucking dare."

"Mark, did you want her to have a choice or not? Are you just kidding yourself? If she loves you, it won't matter who I send, and if she doesn't, are you going to force her?"

"Richard…"

"I feel for you, I really do, and frankly I'm amazed you could stay away for so long. I couldn't have left Leah like that."

"Kelly isn't— it isn't like that. I haven't been lusting after her, not until recently anyway. I've been worried. I want her to be mine, but not for sex." He raked his hand through his unruly hair. Twigs and grass snarled and pulled. "I need a haircut."

"What?"

"Nothing. Kelly is meant to be my mate, I know that. I wanted to let her grow up first though."

"Sixteen is full grown for a wolf, and she's what? Seventeen?"

"She's human and still needs her parents. She

isn't grown. We can't be mates until she can face her parents. It would kill her to sneak away and never see them again, and they would never accept their daughter staying out all night with a guy and disappearing for days at a time."

Mark sat in the bracken beneath the pines and pulled his knees to his chest. "Don't send anyone else. It isn't that I don't want her to have friends, I do, but my wolf can't take it. Accidents happen, and I swear to God, I won't be able to hold myself back if I think one of them might force her."

"Fair enough. You should come home. She's safe. Alfonso and Carlota are checking up on her. She hasn't met them yet or let Andre shift. She's afraid of them, of us."

"I can't… I'll leave her alone, but I can't go. I need to be here."

"Fine, but no more weeks at a time being the wolf. Stay human and stay in control. She might forgive you if you take her in wolf form, but you won't be able to forgive yourself. Stay with the Ramirez's. Leave the house as their dog. Use this time to brush up on the law. It's been a long time since you passed the bar. You're going to need to recertify to become a game warden, and laws have changed since the last time."

"Didn't Arny tell you I'm looking for a place by the college?"

"He did but what are you going to do all day while she's in school? Watch television?"

"I could take classes with her."

"You could, but you shouldn't. Most of those classes you've taken, and she'll feel bad if she can't keep up. Only take classes where you'll actually learn something and don't crowd her. Micheal and Susan will be taking classes and so will six other wolves from the Dakota packs. She can have real friends, ones she doesn't have to hide herself from and can keep when college is over."

"You're right. I'll think of something. Get me a new ID. Mark Miller and make me five years older than her. Make it tight, Richard, so I can buy us a house and sign up for school and get a job. I'm going to keep this ID until she needs to change hers.

"Already did it. I'll send it to Afonso. Tony and Jen Miller are playing your parents, you knew them as Gary and Silvia Franklin of the Plains Pack. They're in Alaska now. Speaking of that, I've been asked to go there and speak with them. They're tired of moving every six years and want advice to see how we manage to stay in one place. Leah and I are planning a trip there in the spring."

"There aren't enough of them," Mark said.

"No, but we were thinking of asking them to join us. I don't want a fight though, I like their Alpha."

"You should invite them to our turf then."

"Don't worry about it. I know better than to even offer in person. I just wanted you to know, Leah and I will be considering it on our visit. Most of the pack is unmated males, and we could increase operations."

"Ahh, I hadn't considered."

"They're a wild bunch, used to living as the wolf and sharing a house. I'm not sure they'll be civilized enough for us."

"Don't mention Kelly," Mark said anxiously.

"No one except us knows of her." Richard snarled softly, and the hair on Mark's arms rose. "That feral's parents will be gunning for you. Rainy called Leah and told her they disappeared. Your trial is clear. As far as the world knows you headed to Florida when you left here, but keep an eye out in case they check there. The attack on Kelly made the news, and while they can't be certain it was their son, they might be checking."

Mark didn't realize he was growling until Richard snapped, "Settle down. They can't know for sure which of you is responsible or that he's dead and not just in hiding. All my lieutenants are on alert. Leah thinks his parents would have gone immediately if they were going to go, and the fact that Kelly survived and is still at home should convince them it was a dog attack, but don't let them get a whiff of you."

"We need to flush them out."

"I'm working on a plan. Don't go off half-cocked either. You smell them around, call for backup, or I'll kick your ass."

Mark huffed, and Richard growled again.

"Fine," Mark bit out.

"I'll call Alfonzo and warn him your coming and, Mark, if you lay one finger on Andre…"

"He's safe from me if he keeps his paws off her."

Richard hung up, and Mark snarled and slashed at the brush with his bare hands. He'd called for reassurance and now had more worries. Andre was a good kid, he wouldn't intentionally force Kelly, but she was undefended here. If any other packs learned of her existence, unmated males would swarm this place and Kelly was beautiful and had no Alpha to protect her.

He growled again and rose stiffly to his feet. He'd need surveillance equipment to watch over her from a safe distance. His scent could lead enemies to her.

Thirty-Four

Mark glared as Andre halted inside his kitchen door and held up his hands. His wide eyes flicked to his father then back to Mark.

Before he could duck back through the door, Mark jumped over the table and grabbed him by the shirt. Without thinking, he snarled and punched him. His wolf wanted Andre dead. Alfonso grabbed his arm as Andre exclaimed indignantly.

Mark shook with conflicting needs. Andre's mumbled complaints settled him. He was neither afraid nor guilty.

"Sorry," he muttered and took a seat at the Formica table.

"Sit," Alfonso said to his son and pointed at a seat across from Mark. "Mark will be staying with us." Alfonso slid a twenty-two to his son. "Carry this. It's loaded with silver bullets."

"I'm glad Kelly has a friend, but you could put her in danger," Mark said.

"I would never—" Andre's cheeks turned red

and he glared.

Mark gave him an insincere smile and waved him to a chair. "I didn't mean that, although you better be careful, but other wolves might not be so gallant."

"I'm not stupid. I didn't tell a soul. Our entire pack knows she's here though."

"I'm not worried about our pack. The feral's parents have disappeared, and Richard thinks they're looking for me. If they show around here, and smell wolf, they might come after her or you."

"You should go," Andre said worriedly.

"I can't leave her," Mark said.

"She loves you."

Mark grinned and then grimaced and ran both hands through his hair. "I love her too, and I can't leave her even to make her safer. I want to, but the wolf won't let me. My wolf hates that you smell like her."

"I'll try not to touch her and wash up if I do. So, what are you going to do?"

"Spy from a distance. Can you get her schedule?"

"Shouldn't we warn her?"

"And say what? Anything we say will scare the crap out of her, and she needs her parents."

"Not as much as you think." Andre held a hand up as Mark opened his mouth. "I'm sure she needed them when you met, and she loves them, but she doesn't need them now. It would hurt her to leave, but she understands she has too."

"I can't force her."

"Look," Alfonzo said and laid a hand on Mark's shoulder. "There's no reason to freak out. We haven't seen a sign of any other wolf, and she's perfectly safe at school and work. Her house is alarmed, and you're there every night anyway. No wolf is going to go there and bust in the door. They'll scope it out first, and she'll smell them and call.

"I'll make sure she calls if she smells a strange wolf," Andre said.

"See," Alfonzo said and squeezed Mark's shoulder. "You can hang way back in the woods where no one can smell you and watch through a scope. My wife and I will make sure she's safe while getting into her car at school and work. Those will be her vulnerable spots."

"Don't forget her runs," Andre said.

"So, you'll accompany her every time, or we'll watch from a distance. Tell her Richard doesn't want her running alone, so she has to run with you as a wolf or runs with her human friends as a human."

"She'll hate feeling confined like that," Mark said.

"Carlota and I can run with her too," Alfonzo said. He rose and poured a cup of coffee.

Mark shook his head when he held it out. Andre accepted a cup and sipped a moment before saying, "She's afraid of us. I'll ask her, but I don't think she'll agree. She should take self-defense classes and carry a gun too."

"Ask her to go with you to the range," Mark said with a twinge of sadness. He'd wanted to take her and teach her to shoot but not for protection, for fun.

"I should have made her take classes when Stacy showed her true colors," Mark continued. Remembered anger clenched his fists.

"Stacy?" Andre asked.

"Her sister. She didn't tell you?"

"No."

"Her sister is a skank and mean, but don't bring her up." Mark pursed his lips and tilted his head, eyeing Andre thoughtfully. "I'm surprised she hasn't approached you. I'd have thought her the type to pursue her sister's boyfriend."

"Well, first, Kelly isn't my girlfriend, we're just friends, and maybe she has. A drugged-out, skanky chick came up to me at the library. She smelled familiar, but mostly she reeked of pot and sex. I was basically holding my breath trying not to smell her."

"She ask you out?"

"Flirted hard but left smiling. She didn't seem angry or disappointed."

"Well, don't fuck her. You'll crush Kelly."

Andre shuddered and made a face. "As if."

Mark snorted with laughter.

Thirty-Five

Kelly gazed up at Andre, grinning from her sprawled position on the blue mat. He offered her a hand to rise.

"That looks fun," Stacy said in an exaggerated drawl.

Kelly jumped to her feet and turned to glare. The gym reeked of sweat and disinfectant, making it hard to sort scents. She hadn't heard her sister approach either. Low music played, but the cement walls echoed with the groans and shouts of her classmates and the instructors offering advice. The meaty smack of flesh on the mats competed with the laughter of those triumphant and the groans of those defeated, masking Andre's low growl.

"My sister," she said for his benefit then, "What do you want?"

"Found a new boy-toy, huh? At least this one looks more your age."

Anger narrowed her eyes, and she had to force back her growl. "What the hell do you want?"

"My, my, afraid I'll poach him?"

"Lady, you don't have a prayer," Andre said in clear disgust.

"She isn't a lady," Kelly said and crossed her arms.

"So, you're with them now? I thought you were better than that. I thought you really loved me." Tears shone in Stacy's eyes as she sniffed and rummaged in her purse with one hand.

"Oh, please, save the crocodile tears. You've gone out of your way to hurt me."

"Because I didn't want that pedophile near you? Look, I'm sorry about the money thing, but I was desperate. And he was a creep."

Kelly sighed hard. "What do you want," she asked in a softer voice.

"Can we go somewhere and talk?"

"No."

Andre grabbed her shoulder and growled softly again.

Stacy gave them a watery smile and said, "Fine, whatever, I just missed you."

"Look, not to be a bitch or anything, but why are you here? You haven't spoken to me in months."

Stacy's gaze flicked from Kelly to Andre, and her eyes hardened. The tears disappeared as if they'd never been. "I just saw you here and thought it was time to make up. Sisters fight, but we forgive each other."

"We aren't making up until you stop trying to wreck my life. Stay away from my school. Do your business somewhere else."

Stacy flushed, then lifted her chin. She placed one hand on her hip and bent a knee in what she probably thought a provocative pose, but it shifted her short skirt releasing a malodorous wave of scent.

"You should hit up a laundromat," Andre said.

Stacy's flush deepened, and she glanced down. "It doesn't have a mark on it."

"It reeks of cigarettes and—" Kelly waved a hand in the air. "It just reeks," she finished.

"You think I like my job? And those stupid boys?"

"You must or why do it? No one forced you. Don't try the pity card with me. Others might believe that bullshit, but I was there and saw how much our parents tried to help you. Is all you had to do was accept their help."

"Everything just comes so easy for you, doesn't it?" Stacy snarled. "All your life you've taken what I wanted. First our parent's attention then—" she clamped her lips hard, and her glare deepened. "Whatever. If you don't want to be friends, we can be enemies." She turned and stumbled over the edge of a mat. When she regained her balance, she tried to march out but wobbled and veered.

"She must be high as a kite," Kelly said in embarrassment. "So, you see why I've never mentioned her."

"I'm sorry," Andre said.

He strode to the window and cupped his hands

to see out. Kelly joined him. Streetlights reflected off the wet pavement. A light drizzle still fell seen more as a softening of the air. They both watched Stacy get into the backseat of a beat-up sedan.

"Must have wanted money," Kelly said.

"Never get in a car with her." Andre gave her a quick hug.

"Isn't that sad, that I have to be so cautious with my own family?"

"I'm your family, and you have more waiting to meet you."

"Mark." She sighed wistfully and again considered calling him.

It seemed silly to wait. She was sure Mark was the one for her.

"I'd call him but I miss him so much I'm afraid my wolf will roll me. I need to finish school first so my parents don't freak.

"Not just Mark, although he'll be glad to hear that, the rest of the pack is your family too."

"Glad to hear it? Do you talk with him?"

Andre bit his lip and looked guilty. She stepped closer to sniff him. "What? And don't say nothing; I smell your guilt."

"Yes, I see him. He lives with me."

"He's still here?" Her eyes lit, and she turned to the door. Andre drew her back. "Go if you want to but think hard first."

"Yeah, you're right. Jesus, this sucks. How is he?"

"Missing you like crazy and worried. Don't call

him if you can't handle seeing him. It's only a few more months." Andre's frown deepened. "It isn't only Stacy he's worried about. You smell any other wolves, call me and my dad; don't hesitate for a second."

"You're freaking me out."

"Sorry. I wasn't supposed to tell you, but Stacy was more, um, off, then I was expecting."

Kelly hid her face in her hands and groaned. "You knew about her," she asked in a strangled voice.

"Mark warned me about her. Don't tell him I told you either."

Kelly glanced around the room, seeing it in a new light. This wasn't a fun exercise to do together instead of running, this was preparation. She snarled low in her throat and tensed.

"Don't freak out. Nothing has changed. We never saw a hint of another wolf, but Mark isn't wrong to worry. You're practically defenseless with no pack to guard you."

"What do I need guarding against?"

"We all aren't as civilized as Richard's pack. Male werewolves outnumber females about two to one. Some packs are small and would fall on an unmated, unguarded female with slavering joy. They wouldn't mean it like a human man would, to them, you would be a dream come true. They would cherish you, I'm not trying to say you'd be treated badly, but you'd have no choice but to be their mate."

"Mark told me wolves mate for life—" she cut off as the instructor rose his voice and the class began doing warm-up exercise.

"Let's go somewhere else to talk." She headed to her locker.

Andre grabbed his bag, and they ran into the drizzle without bothering to change. She got into his car and turned to face him. "Okay, I thought I understood, but maybe I don't."

"We are wolves, and our senses guide us. Smells act on us in ways impossible for a human to understand. You don't really understand because you have no experience with wolves, but pack smells like family, it's an instinct. You might dislike one of us, but we'll still be family."

"Okay, I get that."

"Mates also smell differently. You won't be able to help desiring yours. Even if you don't like him as a human."

"That sounds— unpleasant."

"Without human love to base the mating on, is all you'll have is the sex. Werewolves live a long time and the wolves that mate without love tend to go feral much sooner."

"You kill them," Kelly said horrified.

"No. If you let the wolf take you, and never revert, you age as a wolf. They go to the hills and usually die of old age. Old age for a wolf is about thirteen years. It can happen much faster for an older werewolf though. Sometimes wounds kill them although that's rare. It's the shift that heals us completely. A feral wolf won't shift back even to save his life so, if he's hurt bad, the wounds could kill him before they have a chance to heal.

"But couldn't they stay with a person they did love?"

"Sure, but how do you think Mark would feel if you had sex with your mate and came home to him? You couldn't have sex with him. You could cuddle and kiss and spend all day together, but sex would be out. He wouldn't desire you physically, or I should say it would be hard to desire you physically, your mated smell would see to that. There are ways around it but not easy ways. So, yes, you could still love him but not like you do now. More like you do with me, but you would remember loving him and grow to resent your mate."

"And then the feral thing… "

"My parents are in love and very happy. It isn't all bad. We're a pretty civilized pack. We stay in one place and live in normal human homes. We do have dens in the woods, but we hold jobs and go to school. Richard keeps us safe. Sometimes, if we've been living in the town, he'll send us away for a few years or keep us on the ranch until we can mingle safely again but we'll teach you what to say when asked if you're Kelly when you shouldn't be able to look like you do."

"That must be hard."

"Not really. Audrey is an amazing artist and can make you look any age you need. My father goes to town sometimes and sits in his old bar to talk with his old friends and complains about his cousin's son Alfonso who happens to look just like he used to and it's all good. We change our hair and clothes but mostly we stick together, and that sort of thing doesn't matter to us. We don't need to worry about it because we don't have human friends we run into."

"Still, it must suck having to change careers and names every ten years or so."

"Most don't. And the ones that do don't seem to mind it. I know my mom loved her shop, but she likes the time off with my dad too. Kell, we live so long that we can enjoy what we do without the pressure humans have to reach some career pinnacle. We don't change our given names just the one surname the world knows us by. We use our different names in a pattern. When I need to change my name next, I'll use Garcia. It is my name. We don't live like humans; we aren't human."

"What is your full name and why are you going to law school?"

"My name is unusual for a modern wolf. Normally, parents pick names that would naturally have the same nickname, but my parents picked disconnected family names. My full name is Andre Garcia Emilio Hernando Montoya Ramirez, and all wolves study law. Well, most of us. First, because we take turns being park rangers but more importantly we need to know the human's law so when we break them we do so knowingly. We can't afford to get caught. A wolf that gets jailed either gets broken out or killed."

Kelly shivered. It had never occurred to her how dangerous even a simple arrest could be on the wrong night.

Andre ran a hand through her hair. "Relax. You're not going on a crime spree, are you?"

She smiled weakly at him. "No."

"So, nothing to worry about."

"I could get in an accident or something."

"Sure, you could. But accidental manslaughter won't get you jailed, it will get you parole. And if we thought the charges would stick, you'd disappear safely into the woods somewhere. If you're nervous, stay home the day before and the day of the full moon."

Kelly stared down at the hands clenched in her lap. "How do you kill the ones who tell?"

"I don't. I've never gone on a manhunt, but different ways. We offer silver nitrate or a silver knife to the heart to the wolves who have gotten caught, and we can't get them free, but I've only heard of that happening twice and years ago. We can usually spring them. It isn't that hard to open a cell door and who would stop a dog from walking out?"

Kelly laughed.

"For those like the feral that bit you, we send hunters after them, and they can kill them however they like. Feral's that are in the woods we don't bother with unless they attack humans and then it's likely a bullet. It's never pack killing pack if you're worried I'm going to turn on you."

"We aren't pack."

"But we are friends, and I'm not the type to kill my friends."

She laughed again and hugged him. He'd sounded offended and a bit hurt.

"You're a good man. I'm sorry. I shouldn't doubt you."

"No, you shouldn't." He kissed her temple and ruffled her hair before pushing away. "Want to go for a run instead?"

"No. I'm sort of freaked out. Take me home, please. And tell Mark I'm counting the days." She rubbed the fogged window with her sleeve and spoke with her back turned. "He still wants me, right, or was it his wolf?"

"Oh, he wants you all right." He rubbed his jaw and grinned ruefully.

She smiled at her reflection and rested her forehead on the cool glass.

"Have a good time?" her mother called from the living room when she entered.

"Yep."

"Is he your boyfriend yet?" her father asked as he came in from the kitchen. He grinned and tweaked her hair when she made a face at him.

"No, and he never will be. We're just friends."

"What's wrong with him?" her mother asked, sounding so disappointed Kelly snickered.

"Nothing. He's a nice guy just not right for me."

Kelly ran up the stairs to her room as her mother grumbled to her father. She flopped face down on her bed and growled into her pillow. She wanted to call Mark badly. The wait seemed pointless and dangerous to her now, but she only had three months to go before she graduated. On May sixteenth, she'd turn eighteen and could legally leave her parents. They'd be angry when she moved out, but they would forgive her.

"They're going to freak when I bring Mark home," she said into her pillow. She drifted to sleep trying to think of a scenario they'd buy that didn't make Mark look like a crazy stalker.

Thirty-Six

S he said that huh?" Mark beamed at Andre. "She wants to call, but I told her to wait. Call her if you want but it will push her wolf, and you only have twelve more weeks until she graduates.

"I can wait."

Andre eyed him doubtfully. "You look like you're about to molt. Calm the hell down."

"Ha." I can't wait for you to meet your mate. Let's see you calm down."

"You both calm down," Carlota said and tousled her son's hair. "Go study while I make dinner."

Mark opened Andre's lawbook but couldn't concentrate. He finally slapped it closed and headed for the door.

"Eat first," Carlota handed him a barely browned steak. "Like a human," she said and rolled her eyes as she drew the plate back when he reached for the meat. She pointed at the table. "Sit. The more human you can be, the easier it will be to hold the wolf in check. Don't rush her. Sit."

He sat and used a fork and knife, glaring at Andre who snickered behind his law book.

Dark had fallen while he ate so he borrowed Alfonso's car and left it at Moe's, risking being spotted but not really worried about it. He wore a ballcap and long-sleeved flannel jacket with the collar pulled up. He'd be in the trees on the side of the road before anyone could call out to him and anyone who saw him enter would think he was just taking a piss.

He jogged through the trees and settled on his stomach on the low hillside above her house before taking the night scope from his pocket. Cows milled in the field, and a light flickered on in her parent's room. He couldn't see her room from this angle, but the yard was peaceful.

He relaxed as he stared at the house. She was safe and would soon be his.

Thirty-Seven

March
Two months later

Kelly returned Andre's glare. "So what? The gym is good enough," she snapped.

This was the second time Andre had tried to talk her into going for a run, and she hated to admit how nervous she was now of running in the woods.

"For exercise, yes, but you need to let the wolf out too."

"I do in my room." Guilty exasperation made her tone sharper than she'd intended.

Andre glared at her, his dark eyebrows beetled and his jaw clenched. "That isn't good enough."

"I'm perfectly fine."

"You're stubborn is what you are. Come for a run with me. No one is going to try to snatch you, and I'll stay human. You've got to get over that too, you know."

"Jesus, stop already. I've told you a trillion times. I'm afraid my wolf will want yours. Will it kill you to wait for Mark and me…" She trailed off and blushed when he snickered.

"Stop. It isn't stupid to want to choose with my human side."

His frown faded, and he sighed sadly. "No, it isn't, but your wolf doesn't want me either." He waved his hands and pressed his lips together. "Fine, whatever, we can run wherever you want." He dangled the leash and collar before her.

"No way."

"Kell, we all do it."

"Well, I'm not. No. Just no, okay? Let's go to the gym."

"Join my family tomorrow for the full moon."

"Not going to happen."

She glared out the window angry with herself, but she couldn't stop worrying. The wolf within her pushed for release, her wolf wanted Mark too. The wait was becoming unbearable, and she felt like she was tempting fate. Three wolves had found her already, the one that bit her, the feral Mark had killed, and Mark. Who was to say a fourth wouldn't wander along? It was better to stay inside and not tempt fate by running in the hills.

She'd stayed in her room for three months when she'd first became a wolf and could do it again.

The next night, cool moonlight illuminated her room, and she paced irritably. Her wolf wanted out. Forehead pressed to the window, she closed her eyes and tried to soothe her inner wolf with promises of future runs. When she opened them, the starlight beckoned mockingly.

Her hands trembled as she yanked off her clothes and laid down in her closet. She left the door to her room unlocked and her closet door partway open. The steak she'd left in in the closet occupied her for a little while, but it got harder to stay still as the moon rose in the sky.

The house settled around her. The television quieted, and her parents headed up the stairs, laughing quietly together. She snarled softly and rolled on her back, kicking her feet in the air and wriggling, trying not to hear the soft sounds from their room.

Normally, she flipped on her radio and used headphones when they made love, which they did more than she'd ever imagined, but tonight she couldn't do that, she needed to be able to hear if one rose to check on her. They didn't check her often, but it happened occasionally. So far never on a full moon though.

The soft sounds from her parent's room ceased, and she heard the footsteps approaching. Her glance darted to the window then the door. Her muzzle parted in a soundless snarl of effort as she forced her wolf back. Fiery lances of pain accompanied her transformation, and she trembled as she pulled on her robe

"Oh, you're still up," her father said when he poked his head in the door. "How's the headache?"

"Better. I was sleeping but thought I heard something."

"I'll check, but I'm sure it was nothing."

Her father blushed and hurriedly closed her door.

"Night," he called through the door and practically ran downstairs.

She let her wolf grab her and collapsed to her side, panting hard and trying not to whine. When the pain faded, she raced around her room before settling back into her closet and resting her head on her paws. A whine escaped her and grew in volume, and she had to strain not to howl. When she was calmer, she padded to the window and stood on her hind legs to peer out.

Warm wolf breath misted the window, and she dropped to all fours. Her reflection in her floor length mirror caught her eye, and her hunched, miserable posture shocked her. This wasn't a life for a wolf, caged in a room and afraid of her own shadow. Wolves should run free and be able to hunt and howl, not be constrained. She wouldn't treat a dog this way. She snapped at her reflection and turned her back to sleep in her closet den.

With relief, she greeted the sun and resumed her human shape. She flopped on her bed and had just dozed off when her mother woke her, calling from the foot of the stairs.

"Bad night, honey?"

"Cold coming on, I think." She kissed her mother's cheek and ran out the door.

"Because you never wear your coat," her mother called after her.

Kelly squeezed her eyes closed. She was always forgetting, but she didn't feel the cold much. She breathed out to see if she could see her breath and grimaced at the gray puff that emerged. The snow had melted, and the earth smelled rich and the trees ripe.

"Suck it up," she snarled and started her car. "Just a few more weeks."

The thought of being able to run with Mark beneath the full moon made her stomach tighten and nipples harden. They could make love beneath the trees and drink the cold streams. She couldn't wait.

Her wolf was even harder to hold back on the eve of the next full moon, and she knew she'd have to let the wolf out to run like it or not. She debated calling Andre but was afraid she'd made her wolf desperate for companionship, and it would force her to choose him.

"I'm going for a run," she called to her mother and headed to the woods behind her house, glad it was a Saturday. She hesitated at the foot of the path. The last time she'd run, she'd felt eyes on her but had never smelled or seen anyone.

I'm perfectly safe, she told herself forcefully and headed into the woods.

She spent the day in the woods as a wolf and returned feeling much more relaxed. She'd be able to hold her back when the moon rose and spend the night in her room.

"Andre called looking for you," her mother said when she came in. "Were you in the woods this whole time?"

"Yeah, I ran down to Abby's and was going to knock, but changed my mind."

"You must be starving. There's lunch meat in the fridge."

Her mother followed her into the kitchen and offered condiments while she spoke. "How is Abby? We haven't seen her in ages."

"She's good. If Stacy hadn't approached me in the gym, I might have said hello."

"Stacy's bothering you again?"

"No. I think she wanted money but was embarrassed to ask in front of Andre. He told me she came to the library twice now and hit on him. What's wrong with her?"

"I really don't know. I blame myself. Something must have happened to her, something I never saw. Maybe someone was abusing her or something. Or there was some adult she was afraid of. I realized she was into some dark stuff, all that goth crap and the occult books, but thought it a phase. Other kids seem to come out of it fine. Look at her best friend, Carolynn. She dumped Stacy as a friend years ago, and they both wore the dark clothes and dyed their hair for a year, but Carolynn outgrew it and seems normal. I saw her the other day in the grocery store. She's married now and expecting her first child and was so embarrassed to talk to me."

"Mom, it isn't your fault. Let's not talk about her. I know you hate this too, but I'm set on attending University in Montana.

"I just don't' see why you can't attend Carlton or State."

"Because I want to go farther away with none of my old classmates."

Her mother sighed and slid the folder containing the acceptance letters Kelly had so far received from the file on the countertop. "Fine. I'll send the deposit. We're going to miss you though."

Kelly rose to hug her mother tight. "I know, and I'll miss you too, but we can talk on the phone and visit."

"What about Andre?"

"He can visit too if he wants."

Her mother snorted and flipped the folder open. "There's such a thing as being too picky. Not that I'm rushing you or anything but…."

"I know what I want, and he isn't it. Let's not talk about that either."

With a fingertip, she slid the file across the counter and pursed her lips. She hadn't spoken to Mark about this yet and had no idea how he felt about her attending college. Her cheeks flushed as she considered she didn't really know what he intended. Would they marry and share a home or just meet in the woods as the mood struck him?

"Mom, send them my acceptance but no money yet." She slid the forms back.

Her mother grinned and began filling in the forms.

Kelly gave her a quick hug. "I'm lucky to have such a great, understanding mother."

"Still not taking that crappy car all the way there," her mother called after her, but laughter lined her voice.

The full moon was a week away, a day before her birthday. The last one she needed to get through alone. The thought made her almost giddy with excitement. Her cell trilled but she ignored it and threw on old sweats. The phone rang downstairs.

"Kelly, it's Andre for you," her mother called.

"Tell him I'll call him back later, and I'm going for a run." She didn't want to speak to anyone. She wanted to shift to enjoy a long run and sleep in the woods for a few hours.

"What's got into you," her mother said, laughing at her as she ran down the stairs humming.

"I'm in love," Kelly burst out.

"What?" Her mother's eyes widened in shock, and she clutched her chest. "Andre?"

"No, but I'll bring him home soon."

"Love, huh? You sure you don't mean lust?"

"That too. He's perfect."

"And where did you meet this paragon? And how long have you known him?"

"Later. I'm going for a run and then meeting Abby to talk prom dresses," she lied.

"You're going to the prom?" her mother sounded thrilled now, and Kelly had to turn away to hide her wince.

She hadn't considered going and didn't know if

she could still get tickets at this late date, but Andre would take her to make her mother happy. Her wince turned into a grimace. Her mom would expect her to go with the new boyfriend now. She gnashed her teeth, sorry she'd said anything.

"With the new guy?" her mother asked.

"Later, or I'll be late." She ran out the door before her mother could question her further. She debated calling Abby, she'd cover for her, but hated to impose. The lie had seemed simple, a good excuse to stay out late in the woods.

"Lies are never simple," she grumbled.

Her good mood returned as she ran. Moist leaves silenced her paws and released enticing smells. May sunshine warmed her fur, birds chirped, and squirrels and rabbits bounded among the trees. She snapped halfheartedly and pounced, having no intention of catching anything, but they smelled delicious.

On her stomach, she slunk as quietly as she could beneath the thick pines, her eyes on a brown rabbit gnawing a twig when she whiffed wolf and not a wolf she knew. In a twinkling, terror replaced her joy in the day. Her hackles rose, and she snarled soundlessly, then turned to run. An unfamiliar wolf stood downwind at the top of the narrow path, and she hadn't heard him arrive.

He stared down at her. For minutes, they stared at each other, both motionless. She took a slow step backward, and his ears flicked. She turned and bounded away, running for her life.

Thirty-Eight

"We've got a problem," Alfonso said as soon as Mark answered the phone.

Mark's pulse jumped, and his hand tightened on the phone.

He was on his feet headed to the door as Andre said, "Kelly saw me out running, and I scared her to death. She ran further north. I don't know if she'll try to circle back or keep going."

"Call Andre and send him north to call for her; I'll go to her house," Mark said and ran for Carlota's car. The short drive to Kelly's house frustrated him. He should have been there already.

He left Carlota's car at the top of Kelly's street and ran into the woods bordering the backfield. Dusk darkened the forest, leaving the paths in dark shadow. He called her name, not caring who heard, cursing himself for not making her meet Andre's parents.

"Kelly," he bellowed again and crashed through the trees.

He wasn't sure where she would go if she thought a strange wolf was on her trail. "She'd try to break the trail," he said aloud and began running to the reservoir. Sweat trickled down his back, making dust and foliage stick to his skin. By the time he reached the turnoff leading to the reservoir, he huffed and puffed, worry shortening his breath.

Rocks and shale lined the steep sides of the manmade lake. A narrow dirt road provided access and partially circled the small lake. Since neither fishing nor boating was allowed, hardly anyone came here.

He cupped his hands around his mouth and bellowed, "Kelly!"

A piercing scream of, "Mark," answered him, echoing over the water and he began running again.

Naked and sobbing, she thrashed through the trees.

"Kelly, sweetheart, it's okay. That was Alfonzo, Andre's father. He's sorry he scared you."

She was crying so hard he wasn't sure she heard him. He hugged her close, realizing he'd run from the house shirtless and shoeless when her skin touched his.

"Shh, you're okay," he whispered and ran his hands over her. She twitched beneath his hands. Warm tears cooled on his chest, and her breathing calmed.

"Mark," she said in a tight voice and drew his lips to hers.

He could have kissed her forever. The kiss

engulfed him. Warm and soft, her lips held a world of promise.

He was shocked when she pushed away and slapped him.

She ran from him crying.

"Please, Kelly, you have to come with me. I'll bring you home. I'm sorry I broke my word, but Alfonso said you needed me."

She whirled to face him, brown hair flying about her cheeks and sticking to her tears. "All this time you pretended to be my friend. I thought you liked me!"

Her anger shocked him and left him trembling. It hadn't occurred to him she'd be so mad to see him. "I do like you." He approached slowly with his hands out, not wanting to spook her. "I shouldn't have left you alone like I did, but you were handling it so well, and I didn't want to you to miss out on a normal childhood."

"You're a fucking liar. You let me think—" She clamped her lips hard and spun away. "So, what now?" she asked without facing him.

"You can't go home so upset. I'll bring you home, to my home, and you'll meet the pack. You and Richard can work out—"

"I hate you." She began to cry, deep gasping sobs that shook her shoulders.

Her words struck him like a blow. "Don't say that. You think it was easy for me to leave you alone?"

She spun and glared through her tears. "You led

me on, making me think I was special to you but all that time you were planning to give me away. I was a fucking job to you. You reek of her!"

She screamed and threw her hands up when he took a step forward, then seemed to realize she was naked and crouched, covering her breasts with her hands.

"You smell Alfonso's mate, Carlota, on me. Wolves touch each other a lot. Sniff closer, and you'll smell Alfonso and Andre on me too." He almost sagged in relief. She was jealous, not angry at him. He threw his hands up in exasperation when she continued to glare. "Sweetheart, you were fifteen when we met. Was I supposed to seduce you? I love you."

She shrieked, "Never say that again!" and fell to her knees, curling as tight as she could to cover her face with her hands, leaning over to hide her nakedness.

"Please, just listen and calm down. Wolves mate for life. It isn't a choice, it's biology. Is it wrong to give you a choice, or should I have taken advantage? Fuck, if I didn't love you, why would I hang around in this one-horse shithole for almost three fucking years?"

He almost laughed when she dropped her hands and glanced around as if seeing the woods for the first time.

"Please," he continued in a soft, wheedling voice. "Come home with me, and if, after you meet the pack, you still want me, we'll get married."

The words almost killed him to say, but she deserved a choice.

"You love me?" She crawled towards him on her knees.

"Don't." It was his turn to make a warding off gesture. "You know we have a no contact rule. You touch me while you smell like that…"

She stopped moving and closed her eyes, lifting her face to breathe deeply. When she opened them again, they were golden.

"Fuck," he said harshly and stepped away from her.

"Mmm." She closed her eyes and sniffed. Without opening her eyes, she ran a hand over her breasts. High and firm, they jutted from her chest, the nipples a dark pink and already erect. But it wasn't the sight of her naked breasts that brought him within touching distance but her smell. She wanted him fiercely.

He wanted to ask her if she were sure but words wouldn't form over the lump in his throat. Her skin felt hot under his hand, and her kiss tasted like life itself. He didn't remember removing his clothes, they were just gone and her breasts hard against his chest.

"It will hurt the first time."

He glanced up, but the sun still rode the sky. He knew this was a bad idea, but she'd broken his willpower. He dropped his pants, and she made a small grunting noise. His cocked jumped, eager for her, and he groaned when she touched it. He could smell her excitement and knew she'd be wet for him.

Her breath came hard as she pulled him down to the leaves with her and spread her legs.

"You love me?" she whispered.

"Yes. This is forever between us. Even if you hate me, you won't be able to leave me."

"I love you."

He kissed her softly. Her words eased his guilt. They kissed again. Her hands wandered his body and urged him closer. He felt drunk with desire as if he dreamed the feel of her curves and the soft sounds of her sighs. Moist leaves beneath them warmed with their body heat, the perfect bed.

She groaned when he slid inside her and angled her hips to pull him closer. Her kiss tasted like sunshine and her skin salty as he kissed his way to her breast then took her nipple into his mouth, making her writhe and moan. Sweat beaded on his brow and chest as he thrust, straining to hold himself back as her excitement grew. Perspiration appeared on her forehead and chest, and her nails trailed over his back and dug into his ass.

She thrust with him, her body tensing as her orgasm neared. He wasn't sure he could hold out long enough. Each thrust brought him to the brink, and he came hard when she shouted with her release.

Her scream of pleasure turned to a scream of pain as his cock enlarged and her vagina clamped down. This was new to him too, and he groaned with the sensations.

"Don't pull away; it will hurt more. Relax and let it happen. It will only hurt this one time." She shuddered in his arms and not with passion. The sour scent of fear emanated from her now, but he couldn't stop even if he wanted to. She groaned when he surged.

"It's okay. Wrap your legs around me." He sat carefully, taking her with him and rocked slowly as he surged again. The power of the release caught his breath. He'd known to expect it but hadn't imagined anything could feel this good. He surged again and groaned loudly at her answering burst of wetness that dribbled down his engorged cock. The scent of fresh blood overlaid the sour stench of fear.

Unable to help himself, he bit her neck and licked the blood drops. Her body relaxed against him, and she jerked her hips with his. His tense shoulders relaxed as she did and his next surge was harder. The orgasm continued, his cock swelling and jetting every few seconds. The muscles of her vagina clenched him hard, and she swayed her hips, brushing her nipples against his chest. Only his tight grip kept her upright. Completely limp in his arms, her hair brushed his legs. The wolf within him wanted to bite her and lick her skin, but he forced it back.

He moaned with the power of his release and still his cock hardened and throbbed. Slowly, the sensations eased. Overhead, the sky darkened as night replaced day. Her eyes glittered in the low light. Half-slitted and devoid of human thought, her head lolled as she came with him, nature making her his. When the sensations finally passed, he collapsed backward, holding her tight to his chest. At first, he thought she'd fallen asleep but her heartbeat continued to slow, and her skin grew cold.

Seriously alarmed when she didn't respond to shaking, he scrambled for the cell phone in his clothes, wincing at the blood running down his thighs.

"You on the way home?" Richard answered on the first ring and asked without preamble.

"We made love, and now she's unconscious."

"What?" Richard said in such an incredulous voice Mark almost laughed despite himself.

"Something's seriously wrong with her."

"Are you fucking retarded? Jesus, fucking, Christ! You were supposed to bring her back here first. She's a fucking strong shifter. If she fucking loses control..."

"She doesn't lose control. I've never seen control like hers."

"You, stupid fuck!" Richard breathed hard a moment before saying in a voice of forced calm, "Mating is serious. Why do you think we do it the way we do? It isn't an empty ceremony. She'll fucking need the pack. Her wolf will be strong in her…How are you even calling me? You should be taken by your wolf too. That's probably why she's unconscious. She needs your wolf. You can't fuck like a human; you aren't fucking human." He was quiet a second, panting in anger. "Okay, it's too late to lecture you. We're on our way to you. Keep her with you and keep yourself human until we get there. She'll need food, water, and shelter. Her temperature will drop while she bonds."

Silence descended, and Mark's shoulders tightened even more.

"Jesus, Mark, holding yourself back from the bond… I don't know what it will do to her or you." Richard sounded concerned now, not angry, and it scared him.

The phone became staticky a minute, and voices muffled as if Richard argued with someone with his hand over the speaker and then Leah spoke. Her voice relaxed Mark's tense shoulders, and he wished she were here with him. The alphas' mate had a soothing effect on all the wolves, an effect he didn't realize would translate just from speaking to her, but he was glad it did.

"Mark, don't try to make love to her like a woman," Leah said.

"Too late," he said in a small voice.

"Damn, that first time is painful. I can't imagine how much more if she was really aroused."

"She bled a lot."

"Don't freak out; you know she'll heal. Look, wolf biology is different. Later, when your fully bonded, you can make love human-style but until then come as quick as you can and then hold fucking still. It won't hurt as much the second time, but it'll hurt until she's fully bonded. Your dick has fucking barbs in it. Trying to pull out is a bad idea. Make sure you won't be interrupted and be as, ah, wolfy as you need to. She'll want you to bite her neck and to bite yours. Don't freak her out by getting grossed out or pulling away if she sniffs you, or licks you, or acts like her wolf in any way while in human form."

Again, the phone became muffled and staticky then Leah said," Put it on fucking speakerphone then. Richard wants to know if you told her what to expect."

"Not really. I told her it would hurt, but I think she thought I meant because she was a virgin."

"She's a strong fucking shifter, Leah," Richard said, sounding as angry as Mark had ever heard him.

"He is too," Leah snapped back. "Freaking him out isn't going to help. This is our fault for not insisting he bring her back. We're getting too soft."

"Discuss our faults later," Mark said. "How do I help her now?"

"I'm not sure," Leah said worriedly. "I think you need to treat her as an unwilling mate."

"Rape her, you mean." Nausea burned his throat, and he thought he might vomit.

"Don't think of it like that. She wanted you, right? This isn't a woman who had no choice, but the problem is similar. She doesn't know enough to accept you, so you have to force nature to take over."

"Mark," Richard said sadly. "If you go feral… If

you let her get away…"

"Yeah. You're right, I'm a fucking asshole. I handled this all wrong." The smell of her blood brought tears to his eyes. "Will she die?"

"They rarely do," Leah said.

"Hurry," Mark said and snapped the phone closed.

He was so angry at himself his hands shook. He should have prepared for this, forced her to listen, and kept the hell away from her. He hadn't even made her a den. He was as big an asshole as his father. What did it matter if he loved her if his love killed her?

Limp, Kelly splayed across his lap, her heart beating so slow he was afraid she'd died already. She needed his wolf, and he needed to be human enough to stop her from running and killing. She'd wake ravenous, and he had nothing for her, but this woods was wide and small game abounded.

"And what choice do I have? I'll keep us from killing anyone." He smoothed her hair and leaned closer to breath deep of her scent. Her state dismayed him. He had to close his eyes and pretend she slept to get his body to respond. He nuzzled her neck and licked along her collarbone and down to her breast, using his hand to rub himself hard. The second he slid inside her, his reluctance evaporated.

His wolf knew what it wanted, and he embraced the orgasm. He cried out when his cock engorged, and he bit her neck drawing blood that he licked up, then nipped across her body, leaving small, red welts before collapsing against her. Each pulse of his cock felt like heaven. Her heartbeat accelerated, and she opened her eyes. Her moans joined his, and he screamed his pleasure when she raked her nails across his ass.

When his flaccid cock finally slipped from her body, she licked his neck and curled tightly against him as her heartbeat slowed. He fought sleep, wanting to ensure she was well but he couldn't tell if she just slept deep or was unconscious again. Her heartbeats had slowed lower than a human but so had his. He let sleep claim him and woke to her licking his face. Golden eyes stared from her gray muzzle, and her ears flicked as if each small creak and chirp were explosive.

She continued to lick him, and he wanted to join her, to feel the wind in his fur and run beside her, but he held himself back, not sure he was doing the right thing or not.

"Kelly, sweetheart, sleep beside me."

He glanced at the sky. It was almost dawn, and maybe she'd be able to shed the wolf when the sun shone on her. He figured Richard could be here in about four more hours. Alfonso and Carlota were probably out there but they wouldn't be able to stop him without a fight and Kelly would try to help him and likely get hurt. The thought made him growl, and she jerked away.

"Sleep," he said again and patted the ground beside him. Her whine almost brought his change.

"I want to make love to you," he said in a soft,

cajoling voice and ran his hands over her head to bury his fingers in her ruff. "Tell me you love me. I need to hear it."

She whined again and rolled to expose her stomach.

"We're okay. Tell me you love me. Let me make love to you." He smiled ruefully to himself, sure his words would be more persuasive if he had a hard-on, but he was too worried to be aroused.

She rolled and jumped to her feet.

"Don't leave me!"

She whirled, but before he could rise or transform, she spun back and landed on her human knees before him.

"I love you," she said in a voice that cracked. She crouched and shook, her hair falling about her bare shoulders in a tangled mass.

Her strength of will impressed and dismayed him. That had to hurt, forcing the wolf back so hard when the wolf knew this was her time. She should be free to run with her mate in the starlight.

"I'm so sorry. This isn't how I meant our first time to be."

Her stomach rumbled, and she squeezed her eyes closed.

"We're going to hunt soon." He grabbed her arm and yanked her into his lap when she rose and turned away. "Together. Stay with me." He debated telling her why they were waiting but didn't. It couldn't really help to know and might freak her out that other wolves were coming.

Her heart began to pound hard, and sweat sprang up all over her body. Her familiar smell brought him fully erect, and she straddled him eagerly. He kissed her for a few minutes then turned her until she was on her hands and knees before him. He came quickly. She let out a yelp and fell to her face as his cock engorged.

"God, I pity the humans. You feel so good."

She replied with a low moan that tightened his balls. He'd never imagined it would be this good. He'd heard since he was old enough to care about such things that sex with your mate was much more powerful than with human lovers, and he knew wolves mated like dogs, becoming locked together, but hadn't imagined it could feel so good. Each pulse from his cock was a new orgasm more powerful than any he'd ever had before her. Pleasure washed him in waves as his muscles contracted and released in time with hers.

He bit her between pulses and licked the punctures. Beneath him, her hips quivered and jerked as she made small animalistic grunts and whines. The noises excited him. She was his. He pushed his cock harder inside her, making her scream. He threw back his head and screamed too.

When his cock was finally flaccid, he fell limply across her back and didn't have the energy to move when she squirmed out from under him.

He smiled as she licked his neck and rubbed her cheek the length of his body. He rolled over to hug her close, but she didn't want hugs. Her wolf had caught her.

Her eyes shone with an animal glitter, and she bit his neck hard, growling low in her throat. Without thinking, he smacked her ass, and she released him to rub her cheek against his face, then chest. She licked his lips, then nipples, and sniffed the length of his body, pausing by his cock to sniff him thoroughly before continuing to his feet. She returned to his cock and licked him twice before burying her face in his neck and setting her teeth lightly against his jugular.

He ran his hands through her hair and over her skin until her body relaxed and she drifted to sleep.

A snapping twig jerked him awake. His sleeping mind identified the sound and warned him a human was near. Before he could sit, she'd leaped from his arms as a wolf and pounced on the boy holding the red cooler.

"JJ," he yelled, horrified.

She'd shred him before he could pull her off.

But she turned and snarled at him. Crouched before the child, she showed her teeth and snarled again.

"Don't move, JJ." Mark tried to keep fear from his voice. Not so she wouldn't notice. She'd already smelt his fear, but he didn't want JJ to show fear and trigger her instincts.

"She won't hurt me," JJ said and wrapped an arm around Kelly's chest.

Mark's heart caught in his throat as she hopped forward and snapped at him.

"She isn't used to us. Please don't touch her." Before the words left his mouth, another wolf bowled Kelly over. Kelly howled, then whined and hunkered as low as she could get.

JJ planted his hands on his hips and glared at the wolf. "She wasn't going to hurt me, Mom."

The white wolf snapped at JJ.

"Leave the cooler and go back to your dad," Mark said. He waited until JJ ran from the clearing before dropping to his knees. "Don't hurt her, Leah. She wasn't going to hurt him."

Leah snapped at him, then shook Kelly hard before releasing her to stalk away.

Kelly remained hunkered on the ground. She whined when he took a step closer, and her golden eyes flicked around, searching for an escape.

"It's me," he said in a soft voice and took another step. She whined again and backed away with her tail between her legs.

Thirty-Nine

Mark stilled. Kelly was caught hard by her wolf. Humans were her enemy and the boy a cub she needed to protect. Werewolf children possessed a unique scent that brought out the protective instinct in all wolves. She was probably very confused, seeing a child but scenting a wolf.

He dropped to his hands and knees and let the change take him. When he opened his eyes, Kelly crouched before him and he let his wolf have his way, pinning her down and biting her throat hard until she rolled and showed her stomach.

He snarled and snapped in her face when she tried to rise and didn't release her until she lay still beneath him. When she was still, he stepped away, showing his teeth when she lifted her head.

Immediately, she dropped it again and crawled to him on her belly.

He rested one paw on her back as he cleaned her face and scruff, then sniffed her all over while she sniffed him. Her ears swiveled at every sound, and her nose twitched, her gaze going from him to the trees and back as if she couldn't decide where the threats lay.

The cooler JJ had dropped smelled of raw meat and plastic. She followed him to it and sat while he pawed at the top. He finally pried it open and let her choose first. He hadn't realized how hungry he was until he saw the meat.

While she ripped chunks from the bone she'd chosen, he snarled and snapped over the roast. He'd eaten everything while she still tried to get the small strips of meat from her bone.

She wasn't used to hunting or eating raw meat. The mess she'd made would have made him laugh if he were human. She growled low in her throat when he approached, then whined and dropped the bone to lick his face. He licked the blood and juices from her fur while she gnawed the bone. She needed more food and water. He trotted away, his tail high, and glanced back at the edge of the clearing. She cast a long look at her bone but followed.

The joy of running with her by his side distracted him from finding water. He'd forgotten completely until they crossed a small trickle and she fell behind to drink. The sun warmed his fur, and his belly was full. He settled beside the stream to sleep. He hadn't been sleeping long when she woke him with her whining, and he heard the hunger in it. Water dripped from her muzzle, and she was wet to the flanks. He sat as she tried again to catch a tiny minnow. Tongue lolling in wolfish laughter, he nipped her shoulder and bounded away, nose to the ground and eyes searching for the flick of a gray tail or brown flash of rabbit.

Hunting with her wasn't as easy as hunting alone. She had no idea how to hunt and pounced like a pup at every movement and smell that caught her eyes and nose. Finally, Mark pushed her down and snapped at her when she rose. Her low whine followed him, and she howled when he left her sight and came crashing after him. Snapping and growling confused her. She followed on her stomach with her tail tucked between her legs. Her distress brought him up from his wolf.

She had the instincts of a pup for hunting and couldn't balance that with her mate leaving her. To her, his snaps and growls were abandonment, not wait I'll be right back, and it worried him that her human self was so submerged she didn't see the difference.

He rubbed the length of her body, scent marking her, and let himself resume his human shape. She yipped and jerked away, hackles raised and teeth showing a moment before she dropped to her stomach and crawled back to him. Her cold nose traveled him and her warm tongue tickled across his skin a moment before she heaved a heavy sigh and lowered her head to his chest.

"Will you wait while I hunt?"

Her ears flicked at the sound of his voice.

He lifted her head with both hands and stared into her golden eyes. "Wait here while I hunt."

Golden eyes narrowed as he stood and her head lowered but she didn't move or make a sound when he walked away. The small hairs on his neck rose, but he left her behind, running through the forest as a human.

He debated resuming his wolf shape but it would tire him, and she might need him to be human. He could usually shift three times in an hour with no problem. She seemed to be able to do it at will though, and he didn't want to get caught in the wrong shape for her. Back at their small camp, he grabbed his phone, cursing himself for not calling before running off.

"How's JJ?" he asked when Richard answered.

"Fine. She didn't even scare him. She scared fifty years off my life, but JJ's good."

"Sorry, Richard."

"I should've known better. But I thought she wouldn't see him as a threat."

"It worked." Mark winced at his inane response, but Richard knew he loved JJ too.

"Hmmph. Leah is worried Kelly snapped at you. Her wolf and human are too distinct. She needs to blend them more."

"We need more food. A lot more. She can't hunt and doesn't understand if I ask her to wait."

"Where is she now?"

"I left her at the brook. Send Leah this time."

"What am I, stupid?" Richard hung up on him.

Mark winced and rubbed his forehead. He was inconveniencing a lot of people, but it was too late to worry about it now. He wondered fleetingly what her parents were doing about her disappearance but dismissed the thought. Whatever it was, they'd handle it later. He grabbed their clothes and ran back to her.

Sun dappled her silvery fur. She lay on her side beside the brook and didn't open her eyes or move when he approached. He had to shake her hard to get a reaction at all.

"Kelly, come on, sweetheart. We're okay, and I won't leave you again, but we needed food." She closed her eyes and lay limp.

"Stop it! If you're mad, yell at me."

With shocking suddenness, she resumed her human shape.

"Jesus, I'll never get used to how fast you can do that. Leah will bring us food."

He ran a hand over her bowed head, and she flinched away, crouching to her stomach. Her skin rippled and jumped from his touch. He pulled her tight to his chest, and she began to tremble.

"Kelly, talk to me. I know this is scary. But I'm here, and we can work it out." Her hands clutched him so hard she left bruises behind. His whispered endearments had no effect. Nothing he said or did got a word out of her.

She screamed and began crying when Leah arrived, bearing a bigger cooler and a leather bag. She'd have bolted excepted he was holding her so tightly.

"It's okay, Kelly. My name is Leah, and you and

I are going to be friends. That was my son, JJ, who brought the food earlier, and I'm sorry if I scared you. I was afraid for him, but you wouldn't hurt a pup, I know that now. Don't fight your instincts so hard. We're different but not bad." Leah continued to talk in a soft voice, soothing both of them.

"You'll feel better when you're not so hungry. I'll be close if you need me, but you and Mark need each other now."

Kelly's trembling slowed but she clung to him tighter, and he didn't know if that were good or bad.

Leah ran a hand over Kelly's bowed head, careful not to touch him, and rose. "Eat and sleep and be together. You're private here, and we're guarding to make sure no one gets close. Let the wolf take you. She'll let you come back, and it gets easier to balance with practice."

Leah gave him a worried glance and ran through the trees. Lithe and graceful on her human feet, Mark knew she wouldn't have made a sound approaching if she hadn't wanted them to hear her.

"I need clothes," Kelly said.

Relief made him sag.

"I'll warm you up. Once you eat—"

"I need them," she repeated in a voice laced with hysteria.

"Yeah, okay. Let's see what Leah brought us." Still holding her, he rose and carried her to the cooler. She snatched at the raw meat and ripped off a chunk, then gagged and vomited.

"Don't fight your wolf. It's steak tartare a French

delicacy."

"I'm not human," she moaned.

"You're a werewolf like me."

She moaned again and began to tremble.

He kissed her hands and placed them on his chest. "I love you. What we have is real. I should have brought you to the pack where you could learn to be a wolf."

"Why didn't you force me?"

He winced not knowing if that were blame or curiosity. "I was waiting for you to grow up."

"My father will hate me."

"Did you tell him?" His breath left him hard. Her parents wouldn't keep quiet. It would be a death warrant for all four of them.

"No. I think he saw me though. Sometimes, when I ran at night, I felt someone watching."

Mark exhaled a sigh of relief. "That was me. I watched you every night. He never followed you."

"How could you?"

"How could I not? It took me a year to make friends with you. And every moment of that time I wanted you. It hurt me how hard you tried to be a daughter they could love. I hoped you would realize you needed us. God, Kelly, I didn't want to steal you away like a thief."

"He'll never forgive me. My mother will never let me go home. I've been gone too long this time." Her voice shook with self-loathing when she said, "They'll know what I've been doing; I reek of sex."

"Your home is with me. I want you to come

willingly."

"I don't want to be this— thing." She glanced at the raw meat and shuddered. Her cheeks turned red, and she ducked her head, letting her hair hide her face. "We fuck like animals. I'm an animal."

"Okay, but so what? No one except us sees us. Is amazing sex such a horrible curse to bear?"

She laughed, but it didn't sound happy.

"I get it. Your human upbringing is hard to shake. And maybe a human male would be disgusted; I think he'd thank his lucky stars for such a passionate mate, but so what? What difference does it make what anyone thinks about our sex life except us?"

"It matters to me. I want to make love not fuck."

He pulled her closer. "We will. This is a bonding time. Our hormones will be a bit out of whack while we adjust to each other. The wolf has needs. Right now, we'll let her have her way, and soon she'll be comfortable with me and won't make demands. We'll be able to go slow like the first time."

She shuddered hard, and her breath caught.

"That was a mistake," he said quickly and hid his guilty flush in her hair. I didn't realize it would be worse… I should have finished quicker."

"Can you stop? It feels like we're stuck together."

"Once I come, we can't stop. The wolf takes over, but unlike a real wolf, who has a gland at the end of their penis that gets trapped inside the female, a werewolf also has a spiny-like ridge that cuts into you. The first few times it hurts, but your wolf develops the correct organs for you and the walls of your vagina develop ridges that match me and then it feels good for both of us. Fighting the wolf will prolong the time needed though."

"How long does it take?"

He relaxed and sat back, holding her gently now. She sounded interested and not freaked out.

"Depends. It varies for everyone, and frankly, it isn't something we talk about. Normally, couples go the woods to mate and return in a week or so, but usually, they already know each other and have hunted together and prepared a den. Prepubescent girls are brought to the woods on the full moon until their bodies mature and they choose a mate. The mated pairs make sure they stay safe and unbothered by the unmated males."

"They get to choose?"

A hot flood of guilt rose bile to his throat.

"They can choose who and when they like. Some never pick a mate and keep human lovers although that's rare. Most werewolves can hold back the wolf except for when the moon is full, or they're very frightened. It isn't that difficult to hide yourself away on a full moon. The older you are, the easier it becomes to control your wolf. Lots of older werewolves can hunt perfectly safely with humans nearby.

"But the young ones are dangerous?" She rubbed her thigh. No scars remained from the attack that had turned her.

"They can be. The wolf is powerful. Her instincts are hard to deny especially if you want what she does."

"Jesus, you took such a chance with me. What if I got angry? I could have killed someone."

"You're right, it was stupid, but I wanted you to be happy." He straightened and took a deep breath. "The truth is I wanted to keep you for myself. I wanted you to love me before I brought you to the others so you'd chose me. I didn't think you were a danger to anyone. I swear to God though, I didn't intend this. You fought your wolf so hard. Maybe too hard," he added ruefully. "She wants out now. Mating is a powerful instinct, and she knows you can fight her and win. She'll try to trap you and trick you. Let her have this. Let me have you," he finished softly.

He began making love to her again, but pulled out and knelt at her side. Her eyes widen in surprise. "Watch," he said gruffly.

She made an aroused sound, and he placed her hand on her clit.

"Use your fingers."

Her face flushed but she masturbated while he stroked himself and came on her breast. He pulled her hand away and lifted it to his spurting cock. "Grab the base of my cock."

When her damp fingers touched him, his cock engorged and he groaned, then rubbed his finger in his semen and stuck it inside her.

She hissed and squirmed as her vagina clamped down.

"Okay, let me go," he said between hard breaths. A breeze wafted over them, and he groaned again, this time in discomfort.

She dropped her hand and sat up on her elbows to stare closer. "Does it hurt?"

"It feels great when it expands, like a strong orgasm. It's unpleasant to be outside you though." He batted her reaching hand away. "Don't touch it."

She nodded, her eye's wide and riveted to the small barbs lining the head of his cock.

"Impressive isn't it," he said smugly as he surged and the head of his cock deflated and expanded hard, sending ejaculate a foot away.

"Not the word I would have used." She giggled at his offend expression. "It looks like a sex toy for an s-and-m couple.

She wiggled against his finger.

"It won't last long."

"It feels weird. Not bad, but blah."

He chuckled and kissed her. His cock trembled and spurted again this time staying deflated, and he groaned again. "It's really unpleasant to be cut off like this." She reached down and ran her fingertips through the liquid trailing over his hand.

"It doesn't have a human equivalent," Mark said as he brought her hand to his nose to sniff her fingers. "To us, it smells good, but to other wolves it makes us smell, as you said, blah. It's why we can look at other mated females, smell their arousal, and not be turned on. Naked to us is just naked. The unmated women can arouse unmated males if they tease, but they don't usually do that. It could trigger an attack, especially from young wolves with less control.

She sniffed her finger a moment before snuggling close. He gasped and squirmed when she brushed his cock.

"Sorry."

"It's okay. It doesn't hurt. It's just super sensitive and uncomfortable. It wouldn't expand like that without this. Mark lifted his glistening finger and wriggled it.

She sighed in a mix of relief and disappointment, trailing her damp fingers over the base of his cock.

"Does birth control work for us?" she asked a few minutes later as they both watched his cock surge smaller and smaller.

"I'm not sure. Condoms wouldn't." He grinned and winked at her, sighing in relief when his cock became flaccid. "You don't want children," he asked worriedly.

"Someday. But not yet."

He relaxed and kissed her brow. His palm whisked against her warm skin. The small hairs on her body stood up straight from the contact and her stomach muscles clenched beneath his spread palm. "Werewolf pregnancy is really rare, but we can ask Leah to ask around about birth control, but if you do get pregnant, you'll have lots of help, and I'll be there every second."

"What would I do without you?"

"We'll never know, 'cause you'll always have me."

"I'll be eighteen in a few more days. God, my parents must be freaking out."

"I know."

"I don't graduate for another month."

"You can't go back."

She laid her head on his shoulder.

"Kelly, your control is good, but like it or not we're mated now. My control isn't as good as yours. I can't let you go back. I need you."

"You love me?" she asked so low he could barely hear her over the wild thumping of her heart.

"I've loved you for years, and I'd do anything to make you happy."

She kissed his neck then turned away to peer doubtfully at the meat. "Can we cook it a little?"

He laughed and snuggled her closer, breathing deeply of her scent. "I can call Richard and ask him to leave a forged note for your parents. Where do you want to say you are?"

"'With you."

"Kelly…"

She straightened and pushed away. "Tell them we eloped and aren't coming back until I'm eighteen."

He reached for his phone. "I'll tell them whatever you like, but that won't make them love me."

"I love you," she said so tenderly it brought tears to his eyes.

He made the call.

Leah had brought blankets and soap. He wrapped Kelly in the blankets and gathered kindling. She lay propped on one elbow, watching his every move.

He laughed and dropped the sticks, speaking over his shoulder. "Stop it, or you're not getting cooked meat."

"Stop what," she said in a teasing voice.

"I can smell your desire."

"You can?" She sat and gripped the blanket tighter.

He laughed again at her wide-eyed expression. "Can't you smell mine?"

She closed her eyes and drew in a deep breath. A soft smile crossed her face, and she dropped the blanket and held out her arms. He didn't wait to be asked twice. He entered her fast and pumped hard and screamed in satisfaction as he spurted and his cock engorged.

"That feels amazing," she said and shivered against him.

"Let the wolf out. Bite my neck if you want to."

She giggled and nipped him, then growled and really bit him, drawing blood that she licked up. In moments, they were growling and shivering caught in their wolves, mating like animals, using their nails and teeth and crying out with each ejaculation.

A distant part of him wondered if Leah or

Richard watched, but he couldn't bring himself to care.

Kelly would care though. *I'll make sure the pack gives us a wide berth*, he thought as his hips jerked again. *This would be boring as fuck to watch though*. For over an hour his cock ruled them, jerking spasmodically, each ejaculation sending orgasmic waves over them. They held each other in a tight embrace, barely moving.

She growled and shivered beneath him. Wetness dribbled down his thigh and over his balls as she came in spurts with him. The smell of sex covered the smell of meat and damp leaves, and he forgot himself completely only regaining human thought when she drew her knees to her chest and fell asleep with her ass tucked tight to him and his body curved around her. He vaguely remembered her licking his balls, and the taste of blood and her come as he cleaned her, but it didn't matter to him now. He fell asleep to her rapid heartbeats and smiled. Her heart beat fast like the wolf she was. Surely, she would come away with him now.

Forty

One week later

A week later, Kelly knelt before her mother and took her hands. She glanced back at him and gave him a worried smile.

"Just listen, Mom. This isn't Mark's fault."

Alice snorted harshly and yanked her hands away.

"We'll listen," John said, but he didn't lessen his glare at Mark.

"Mark didn't know my age. He thought I was nineteen. I lied to him."

"You lied to us, told us you never saw him, that there was nothing between you." Alice's glare ratcheted up a notch.

"There wasn't. When Stacy threatened him, I felt like I should warn him, so I went to his house. The man there gave me an address. I wrote Mark, and he wrote back. We began emailing and texting and then talking on the phone. This was my idea. I asked him. I pursued him. He knew I was young, so I lied."

"How old are you," John asked gruffly.

"Twenty-three, sir." The lie tripped easily off his tongue. He'd wanted to take the blame, but she'd insisted.

"I'd have thought older, but you look the same as I remember." John pursed his lips, but his stance lightened.

Mark relaxed a little and turned back to her mother. Alice still glared, and Mark couldn't blame her.

"He talked you into running away. We were worried sick."

"I talked him into it." Kelly took a deep breath and smiled at him over her shoulder. Mark smiled back, unable to help himself.

"We got married," Kelly said.

"What!" Alice exclaimed as John took a half step forward, then lowered himself slowly to a kitchen chair.

"We got married, and I didn't tell him the truth until after our wedding night."

"Oh, dear God." Alice rubbed her face hard and stood. "You'll just have to get it annulled then."

"We won't. I'm sorry to hurt you, but I love Mark, and he loves me."

"I'll take good care of her," Mark said and winced when her father growled.

"What about school? She didn't even graduate high school."

"Mom— you know school means nothing to me. I can get my GED if they won't give me a diploma and still go to college."

"Kelly, honey, it isn't that simple," John said and rubbed the bridge of his nose.

The mannerism was so like Richard's it made Mark smile.

"College costs a lot of money. If you aren't a dependent, you can't get the loans. Where will you live?"

"I can support her and pay for any college she wants to go to," Mark said quickly. "We can live wherever she wants."

Her mother rose an eyebrow, clearly not believing this boast. "What do you do now for a living, Mister Miller. Last I knew you were a carpenter."

"Call me Mark, and I was, but I don't need to do anything. I have an inheritance. Right now, I work at a wildlife conservotory."

Her mother sniffed and sat. "Alaska! Humph, that explains that, I suppose."

Kelly giggled and rose to hug Mark. He lowered his head to breath deep of her scent and rested his lips on her neck. Warm and soft she relaxed against him. His eyes fluttered shut, springing open when her father cleared his throat.

"You're wasting your breath," he said to his wife as he stood. "Look at them. They're in love. They'll have to learn the hard way, I guess." He offered his hand to Mark who hesitantly shook it.

"Take care of my daughter."

"I will, sir."

Kelly's mother made an unhappy sound. "I still

don't like all this sneaking around. I really thought better of you, Kelly."

"I'm sorry, Mom, but I knew you would hate the idea."

She sighed and gave Kelly a quick hug. "What's done is done. Maybe you can still graduate with your class. I guess we could call the school and see if you can do makeup work."

"I'm not going back. Mark and I are going to visit his family in Alaska. He has money but not so much that losing his job is a good idea."

"Alaska…Honey, that's so far away and cold." Tears filled Alice's eyes. "When will I see you again?"

"We can video chat, but, Mom, you knew this separation was coming. I was leaving for college in a few months anyway."

"I guess."

Her father hugged her mother, saying gruffly, "We knew you would leave us but this is so sudden it will take time." His eyes narrowed on Mark. "I'm not sure I believe this was all her idea, but I can see she loves you. You hurt her, and I'll track you down, boy."

"I would never hurt her. She means the world to me. Your daughter is an amazing woman, and I'm gladder than I can say that fate brought us together. She was heaven sent just for me."

Kelly giggled and kissed his cheek, then moaned softly. She hastily cleared her throat and released him.

"I'm sorry we can't stay longer, but we have a plane to catch," she said.

"You're leaving now?" Alice asked incredulously. "You just got back."

John glared again and crossed his arms. "Your timing is suspicious, young lady. Are you pregnant?"

"Not yet." Kelly turned to wink at him.

Alice inhaled sharply.

"I did time it, Dad," Kelly said in a soothing tone. "And it was cowardly, but I knew you could talk him out of it. So, I told him I'd finished classes in May, he thought I meant college classes, and convinced him to elope, but I had to wait until I was eighteen to legally sign the papers so I, uh, stalled him. He'd already bought our return tickets and didn't realize I'd stall him and here we are."

"This is my fault. I let her convince me," Mark said hurriedly when John turned his glare on Kelly. "I should have asked first, but I knew you wouldn't approve."

"Hmmph." John pursed his lips, but half-smiled.

"Kelly, honey, your father and I were frantic. You left without packing a thing. We thought you'd been kidnapped."

"We called the police and everything, and I've never been more embarrassed in my life then when Andre told us where you were and I had to call them back and say you ran away with a man." John sighed hard and slumped back in his seat. "Well, that isn't true, Stacy embarrasses me more daily, but

I didn't appreciate having to make that call."

"I'm sorry, Dad, I really am. I actually didn't intend to leave so soon, but then Mom asked me about the prom, and I called Mark and almost told him the truth, but I chickened out, and instead, somehow, I talked him into coming for me sooner."

Kelly kissed Mark's cheek, then her father's before turning to grin at him over her shoulder.

"I'm just going to go pack a bag. Mom, can you give me a hand? You'll have to send the rest of my stuff when we get settled."

The two women left the room, leaving Mark in uncomfortable silence with her father.

"So, how much of that was bullshit," John finally asked.

"A lot of it," Mark admitted. "She's worried you'll hate me, think I'm a pedophile or stalker, but I swear on my soul her age isn't what drew me to her, it's what held me back. Hell, I wished she were older and left her alone. I know she was too young for me. But your daughter has grown into an amazing woman. Her strength of character, how deeply she loves you, is one of the things I love most about her."

"Kelly is an amazing young woman, too young to be married." John held up his hand as Mark opened his mouth. "No, I'm not saying you should divorce her. I can see that would break her heart. I'm worried that what you have is lust."

A flush burned across Mark's cheeks. "I like to think I know the real, deep-down her."

Her father snorted. "How could you? You've known her, what? A year? And all from long distance. Or was that bullshit too?"

"We've been in touch since we met, but it wasn't until recently that we admitted we were in love and this week was the first time we ever touched." Mark smiled sheepishly and spread his hands. "I offered to come for her sooner or move back to town, but Kelly asked for time apart. She wanted to know if what she felt was real. I sent Andre to check on her, and it killed me when they became such good friends. I'm more grateful than I can say she loved me enough to hold on even when we were apart."

John sat straighter and looked surprised. "I didn't realize you knew each other. I thought Andre was her friend."

"He is. I've known Andre his entire life though. He's like family. Not that, that stopped him from trying to steal her away, but she really does love me." He couldn't help sounding smug, and John chuckled.

"Well, that puts a new light on things," he said. "I still hate all this secrecy."

"She did too. She really hates the thought that you'll disapprove of her and turn your back. She sees Stacy clearer now though and realizes the distance between you is Stacy's choosing, but for years she was terrified she'd do something wrong, and you'd turn her out."

Her father paled. "We love her."

"I'm not saying you don't. Kelly thought your

love was conditional on her being good, on choosing what you wanted, not what she wants. Just choosing a sport to play caused her months of angst."

"I had no idea she was so insecure …"

"I'm not saying this to make you feel guilty just explain why she hides parts of herself. Kelly is more of a, um, free spirit then she thinks you can accept in a daughter."

"She doesn't want to go to college?"

Mark shrugged, resting one hip on the table and turning to peer at the stairs. "I have no idea. Sometimes, it feels to me, like she's talking herself into wanting it. I know she wants to go away and travel. She hates this town. Sometimes, I think she picked me because I live so far away…that, and I love the outdoors as much as she does."

John smiled ruefully. "I did realize she enjoys being alone in the woods, and I know she wished she could spend more time there but didn't because it made her mother uneasy. And not just because Kelly is a beautiful young woman but because twice she's been lost in the damn woods. Frankly, I don't understand why she still enjoys it so much. You'd think she'd be afraid, but every chance she gets, she's outside."

"I'll make sure she has everything she wants. We plan to do a lot of hiking and camping this summer. Cell service is crap in the mountains, but we'll call as often as we can."

"As we can what?" Kelly asked as she entered

the room. She clutched the handle of a battered suitcase, and her bulging book bag hung over her shoulder. Alice followed carrying another stuffed bag that she set beside the door.

Mark straightened and reached for the bag. "I was just telling your father we plan to spend the summer hiking and camping and would have bad cell service."

"Harrumph," her mother said crossly.

"I'll call when I can though." She handed Mark the suitcase and bent to kiss her father. "Thanks for being so understanding. I really want you to love Mark too." She turned to her mother and gave her a hug. "I love you guys so much." She pulled away and wiped her eyes. "Call Abby for me, would you."

"She doesn't know either?" Alice asked in a more cheerful voice.

"No one knows. I love you guys," she repeated, in a voice thick with tears.

Mark pulled her close and growled softly. She tried to give him a cheerful smile, but he smelled her anxious sweat.

"I'll call you," Kelly said as she dragged him from the house.

In the car, she hugged him tightly, taking his hands and putting them beneath her shirt on the skin of her waist. Her body trembled, intensifying his need to comfort and protect.

The brief separation had really stressed her, or maybe it was leaving her home. They needed more time in the woods. He'd known they'd left much too soon, but her anxiety over her parents had made it impossible for her to relax. They still had a way to go, he had hard truths to tell her, but at least this hurdle had been overcome.

He started the car and laid his hand on her neck. "You did good. They believed it and forgave you."

"I feel so bad for them."

"I know you do, sweetheart," he said sadly and ran his hand through her hair.

"How long until I have to permanently disappear?"

"Maybe you won't have to. Let's see how your parents take this separation. Let them realize you're an adult and maybe we can tell them without them wanting to help you."

She snuggled so close she was practically sitting on his lap.

"Just a few more minutes," he said in a choked voice.

"Will it always be like this?"

"I hope so."

She grinned and kissed him, and all he smelt now was her arousal. The wolf within him settled down, leaving him feeling relaxed and content in a way he'd never felt before. She seemed to feel it too. Her body relaxed against his, fitting perfectly as if made him.

And she was, he thought happily as he kissed her brow. Her presence was a miracle he'd never thought he'd have nor imagined in his wildest dreams could be so good.

"The moon might have caught you for me, but you are Heaven sent."

"The moon didn't choose, I did," she assured him and kissed his neck.

He smiled, not caring one whit how he'd gotten this lucky.

The End

C. M. Conney, a *non-de plume* for S. M. Savoy, lives and works on the family farm in New England alongside her husband and two grown children. She loves animals and owns more than she'd like to admit. Most days, when she isn't baking or planting, she spends her time writing. An avid reader since childhood, she appreciates work in all genres and likes to mix it up a bit in her own work.